Spoilers

The Rise & Fall

Marsha Thompson

In memory of my mother, Golda Thompson

and father, Arnold Thompson.

To my sons, Emmett Hagood, Mark
Hagood and brother, Leonard McReynolds.
You never doubted.

For Janae, granddaughter. Your enthusiasm.

CHAPTER ONE

Fall winds engulfed colorful leaves, tossing them up and down, creating a mystical illusion, outside a six story historical brick building located in New York's Upper East Side. In front of the building, a sign attached to a pole swayed back and forth. Engraved on the sign in bold black letters was *Charlton Academy*.

Several concrete steps led up to a large mahogany door; inside was one of New York's most elite preparatory schools. The school had a waiting list of two to three years. In order for a student to be added to the list, the student's parents had to go through a rigorous screening process.

The criteria were based on wealth, social status and fame. If the family had achieved a place in any of these categories, their son or daughter would be placed on the waiting list.

The Board of Directors recently approved a decision made by its headmaster; in order to present the school as a more compassionate institution, they would admit a few disadvantaged students. However, those students must excel in certain areas so the school would maintain its prestigious reputation.

Three gifted students were chosen for a final interview and were asked to come to the school with their parents to meet with the dean. The three students were Mia Britt, fifteen, African

American, who excelled in science; Lee Chang, fifteen, Asian descent, with advanced technology skills; and Lance Mahoney, fifteen, Irish, with extraordinary math and physics abilities.

The Board of Directors felt these three students were an excellent choice. Not only were they exceptional, they came from working class families. The three students waited with their parents in the Dean's reception area. It was a very plush room surrounded by shelves with leather-bound books. Beneath their feet a Persian rug covered a shiny maple wood floor.

The Dean of the school was Dr. Zachary Bloom. He was a rather odd-looking man, in his fifties, poor posture, with thin brown hair partially covering his head. He had an uncontrollable eye twitch seen through his narrow reading glasses that sat on his oversized ears.

His receptionist, Miss Finney, thirties, was a very attractive woman. She had emerald green eyes, greener than most—very piercing. She could have been a model at one time, with her lean body. She was fashionably dressed, a shimmering hair clip kept her shoulder-length black hair out of her eyes. She sat poised behind her desk typing on a keyboard.

Miss Finney glanced over at the new students. It's a big mistake to admit these students from public schools to their prestigious academy. Students from inner city schools cause havoc, she thought. She had previously made her feelings known to Dr. Bloom.

"Are you sure, Dr. Bloom, you're doing the right thing by admitting these students to our school?"

"Trust me, Miss Finney. These students are brilliant. It took me months to convince our headmaster, Dr. Woodman that we need to reach out to underprivileged students. It was the only way I could get these students here."

"You know our future depends on their capabilities. If they fail, so do we."

"We're not going to fail, Miss Finney. I hand-picked these students myself. They have already proven to be experts in their field. They will fill the needs of the school and secure our future."

"I hope you're right."

"Don't worry, Miss Finney, my students will be under my control."

Lance's mother nervously flipped through magazines, she wanted more than anything for Lance to be accepted into Charlton Academy. She knew his father would be very proud of him.

"How do I look, Lance?" Irene asked. "I want to make a good impression."

"You look great, Mom. Stop worrying."

"It's just this school is the best."

Lance glanced at Mia. He was amused by the look of boredom on what seemed to him to be a very cute face. He felt, she definitely doesn't want to be here. I don't blame her. I'm still trying to figure out why I was recruited. There are a lot of students good in math and physics. Well, maybe not as good as me.

Mia sat with her legs crossed, her face rested in her hand, and her glasses stood on the rim of her nose. Her school counselor told her she would only be in high school another year. She had already tested out. But she never thought, she would end up in a snobby school for the rich and famous. Her feeling was that life sucked.

Mia looked at her grandmother, Beverly. "Are you sure I should go to this school?"

"Yes Mia, I really do believe this is a good opportunity for you."

"I hope you're right. This school seems sort of stuffy."

Beverly placed her hand in Mia's hand. "All I'm asking is you give it a chance."

Her grandmother knew kids who graduated from Charlton Academy went to the best universities. It was mentioned in the school's catalog. She hoped Mia would get a full scholarship.

"Okay, Grandmother, I'll give it a chance." Mia squeezed her grandmother's hand tightly.

"Now sit up. Remember, first impressions count," Beverly said.

Mia straightened up in her chair and looked over at Lance. She wondered if he played basketball. He did tower over most boys his age but she wasn't sure Charlton Academy had a basketball team. She thought, maybe he's a musician, he had the look—tall, thin, long blond hair. The girls would really like him. She hoped to make the gymnastics team. She had been taking classes for eight years and was pretty good. She loved to compete.

Lee wore a New York Knicks cap turn backward on his head, a black leather jacket, and Retro Nike Jordan's. He was busy trying to calm his parents down. They seemed to be having some type of disagreement.

"Could you guys please speak English?" Lee whispered, with his head bent, slightly embarrassed.

"You see? He's ashamed of his culture," Lee's mother said.

"I'm not ashamed of our culture. It's just that people don't understand what you are saying. They think you're arguing —which you are."

"You see?" Lee's father said to his wife. "Lee's a good son. You make too much fuss."

Miss Finney stopped typing and looked up at the students and their families. She took a few sips from her coffee drink. "Dr. Bloom is on a very important conference call. Keep your voices down," she said in an unpleasant tone.

Everyone looked at her. They couldn't believe she spoke to them in such an impolite way.

Mia felt she was rude. "Did you hear the way she talked to us, Grandmother?"

"Just ignore her. Remember what I taught you. Tolerance is a blessing"

"Mia Britt, you can go in now," Miss Finney said, holding her drink in her hand. She pointed to Dr. Bloom's door and rolled her eyes at them.

Mia and Beverly walked past Miss Finney to Dr. Bloom's door. Mia paused. She stared at the cup Miss Finney held in her hand. The cup shook vigorously, splashing the coffee all over her designer dress. She jumped up and grabbed some tissues from a box on her desk and wiped her dress off.

"Oh no!" Miss Finney cried out. "My dress! How did this happen? I was just holding my cup in my hand and it started shaking. I couldn't control it. Something very strange is going on." She looked around at the people in the reception room. "It wouldn't surprise me if one of you had something to do with this. Oh, just forget it. I have to go home and change my clothes."

Everyone looked at each other puzzled by her outburst and ridiculous accusation. Lance and Lee found it amusing. They glanced at each other and chuckled. They all watched her rush out of the room.

Dr. Bloom was seated behind his polished desk. His long legs could barely fit underneath it. He was the size of the basketball players who came to the youth center in Mia's neighborhood.

Dr. Bloom reassured Beverly that Mia would do well at Charlton Academy and with his guidance, she would excel in science. He would personally make sure of it.

Meanwhile, Mia sat patiently looking around the room. She saw pictures of Dr. Bloom on the wall, one of them with the Governor and another with a Senator. She also recognized a few pictures of him with movie stars. She thought, *No family pictures. Maybe he couldn't find anyone to marry him. He is pretty big. Or it could be because of his big pointed ears. Well anyway, he seems to be a nice enough person—not at all like his uppity receptionist.*

CHAPTER TWO

One day the three teenagers ended up at the same table in the school cafeteria—it was the beginning of their friendship. The three of them became best friends.

Lance, dressed in his blue pants and white shirt, the school uniform, rushed into the noisy cafeteria filled with students. He brushed shoulders with another student. "Excuse me," Lance said.

"No problem," the boy said, walking briskly away.

Lance wasn't paying attention to where he was walking. His mind was on his fencing class. He was going to have his first fencing match after lunch. He pushed his shoulder-length hair from his face and grabbed a tray. He placed a hot dog on it, fries, and packages of mustard and ketchup. He picked up a small carton of milk and moved to the cashier to check out.

Not far from Lance in the line was Mia. She leaned forward to get a closer look at the food in the bins. She pushed her glasses back on her nose. She was delighted they had spaghetti, even though it wouldn't taste like her grandmother's.

Standing next to Mia was her classmate, Ivor. He had bright red hair and spoke with a British accent. Mia loved to hear him talk. She turned to him. " How's everything going, Ivor?"

"Quite well. I can't complain... except for the food," he said smiling.

Mia had always been fascinated with British people, because they still had queens, kings and especially princesses. Perhaps it was something that spilled over from her childhood. She enjoyed watching their elaborate weddings on television. She would pretend to be a princess, placing a tiara on her head and sashaying around her room in a long, glittering dress. She would use her powers to close her window. The noise from Mr. Sanchez's market interfered with her fantasy.

Mr. Sanchez owned a produce market next to her building. He would place his vegetables and fruits on a stand in front of his store. Every day, the same group of neighborhood boys would pass by his stand and grab apples or a handful of grapes and run down the street.

He would run out of his store in anger, shouting words in Spanish. Mia didn't understand what he was saying. She repeated a couple of his words to her grandmother. She got very upset and told her not to ever repeat those words again. She asked one of her Spanish speaking friends what the words meant, and then she understood why her grandmother reacted the way she did. She wondered why Mr. Sanchez just didn't put extra fruit on his stand.

Mia and Ivor checked out of line. Ivor saw some of his friends sitting at a table. They waved to him to join them. He hurried over to them. Mia looked around to find a seat. She saw Lance sitting alone at a table, eating a hot dog and flipping through a fitness magazine. She walked over to him and placed her tray on his table.

"Anyone sitting here?

"No one," Lance said, absorbed in his magazine. He looked up, surprised to see it was the cute girl—the one he saw in Dr. Bloom's reception room. He quickly closed his magazine and stuck it in his backpack on the floor next to his chair. He gave her his full attention. But before she could sit down, Lee rushed over to the table carrying his laptop and holding an energy drink in his hand. "Do you guys mind if I sit here? The noise is blown out at the other tables and I have a report to finish before my next class."

"Sure, have a seat. It's not like we're a five-star restaurant," Lance said jokingly.

Lee introduced himself while opening up his laptop. "Oh, by the way, my name is Lee."

"I'm Mia."

"I'm Lance... I think we all saw each other in Dr. Bloom's waiting room."

"That's right," Mia said. "We did... we are the chosen ones." They all laughed.

Lance was slightly shy and limited on words until his conversation turned to fencing. His face would light up, like someone flipped a switch. After watching the movie *Star Wars*, he became obsessed with the art. He vowed that one day, he would win a gold medal in the Olympic Fencing Competition. He wanted his mother to see him compete against the world's best, just like his father had competed against some of the world's best boxers.

Lee was very confident about his computer skills. He would occasionally mention one of the many offers he'd received from major computer companies to join their team.

Lance and Mia asked him why he didn't take one of their offers and skip school. He told them that he and his grandfather had made an agreement. He would earn a college degree, even though he felt he didn't need one. In exchange, his grandfather would teach him martial arts.

His grandfather held high honors in the field. He had studied under some of the best. Lee had earned a Black Belt in Tae Kwon Do. Now, his grandfather was teaching him Jeet Kune Do, the style created by his hero, Bruce Lee. They would practice in the alley behind their family's restaurant. Sometimes they would draw a crowd, mostly boys in the neighborhood.

Mia's long braids were pulled back with several clips to keep them from flopping in her face. She constantly pushed her glasses back on her nose. She was very outspoken and witty, with an enormous sense of humor brought on by her ability to entertain herself using her special powers.

She carried a backpack slung across her shoulders, with bright colorful letters that spelled out the words, *Fight the Power.* She explained to her friends that she cut the letters off one of her mother's old jackets and it meant to fight for what you believe in. This was Mia's way of holding onto her mother's memory.

Sometimes at night, while lying in her bed, she would think about her mother. She remembered listening to her read stories. She would change her voice to imitate the characters in the book. She was very funny.

Mia believed her mother knew she had powers, too. One night, her mother had taken her doll from her and placed it on a shelf. When her mother left the room, she used her powers to make the doll come to her. Her mother came back into the room. She saw her holding the doll. She just stared at her for few minutes and left the room with a strange look on her face.

Her father would take her to the park and show her frogs and insects. She spent all of her time playing with them and very little with the other kids. Her interest in science started there. She earned many science awards, including the Intel Science Fair.

Mia practiced gymnastics every day in the gym with her teammates and coach, Miss Wilson. Mia was very fond of her. She was a young woman in her twenties who was easy to talk to, or at least willing to listen. She had won an Olympic Gold Medal in gymnastics when she was fourteen.

Miss Wilson was determined to get the best performance out of her team. Her students didn't mind her rigorous training schedule because they felt she was cool. Miss Wilson helped Mia make the transition to Charlton Academy.

Mia was ready to return to her previous school after just a couple of weeks at the academy. But Miss Wilson spent extra time with her. They would occasionally have lunch together and go window shopping.

Miss Wilson knew there was something unusual about Mia because she distance herself from her classmates. She wondered if Mia felt out of place because her family wasn't wealthy like the other students. Or if Dr. Bloom was putting too much pressure on her to maintain her high GPA. He wanted to impress the Board of Directors because he wanted to be the next headmaster of Charlton Academy.

Miss Wilson felt Mia deserved to be a normal fifteen-year-old girl, having fun with her classmates, instead of spending her free time working on science projects. What she didn't know was how different Mia really was from the other students or why she couldn't allow herself to become close to them. They already felt she wasn't one of them because she came from a different background. If they knew her secret, they would think she was some kind of freak.

She didn't even tell Lance and Lee, her best friends. She had made a promise to her grandmother that she wouldn't tell anyone about her special powers. She had telekinetic powers, the ability to set things in motion with her thoughts and emotions. During a gymnastics practice she fell off the pole and hit her head on the gym floor. The pain caused a strange sensation in her head. Miss

Wilson and her teammate Daily ran over to see if she was injured. They helped her sit up.

"Are you okay, Mia?" Miss Wilson asked.

"Just a little dizzy," Mia said, with her hand pressed against her forehead. She tried not to panic. She took a deep breath. She knew when she hit her head on the floor it triggered her powers. *Stay calm, stay calm,* she told herself. She had to leave right away, before something terrible happened and everyone learned her secret.

"Let's get you to the nurse," Miss Wilson said, looking her over.

"Miss Wilson is right. You could have a concussion. My dad is a doctor. He says if you hit your head, always have it checked out," Daily explained.

Mia stood up. She said, "Okay, I'll go see the nurse, but I feel fine now."

Miss Wilson said, "Daily, please go with Mia."

"Sure," Daily said, holding onto Mia's arm. The two walked out of the gym.

Mia tried hard to keep her powers under control. She felt a rush of energy building up inside her—like a balloon filling up with air. The restroom was just a few feet ahead. She told Daily she had to go to the bathroom. Daily followed her.

Mia darted quickly into one of the stalls. She sat on the toilet seat, bent over and placed her head in her hands. "Please...please go away," she repeated quietly to herself.

Meanwhile, Daily peered at herself in the mirror above the sink. She flipped her hair back with her hands. She was taking gymnastics to please her parents. They insisted she be well-rounded. Her desire was to be a lead singer in a rock group, something her parents were totally against.

Daily made sure she looked different from the other girls at the school. They all wore the typical white shirts and blue and green plaid skirts but she added colorful extensions and a flower to her hair. On her wrist she wore multi-colored bracelets.

The school ignored her appearance because her family made generous donations to the school. Mia couldn't understand why the school named the library after them—that was the last place you would find Daily.

After school, Daily made a complete metamorphosis. She would dress in denim, boots and tinted glasses. She would sit in her spacious room for hours, playing on one of her guitars that lined the wall. Her room was her stage. Her audience was the famous bands pictured on her wall, Guns N Roses, Aerosmith, Metallic, Black Sabbath...

The bathroom shook, causing the stall doors to open and close, making loud banging sounds. Daily held on tightly to the sink. "Mia, are you okay? What's going on?" she shouted.

After a few minutes, the room stopped shaking. Mia came out of the stall. She went to the sink and splashed cold water on her face and dried it with a paper towel. "I'm going to have to find away to control these feelings. Maybe I am weird," she mumbled under her breath.

Daily was shaken and confused by the disturbing events. "What just happened?"

"It must have been a tremor," Mia said. "It's over now. Let's get out of here."

The school bell echoed loudly. They walked out into the hallway. It was chaotic; the students were nervously rushing through the hallways. They were anxious to leave the school and go home before another tremor hit. Mia told Daily to go home and not to worry about her. She felt just fine.

"Are you sure? My driver can wait," Daily said, showing concern.

"Thanks, but I'm good. My grandmother will take me to the doctor if I need to go."

"Okay, if you're sure."

Miss Finney stood by the large open door monitoring the students who swiftly passed by her, out of the building, and down the steps. Mia stood on the sidewalk. She watched some of her classmates enter fancy chauffeur-driven cars. She wondered if they had ever ridden the subway. It would be very sad if they hadn't. After all, life is about experiences.

Daily shouted to Mia from the backseat of a car, "See you tomorrow." Mia smiled and waved back at Daily. What a close call she had today. She took her cell phone out of her pocket to call Lance and Lee. She wanted to know if they were on their way. Sometimes Lance had fencing practice after school, and Lee would get hung up in the computer lab.

Just about all the cars had left the school. Only a couple of students were coming down the steps. Mia saw Lance and Lee, with their backpacks on their shoulders. She waved to them. "Finally you showed up," she called out.

They waved back at her and rushed down the steps. Lee, medium height, wore a new short faded haircut, which he felt was very in. He carried a backpack filled with the latest tech devices: a laptop, tablet, and a couple of cell phones, all given to him by companies, to see how he could advance their technology. He was definitely a computer geek.

"What took you so long?" Mia asked. "You're the last ones. I've been waiting like forever."

"Don't look at me," Lee said. "I was waiting for Lance. You know he always has to go back for something."

Lance said, "I left my iPod in the gym."

"What else is new? Last week it was your phone," Lee said.

Lance examined his iPod to make sure no one had tampered with it. "I was distracted by all the weird stuff going on last period.

I set my iPod down on the bench in the gym next to me when the building started shaking. I totally forgot it was there."

"It was just a tremor," Mia said. She had to convince her brainy friends that's all it was. She didn't want them to become suspicious and find out it wasn't a tremor that caused the school to shake.

"Well, I called my mother. She didn't feel anything," Lance said.

"It's only logical. It had to be a tremor. Remember, it's only been a few weeks since the last quake. Geologists predicted there would be more," Lee explained.

"Well, its over," Lance said. "Let's go to the restaurant where my mother works. She's treating us." Lance took his cap out of his backpack and placed it on his head.

"Sounds like a plan to me," Lee said. "My mom's a good cook but try eating the same thing day after day. You get food fright."

It started to rain. Mia pulled her jacket out of her backpack and wrapped it around her shoulders. "Maybe we should flag a cab," she suggested.

They watched people squeeze themselves into cabs already occupied with other people. It would be impossible for them to catch one before they got soaking wet.

"Everyone seems to have the same idea," Lee said, looking around. "We might as well keep moving."

"You're right," Mia said. "We're not going to get a taxi anytime soon."

The sky darkened, clouds formed, thunder roared, and a flash of lightning crossed the sky. The teenagers walked swiftly down the crowded sidewalk moving between people rushing to their destination. Their shoes, hitting the wet pavement, made splashing sounds. They turned onto Broadway St. to the corner newsstand. Sam, the owner, with a Yankee baseball cap on his head was putting a plastic cover over his stand to keep his magazines and papers dry. The teenagers moved quickly to help him.

Lance saw a man sitting against a building. His face was covered with a newspaper. An oversized coat covered his body. "I think that's Moody. I haven't seen him in a few weeks," Lance said anxiously. He rushed to the man. "Moody," Lance called. He removed the newspaper from the man's face.

The man was upset. "It's raining out here. Give me back my paper...Do I look like Moody?" He snatched his paper out of Lance's hand.

"I'm sorry. Moody is usually in this spot... Have you seen him?"

"Not since the earthquake. Now, leave me alone. Strange things going on...people missing."

Lance handed the man some money. "Here, take this money and get out of the rain. Buy yourself something warm to drink. If you see Moody, tell him Lance is looking for him."

The man grunted and took the money from Lance. He pulled himself up and headed to the nearby convenience store. Lance walked back to join Mia, Lee and Sam. They had moved the newsstand close to the building to protect it from the storm.

"Look Lance," Sam said with a thick Greek accent, "you won't get much out of that homeless man. He's in a world of his own." Sam took off his hat, scratched his head and put it back on.

"It's just his way of coping," Mia said. She watched the man disappear into the convenience store. She wondered what happened in his life that brought him to the streets. What was his story?

"I guess you're right, most of the people living on the streets have a problem, or just bad luck. Some people want help, some don't. So what do you do?" Lance asked.

"You don't give up on them," Mia said. She was worried about Marge, one of the street people. Marge was in her thirties with straggly blonde hair. People in the area called her the push cart woman. They would avoid making eye contact with her— perhaps she stirred up something inside of them. They knew if it happened to her it could happen to them.

Marge was a successful Investment Banker on Wall Street. She was also a single mother, who enjoyed raising her energetic six-year-old adopted daughter Hanna. Marge was sitting on the steps of her brownstone working on her computer and watching Hanna roller-skate. She glanced up and saw Hanna had taken off her helmet. It was too tight Hanna told Marge. But, Marge insisted she put it back on.

Marge told her to wait on the steps. She was going into the house to get them some water. While in the house Marge received a phone call that delayed her going back outside. Like most kids, Hanna became impatient. She decided to continue to skate. She placed her helmet on her head, but forgot to fasten it. She skated speedily down the street, navigating around a group of kids playing on the sidewalk. She hit a large crack in the sidewalk and lost her balance. Her helmet flew off and her head hit a pole. She was knocked unconscious. She was taken to the hospital but never awakened.

Marge blamed herself for the loss of her daughter. She became very depressed. She lost her job, then her home. Mia found these things out from her friends who would occasionally come looking for her. Mia was hoping she would leave the streets and go back with them, but Marge wasn't ready to face the world without her daughter.

Mia looked up and down the street through the crowd of people, hoping see Marge. "You know, I haven't seen Marge in a while, either."

"You guys are starting to freak me out; chills just went through my body," Lee said.

"Ah, I wouldn't worry too much about your street friends," Sam said. "They probably moved to another location."

The teenagers continued down the street. The rain poured heavily. They could barely see in front of them. They passed by one of Mia's favorite boutiques. The salesclerk was putting a new dress on one of the mannequins. Mia ran over to the window. She wiped the rain from her eyes to get a better look at the dress. She spoke softly to herself, "I wish I had that dress. It's so cute."

The salesclerk waved at her and went back into the shop. While Mia was admiring the dress, the mannequin fell over. Mia turned to see if anyone was looking. A couple of people walked by holding their open umbrellas. Lance and Lee had already entered the restaurant.

Mia stared at the mannequin, causing it to stand up. She paused for a moment to get another look at the dress, when a flash of lighting lit up the sky. She quickly moved on to the restaurant, where Lance and Lee stood inside dripping water on the floor mat.

CHAPTER THREE

Lance's mother was busy taking an order from a customer. Her long blonde hair was stuffed under a net. She wore black pants and a white shirt. She glanced up and smiled when she saw Lance and his friends standing in the entranceway of the restaurant. She motioned to them to sit at a table in the back of the room. Mia and Lee followed Lance.

Irene came over to their table. Lance hugged her. He gave her a kiss on her cheek. Irene looked up at him. "Okay," she asked, "what's that for? What have you done? There better not be any strange person sleeping on my couch tonight."

Lance laughed. He knew if he had found Moody that's exactly where he would be. He and his mother had developed a close relationship, since his father suffered a fatal heart attack during a boxing match. His father had earned quite a reputation in the boxing industry. He had the potential to become the next Lightweight Boxing Champion.

Lance was proud of his dad, especially, when he took him to his gym. Everyone was so friendly. The boxers would come over and shake his dad's hand. They'd pat Lance on his head and ask him if he was going to be to a boxer like his dad. In a strong voice his father would say no. He told them his son was too smart for his head to be used as a punching bag. He believed Lance was a genius because at the age of four, he could add faster in his head than he could on a calculator.

One night, Lance's dad returned home from a long day at the gym. He looked into his bedroom and saw him with his blanket pulled over his head. He called out to Lance and asked him what was wrong. Lance told him he was afraid of the monsters. He had a bad dream. Lance's dad sat down on the bed next to him and pulled the covers from over his head.

Lance never forgot what his dad told him. He said if he was ever in a threatening situation, not to show fear, to look directly into the eyes of the person or thing. Once it knows you're not afraid, it will lose confidence and be thrown off guard. From that night on, Lance was never afraid of anything.

Irene worked very hard at the restaurant to support the two of them. Her dream was to land a part in a Broadway musical, a dream Lance shared with her but for now, she was happy knowing Lance was attending Charlton Academy. She would tell the other waitresses her son was the smartest kid in New York City and one day he was going to be a math professor at Columbia University.

Irene didn't understand why in this modern time, Lance was so enthusiastic about fencing. But she never understood, either, why her husband wanted to be a boxer. She believed he would still be alive if he hadn't been boxing.

Irene was always happy to see her son and his friends. She knew Lance liked Mia a lot. He was always smiling when she was around. "How was school today?" she asked.

"Good, if you don't think the school shaking was unusual," Lance answered.

"I thought it was pretty cool," Lee explained. "It was a tremor."

Mia quickly changed the subject. "Oh, thanks for inviting us to lunch, Ms. Mahoney."

"You're welcome. I'm glad you guys could make it. You know, we didn't feel anything over here. But then, we have all that construction going on across the street."

"We're starving, Mom," Lance blurted.

"Okay, what will it be, burgers and fries?" Irene asked.

"Yeah," they replied.

"And three Cokes, Mom," Lance added.

The three waited patiently for their food to come. Mia looked out the window at the rain that didn't seem to be letting up. "I hope it stops raining. I have to take my grandmother to the doctor."

"Is she sick?" Lee asked.

"I'm not sure. She's been very tired lately," Mia answered.

"One of my teachers has the flu," Lance said.

"Maybe my grandmother has the flu… I hope the doctor can give her something to make her feel better."

The three ate their burgers and fries. Mia took the last bite of her hamburger and swallowed down the last of her Coke. She grabbed her backpack and told Lance and Lee she'd see them tomorrow. She darted out of the restaurant onto the wet sidewalk to the subway station.

Mia was worried about her grandmother. She feared she might lose her too. She wouldn't know what to do without her. She made her way through the crowded, noisy subway station. Many people scurried to catch their trains. Mia could see her train at the platform. There were several people ahead of her at the gate.

Finally, it was her turn. She swiped her card and ran to the train. It was too late. The subway door closed. Mia stared at the door, opening it. She entered the crammed car. A few people standing by the door looked puzzled by the bizarre occurrence.

Two large men cramped together on two seats looked suspiciously at Mia as they whispered to each other. Mia felt she had to say something, although most of the people in the subway car had their eyes closed or were on their cell phones. "I think I heard there's a problem with some of these doors opening and closing."

An elderly lady, with a flowery scarf tied around her head, held on tightly to a pole with one hand. In the other hand, she held onto a shopping bag. She stood close to Mia.

"You'd think with all the taxes we pay, everything would be in working order," the elderly lady murmured.

A few people overheard the elderly woman. They nodded their heads in agreement. The train pulled into the next station and stopped. Mia exited the train. She waved goodbye to the elderly lady. She smiled and waved back at her.

The two men seated next to the door looked through the window at Mia. They watched her move vigorously down the platform.

Mia inserted her key into the lock on the apartment door and entered the room. Beverly sat comfortably on an old, worn brown recliner with a blanket covering her legs.

"How was your day, Grandmother?"

"It was good. How was yours?"

"The usual," answered Mia, grabbing a shiny apple from a bowl on the table.

"Did you make any new friends today?"

"No, Grandmother, I didn't. I have two best friends, Lee and Lance. You remember, I brought them by to meet you."

"Yes, I remember them, Mia. They seem very nice, but you should have at least one girlfriend."

"There is one girl I think is pretty cool. Her name is Daily. She plays the guitar. She's really pretty good. All the other girls spend their time texting and talking on their phones."

"Well, it's nice you have a friend that's a girl. But I still think you should have more friends."

"Okay grandmother. I'll try to make more friends at school who don't mind befriending the poor."

Beverly shook her head. She told Mia she had a lot of her mother's ways, especially when it came to her mouth. Beverly seldom talked to Mia about her parents. She didn't want her to build up her hopes, thinking she might see them again, and be disappointed.

Beverly had explained to Mia that her mother Erica had an opportunity to attend a good school on the Upper East Side but she wouldn't go. She was afraid someone would discover her powers.

She had taken her to a psychologist. He wanted to place her in a facility where he could observe her behavior. She ran out of his office crying. From that day on, she shut out everyone. She was afraid people would think she was different.

She met her father, Aaron Britt, when she was nineteen. He was a few years older than her, a nice enough guy, very protective. She felt safe with him and trusted him with her secret. They got married. She was born a year later. Her mother and father spent most of their time traveling in and out of the country. Her father worked for the government.

His last assignment brought them back to New York City.

She came home one day to find them rushing around the apartment, throwing clothes in a bag. Something very important had come up. They had to leave for Washington, DC right away. They asked her to take care of Mia until they returned. That was ten years ago—the last time she had seen them.

She tried to find out what happened to them. She went to Washington to see the agent they told her to contact in case of an emergency. The agent said he would call her if he found out anything. They kept in touch for a few years but there were no leads, nothing—it was like they just disappeared without a trace. The government wouldn't say whether or not they were still alive.

Beverly wondered if someone found out about Erica's powers and was using her in some way. She knew Mia's mother and father loved her very much. Something or someone had to prevent them from coming back. Beverly told Mia that's why it was so important no one knew about her powers.

"Well, it's getting a little chilly. We better get going. It's going to take us a little while to get to the doctor's office," Beverly said. She grabbed her sweater from the chair.

Lee hurried into his family's busy restaurant. He greeted a few customers waiting in line for their orders. Some of them expressed their dissatisfaction at having to wait. Kim, Lee's sister, a year younger than him, was taking an order from a customer. She hollered at Lee in Mandarin.

"You're late. Do you think you're a prince because you go to that school for rich kids?"

"You're crazy, girl," Lee said, chuckling.

Kim took off her apron and threw it at him. "You wait on these impatient people." She snatched her purse from behind the counter and stormed out of the restaurant.

Lee's mother and father rushed out from the kitchen when they heard the commotion.

"What's going on?" Lee's father asked in Mandarin.

"It's your daughter; she's crazy. But I've got everything under control, Pop."

"I've got it under control, Pop," Lee's mother said, throwing up her hands. "What kind of talk is this? He goes to the best school in New York and he talks like this. It's your fault we have two crazy kids."

Later that evening, Lee participated in a karate competition. His grandfather had taught him well. So far in his division, he remained undefeated. His moves were swift and his jumps high, as if he was propelled into the air by some unknown force. He kept his opponent bewildered and off guard.

Lance watched Lee. He was amazed at how his computer geek friend had changed into a fighting machine. Lee dominated the match. He gave his opponent a swift kick, sending him whirling across the floor, ending the match. After being declared the winner, Lee shook his opponent's hand. His grandfather told him it was a form of courtesy essential to the game. It showed respect to the opponent and officials.

Lance was very proud of Lee. He'd never seen him in action before. He gave him a high-five. They walked out onto the street. Lance smiled and patted Lee on his back. "Man, you were awesome, another Bruce Lee in the making," Lance said. "You know, I was just thinking. You ought to invite Mia to come to one of your Karate competitions. She loves action."

"I never thought about it. But you're right...she's pretty cool." Lee replied. "I checked her out during her gymnastic practice. She's really good...You know she likes you."

"I know she likes me. She likes you too." Lance said.

Lee grabbed Lance's shoulder. "Let me put it this way: she likes you in a boyfriend-girlfriend way. When she's with me, she talks about you, and when you're with me, you talk about her. You should ask her out. Maybe to a movie."

"Are you sure?"

"Of course I'm sure. I know all about girls."

"You must have learned about them from your robotic computer." They both laughed.

"Well, I'd better get home. I've got a math test tomorrow."

"Since when did you start studying math, Lance?"

"I didn't say anything about studying. I found a shortcut to one of the formulas. I thought I'd spring it on the test tomorrow. Mrs. Pleasant will really be confused." Lance grinned. He had a mischievous look on his face. This was his way of challenging his teacher.

"Have you tried out my new fencing program?" Lee asked.

"Not yet, but I plan on installing it tonight. I'll let you know if I have any problems... I knew you would come in handy," Lance said, smiling.

"Right," Lee said. "I'll see you tomorrow. Don't forget to call Mia," Lee shouted. He walked briskly away in the opposite direction. He decided to treat himself and take a taxi. He stepped out onto the street and waved his hand. Several taxis sped by him with passengers. Finally, one swerved over to him. Lee opened the door. "West 34th street," he told the driver.

The taxi took off, veering in and out of lanes. Without any warning, a man jumped out from between two parked cars. The taxicab driver hit his brakes but it was too late. The taxi hit the man, knocking him onto the cold pavement.

Shaken, Lee hollered, "Oh my God! The man!" Lee and the taxicab driver quickly exited the taxi and ran over to the man lying on the street. A crowd of people had gathered around him. Lee took out his phone to call 911. The odd-looking, man, with heavy eyebrows and a blotched complexion, sat up. He reached for his hat and placed it on his large head.

"I'm fine, no need to call anyone. It was my fault. I didn't look," uttered the man.

"Are you sure?" the taxicab driver asked. "I should get your information. You may need medical attention later... I should report this."

"No need to worry... I'm fine," the man said. He stood up a little unsteadily.

The taxicab driver pleaded, "Come with me. Get into my taxi; I'll take you where you were going, no charge."

"You should really come with us. You could be in shock," Lee said.

"No thanks," the man said, brushing off his long coat. He turned and walked away. The wind picked up, blowing the man's coat open. He pulled it together and held it tightly.

Lee tried hard to understand what just happened. He couldn't believe this man just up and walked away as if nothing happened. He and the taxicab driver got back into the taxi. They continued on their way. They could see the man walking a short distance ahead of them. He was slightly hunched over but able to move on his own. Lee looked back at the man as they passed by him. *It's incredible,* he thought.

Lance followed the sound of music coming from the living room. Irene was dancing. She stopped and turned down the CD player. "You won't believe it. I got a call back. I'm so excited." She made several turns moving to Lance. "This could be it, Lance." She said glowing.

"That's great, Mom." Lance said with a big smile on his face. "I'm sure you're going to blow them away. Let me know what happens. I'm going to practice my fencing."

"Just keep in mind, you're going to be a math professor." Irene turned the music back up and continued to dance.

Amused by her persistence, Lance shouted, "Yeah, Mom ... a math professor."

Irene shouted, "Your dinner is in the fridge."

"Thanks, Mom," he said.

Lance went into his small bedroom and turned on the computer. His room was full of books stuffed on shelves and piled up on the floor—mostly math and physics books. A chalkboard with formulas scribbled on it stood in the corner. On his wall hung an International Mathematical Olympiad gold medal.

He inserted the fencing program on his computer. He took out his sword and positioned it to fight against his opponent on the screen. Simon, his cat, peeped up from underneath his bed. Nervously, he watched Lance waving his sword. Lance's phone rang. He looked over and saw Lee's name on the screen. He put his phone on speaker. Simon seized the moment to make a quick dash from underneath the bed and out of the room.

"What's up?" Lance asked.

"You won't believe what happened. The taxi I was riding in hit this man. By all logic, the man should be dead, or at least injured. But the dude gets up and walks away with no injuries—unbelievable."

"That is weird. Maybe he's like a cat and has more than one life."

They both laughed. Instead of returning to fencing, Lance decided to call Mia and talk to her about Lee's experience. It would be the perfect time to ask her out. "Call Mia," he instructed his phone.

There was a large poster of Isaac Newton on Mia's bedroom wall. She believed he would have had a scientific explanation for her powers. She was sitting at her computer researching information for her science project.

Dr. Bloom had discussed with the teenagers how important it was to advance satellite capabilities. He told them it was the future, and it would make an excellent science project. They took Dr. Bloom's advice and worked together. With their combined talent they were developing a device called the Enhancer. It would have the capacity to strengthen a satellite's signal to more than a hundred times its present capability. Dr. Bloom was thrilled with their project and told the school to spare no expense for the materials they needed.

One of Mia's favorite songs played from her computer. She turned the volume up and moved her body to the beat of the music. She looked at her stuffed animals lying on her bed and used her powers to make them dance. She stood up and danced with them. Her phone rang. She turned to her computer and saw the call was from Lance. The stuffed animals fell on the bed. She stopped the music and hit the video cam. Lance appeared.

"Did you talk to Lee?" Lance asked.

"Yes, that was really wild. I guess the man was just crazy." Lance paused for a moment. He decided to ask Mia out. *What's the worst thing that could happen?* He asked himself. *E will still equal mc^2.*

"Do you want to catch a movie this Saturday?"

"Sure, what did Lee say?"

"I'll get back to you," Lance said.

"Over and out," Mia said.

Lance sighed. "Now what?

CHAPTER FOUR

Mia, sat at a table in the school library with Lance and Lee. Lee read from his laptop. Mia flipped through a book looking for ideas for her English Literature paper. They both looked over at Lance, whose head rested on the back of his chair. His eyes were closed. He appeared to be sleeping. Mia turned to Lee with a sneaky look on her face. She balled up a piece of paper to throw it at Lance. "Should I?"

Lee smiled. He balled up a piece of paper. "Let's do it," Lee said. They threw the balls of paper at Lance. Startled, Lance sat up abruptly. He grabbed his chair to keep from falling. He smiled, picked up the balls of paper and threw them back at Mia and Lee, missing them but hitting a student studying at another table.

The students at the other table laughed. They balled up paper and fired back at them. Another table nearby joined in the paper ball fight. Paper balls flew back and forth across the room. The students stopped when they saw the librarian, Mrs. Beasley, short with gray hair pulled back in a bun, walking swiftly toward them. She had a stern look on her face. They scrambled to pick up the balls of paper on the floor.

Mia stared at some books on a shelf, causing them to fall on the floor. Mrs. Beasley, distracted by the falling books moved quickly over to the bookshelves to pick them up. Mia rushed over to help her.

"I'll pick them up," she said in a low voice to Mrs. Beasley, feeling guilty for having caused them to fall.

"Thank you. I'd better get someone to look at these shelves. They must not be level," whispered Mrs. Beasley.

"I wouldn't worry too much about these shelves. It's probably one of those bizarre things that will never happen again," Mia said. She looked back at her classmates picking up the last balls of paper and returning to their seats. They laughed among themselves unaware of Mia's part in distracting Mrs. Beasley. Lance joined Mia and helped her pick up a few remaining books lying on the floor.

"Mrs. Beasley, where can I find the rare historical book collection?" Mia asked.

"Follow me," Mrs. Beasley said.

"If you don't mind I'd like to come too," Lance said. "I have no idea what subject I'm going to write about for my lit term paper."

"You just want to see what I'm writing about," Mia said grinning slightly.

"Oh, I can't have my own ideas?"

"You could possibly have one, maybe two," Mia answered sarcastically. She turned her head so Lance couldn't see her smiling.

They followed Mrs. Beasley down a narrow hallway. She stopped in front of a room, opened the door and pointed. "You can go through the collections in this room but the other room across the hall is off limits to you." She walked away quickly.

They entered the stuffy room. Mia went over to a window and tried to open it, but the window was nailed shut. She looked closely at the books on the shelves and read the titles out loud. She picked up one of the books. "Unbelievable...look, Lance... this book, *A History of Rome*, received the Nobel Prize for literature. This could be just what I need." She turned to show Lance the book, but he'd left the room. She walked to the door and looked down the hallway. The door to the off-limit room was slightly ajar. She moved quietly to the room, making sure no one saw her.

The room looked like a replica of an eighteenth century room. An antique chair sat in the corner of the room with old newspapers stacked on it, and shelves were full of old dusty books. There were even a few dried-out ink bottles and a couple of old ink pens sitting on a table.

Mia sneaked up behind Lance. He was glancing through one of the old books. She poked him with her finger. Surprised, he turned quickly around, making a loud sound. Mia placed her hand across his mouth so he wouldn't make another sound. "Shh!" she said, giggling. "You should have seen the look on your face when you turned around. It was priceless. I should have taken a picture."

"I'm glad you're amused. You scared the daylights out of me," Lance said.

"I know. I shouldn't have surprised you like that, but I just couldn't help myself," Mia said smiling.

For a moment everything was silent. Neither of them said a word. They just looked into each other's eyes—a definite connection. It was the first time the two of them had been alone together. Lance thought he should let her know how he felt. He reached his hand out to her but dropped the book he held in his other hand. Lost for words, they both bent down to pick it up.

"What are you doing in here?" Mia asked.

"Trying to figure out what makes this room so forbidden," Lance said. "Apparently no one has been in this room... like in a hundred years. Why would they keep this stuff anyway?" He examined an old ink pen. Mia looked around the room. She saw a stack of paper notebooks on top of a desk next to an ancient computer. She picked up one of the paper notebooks and glanced through it. "Look Lance, a sketch of the school."

Lance looked at the picture and read a few notes scribbled underneath it. "Nothing unusual here. It's just a small drawing of the school." His focus turned to a large rolled-up paper sticking out of a basket next to the desk. He picked the paper up, blew off the dust and spread it out on the desk.

"What is it?" Mia asked.

"It's faded, but it looks like a map, a sketch of the tunnels in New York. It's a few centuries old," Lance said, sneezing from the dust particles.

Mia looked closely at the sketch. "It must be plans for the subway system, sometime in the late 1800s. I think it was about the same time this school was built. I'm not sure about the date of the school."

"Well, I don't have a clue when the school was built; when Dr. Bloom said 'welcome students,' I left. I wanted to check out the school for myself. I don't think its plans for the subway system; from the measurements it would be too narrow," Lance said.

Mia pointed to one of the tunnels sketched on the drawing. "Look at this small area. It connects to a tunnel leading to our school."

"That's not so unusual. There're lots of tunnels and openings beneath the streets. Maybe they started to build something and stopped," Lance said, looking at the map, trying figure where the school and tunnel connected.

"You're probably right," Mia said.

Lance sat down in front of the computer and powered it on. He needed a password. "If we can get into the computer, we might be able to find out more," Lance said.

"We need Lee," Mia said.

"I'll get him," Lance said.

"Be careful, don't let Mrs. Beasley see you. Hurry! Hurry!"

Lance stood in the hallway and peeped into the library. He saw Mrs. Beasley at her desk helping a student. He waved to Lee to get his attention. Lee stopped typing, closed his computer, grabbed his belongings and rushed over to Lance. "What's up?" he asked.

"Give me a second," Lance said. He rushed back to the table, picked up Mia's and his backpacks and returned to Lee. "We need your help to get into a computer."

"So now what... I'm the friendly neighborhood hacker?" Lee said, smiling.

"You said it, not me," Lance said grinning.

They quietly made their way back down the hallway to the room. Mia was reading from one of the notebooks.

"What are you guys trying to find out? Lee asked. "What is this room?"

"We'll fill you in later... We don't have much time," Lance said.

"This room is off limits to us. We aren't supposed to be in here," Mia said. "We really don't know what we're looking for. It's just so mysterious that someone from this school was researching tunnels, one of them leading into the school."

"The school is pretty old. The question is which came first the school or the tunnel? If the school was built first, why would they need to connect a tunnel to it?" Lee asked.

They gathered around Lee seated at the computer. He entered a password and got in on the first try. "Bingo... we're in," Lee said, watching the computer accept the word. "Way to go, Lee," Mia said, patting him on his back. She turned to Lance. They were dumbfounded. It took Lee two seconds to get in.

"I wish I could contribute this to my exceptional tech skills, guys but the password was simply, Charlton." Lee said trying to be modest.

Mia and Lance watched Lee scan through the different sites. "There's not much on here, just a list of names, addresses and dates of teachers who once taught at this school...Quite a few of them," Lee said, looking closely at the computer screen.

Mia saw an old album underneath some books on the desk and pulled it out. She opened it up and looked closely at the old black and white photos of men and women. She showed the pictures to Lance and Lee. "Look at the people in this picture. There's something unusual about them. They don't look real... I guess it could be the way the old cameras made you look," Mia explained.

"Wow, you're right. They look stiff—like statues. Some of their heads and ears seem to be larger than normal. They could belong to the same family," Lance said, amused. He looked over at a disk sticking out between two books. He took it down, wiped the dust off of it and placed it into the computer. "Open this up, Lee. Let's see what's on it."

Lee opened up the disk. He focused on the screen. "It's some type of census report. The number of people in households all over the country. That's interesting, a school needing that info."

"Why would they need that information?" Mia asked, pushing her braids out of her face and reading over Lee's shoulder.

"You got me," Lance said.

The teenagers couldn't make a connection. Frustrated, they continued to look through books and papers. Mia, hands on her hips, turned to Lance and Lee. "This is a waste of time."

"I know what we can do," Lance said.

"Okay, Sherlock, let's hear your idea," Lee said.

"Let's find the tunnel," Lance said, stirred up.

"Then what?" Mia asked, checking the hallway to make sure no one was there.

"I don't know," Lance said, "maybe there's something hidden in it, or something they don't want us to know."

They moved quietly out of the room down the hallway. Lance was in the lead with the map in his hand. They reached the area where Mrs. Beasley sat helping a student. Mia went over and stood behind the student to block Mrs. Beasley's view so she couldn't see Lance carrying the map out of the library. Lance and Lee moved to the stairs, where Mia joined them.

They took the stairs to the basement. Lance figured out one of the rooms down there led to a tunnel—but which one? They went quickly in and out of the rooms until they heard a jingling sound. Someone was coming down the hallway toward them. They ducked into the closest room—a laboratory. Once inside, they hid behind a counter full of large containers filled with some kind of green substance.

A maintenance man entered the room. His keys were attached to a belt around his waist jingling when he walked. He turned on a small television set, opened a drawer and took out a small bottle. He took a few sips from it and placed it back in the drawer. He plopped down in a chair to watch a program on the television. He smacked the old TV a couple of times to get a better reception.

The three teenagers looked at each other, wondering how long they were going to be stuck there. After about fifteen minutes, the maintenance man's phone rang. He reached in his shirt pocket and took out the phone.

"Okay," he said, and turned off the television. He walked to the counter where the jars rested that concealed the teenagers, pulled open a drawer and snatched a couple of tools from it. Then he turned around and walked toward the door humming a tune.

Mia felt something crawling on her leg. She brushed off a spider. The maintenance man heard the sound and paused for a second. He looked around to see where the sound came from but saw nothing unusual and walked out of the room.

The teenagers were relieved. If caught, they would have no explanation for being in that room. They looked at the large jars, trying to figure out what type of chemicals they contained. Lance picked up one of the jars to get a closer look. He unscrewed the top and smelled it. "Gross! It smells like rotten eggs."

"Be careful, you don't know what kind of elements are in that jar," Mia said cautiously. "They could be harmful."

"Hold on," Lee said. He reached into his backpack and removed his tablet. He had installed a program on it that could analyze elements in the environment. He scanned the container. "That's weird. It can't identify the elements."

Lance examined the bottle. He shook it. "I've worked with a lot of chemicals but none that would produce this color or consistency."

Mia felt a draft coming from the back of the room and followed the cool air to a door in the back of the laboratory. She placed her hand on the door and called Lance and Lee. "Feel the door; it's cold. It must lead to the outside or possibly the tunnel."

"You're right," Lance agreed, placing his hand on the door. "This has to be the one." He turned the doorknob but it was locked.

Lee saw a small screwdriver on a counter. "Hold on," he said. He snatched the screwdriver and tried to loosen the screws on the doorknob but the screws were too old and rusty.

Mia knew she could open the door. But, she had to distract Lance and Lee. She turned to the door where they entered. "Did you hear that? It sounded like the jingle made by the maintenance man's keys."

Lance and Lee rushed over to the door and peeped out to see if the maintenance man was in the hallway. They waited for a few minutes to make sure he wasn't out there.

Meanwhile, Mia stared at the door and it opened. Lance and Lee returned surprise to see the door was unlocked.

"Look, the door is unlocked," Mia said. "It just came loose."

"How did that happen?" Lee asked, examining the lock.

"This whole thing is pretty spooky if you ask me," Lance uttered.

They pulled the door open hesitating for a moment. It was so dark they couldn't see anything. Lee flashed the light on his phone. "Nothing unusual," he said. He looked at the concrete walls and dirt beneath his feet. They walked through the dark tunnel. Up ahead they could see an entranceway with slabs of wood nailed across it. They went quickly to it.

"This is it—the area we saw on the map," Mia said excitedly. "But why is it boarded up?"

"There must be a reason," Lance said.

Lee peeked through the cracks in the wood. "Maybe it's not safe to go in there," he said.

"We have to look inside. It's the only way to find out what's in there." Mia insisted.

They pulled off one of the slabs of wood. Mia glanced at her phone. "We have to leave, now! We'll going to be late for our next class!"

The three paused for a moment and ran back to the school. They wondered if they would ever find the answer to this mystery. Why was that part of the tunnel boarded up?

CHAPTER FIVE

After school, Mia waited in her usual place for her two friends. Once they arrived, the three made their familiar walk down Broadway Street.

"You seem to be in a very good mood today," Lance said to Mia not realizing she had earplugs in her ears. She sang to the music from her phone. She saw Lance's mouth moving. "What did you say?" she asked removing her earphones.

"I said, you are in a good mood today."

"I am in a great mood. My grandmother is going to be fine."

"That's cool," Lee said. "I know you were really worried. Sometimes I worry about my grandfather. He's getting old too."

"The doctor said her iron is low and he gave her some pills to take. That's why she was so tired. She should feel better in a few days."

"That's great," Lance said, smiling.

They approached Sam's newsstand. Lance looked over at Sam who was busy stacking newspapers and magazines on it.

"Haven't seen Moody yet," Sam hollered.

Lance turned to Mia and Lee. "Let's go through the alley. It's connected to a tunnel. They could be in there."

Mia and Lee agreed with Lance. They walked a short distance through the alley and went d o w n i n t o the tunnel. They could see the damage caused by the previous quake. Mia saw a slightly bent shopping cart resting against the wall of the tunnel and rushed over to it. Lance and Lee followed. She rambled through the dirty shopping cart filled with debris from the earthquake. "This is Marge's cart. She wouldn't go anywhere without it!" Mia sighed.

"How can you be so sure it's hers? Lance asked.

Mia grabbed a dirty cup out of the cart. "Because I gave her this cup. Something must have happened to her and maybe Moody too. "

They took a few steps forward. The ground beneath them rumbled. They grabbed onto each other.

"We're having another earthquake," Lance said anxiously.

"This isn't good." Mia stated nervously. She shifted from one side to the other trying to decide which way to go.

"I agree. We can't stay here. This tunnel may give way! Lee spoke out.

They ducked and dodged pieces of concrete falling from the top of tunnel. Lee rushed over to an opening in the tunnel. "Over here. Come on... hurry!" he shouted. A piece of debris hit him on his forehead. Stunned, he placed his hand on his head and staggered. Mia and Lance latched onto him. They all stumbled into the opening, where a powerful force from within carried them downward through the earth. Three thumps were heard when their bodies hit the ground.

"Is everyone okay?" Mia asked, taking a deep breath. She felt her glasses on her chest. She put them on but it was too dark to see anything.

"Oww, I landed on my butt," Lee said, pulling himself up.

"I think I'm still alive. What a ride," Lance said.

They were surrounded by darkness. They felt for their backpacks, embedded in the dirt.

"Hold on…I have my backpack. I've got my phone," Lee said. He shined the light from his phone on the ground. Mia and Lance picked up their backpacks. They scrambled for their phones and tried to dial out but there was no signal.

"Where are we?" Lance asked.

"I haven't a clue," Mia said. "I hope it's not hell. My grandmother said that's the last place anyone wants to go"

They looked around the dark, dreary enclosure where plants grew out of the walls and strange-looking insects crawled around on a reddish dirt floor.

"Maybe we're just in another tunnel," Lance said, looking around.

"This is a cave, not a tunnel," Mia said, rubbing her fingers against the dirt wall. "I've never seen dirt like this before."

"Me either," Lance said. He rubbed his fingers in the dirt. "It feels like clay."

"Hold on for a second," Lee said. "I'll scan the area. It might help us find out where we are."

Lee reached into his backpack and took out his tablet. He scanned the area. "Wow," he said, turning to his friends to show them the results.

"What does it say, Lee?" Lance asked.

"Some of the elements are unrecognizable." said Lee.

"Interesting," Lance replied.

Mia suggested some foreign elements may have invaded their atmosphere like the unknown substance found in the containers in the school's lab.

"One thing I do know. We are definitely not in the city."

"There's only one way to find out where we are," Lance said. "Keep moving."

They reached the end of the cave, which led to a vivid forest seen through a heavy mist. They continued to walk down a path through the forest. "This is too strange," Mia said. "The environment is altogether different." She could barely see between the dense trees in the forest. She couldn't tell where one ended and another began.

"Maybe we're on an island," Lee said.

"How would we get on an island?" asked Lance, pushing his hair out of his grimy face.

"Who knows? None of this makes any sense," Lee said.

They could hear the sounds of animals close by and the hissing of multi-colored snakes wrapped around trees. A rainbow of birds flew from one branch to another to get a better look at them. Mia stopped. She saw something in the forest. "Hold on! Did you see that?" She asked.

See what?" Lee asked. He flashed the light from his phone into the forest.

"Something's out there. It's following us," Mia warned them. She looked to see if she could see it again.

"It's probably the shadows from the trees. I don't see anything," Lance said. "Let's keep moving."

"There's something out there," Mia insisted.

The three approached a clearing. A piercing sound resonated from above. A dark, shadow engulfed them. They looked up to see a vicious giant gray bird, with exceptionally wide eyes, oversized wings, and pointed sharp claws, flying toward them. Suddenly, something or someone pulled them into the bushes. Speaking in a low voice, a man told them not to make a sound. The giant bird would capture them. Another person, barely seen through the jumbled tree branches, motioned to them to come quickly. She called out to them in a faint voice to follow her.

The loud, scary sounds made by the wicked prehistoric bird could be heard as it trailed them from above. The animals in the forest sensed danger. They scattered behind rocks and trees. The bird flew closer to them. Mia tried to focus on the bird to use her powers to stop it but she couldn't get a clear view of it through the branches.

The teenagers were apprehensive about following the strangers, but more frightful of the bird. They followed the mysterious people. The faces of the man and woman were covered by hoods.

They led the teenagers down a path through the forest. Mia glanced at Lance and Lee. They wondered where the strange people were taking them.

Finally, they reached a cave. Inside, Nadia, a fifteen-year-old girl, olive complexion and long black hair, swept the floor using a stick with bushes tied to it. She wore a short wrap made out of animal skins. She turned around, and stared through the particles of dust. She was surprised to see three new people enter the cave with members of her group. She rushed over to greet them knowing they must be scared and confused.

"Don't be afraid, you're safe here with us...my name is Nadia," she said in a low voice.

The three teenagers looked puzzled and bewildered but relieved they were among friendly people.

"I'm Lee. These are my friends, Lance and Mia. Somehow, after a wild ride, we ended up here."

Lee looked around the cave. A fire burned in the middle, surrounded by piles of rocks. Animal skins hung from the top of the cave and long robes lay drying on rocks.

"We came from New York...the city," Lance said, baffled by his surroundings.

"So did my brother and me," Nadia said.

"Where are we?" Mia asked.

"You're far from New York... You're in another world—one beneath your world." Nadia explained.

Mia asked Nadia, "What do you mean another world? You sound as if we're in some science fiction movie."

"I'm afraid it's worse than that. A movie ends and you return to reality but this is a nightmare you can't escape."

Mia trembled hearing what Nadia said. She couldn't control her emotions. She stood in a trance, her eyes fixed. Her power sent chunks of dirt flying through the cave. Everyone except Lance and Lee took cover behind big rocks.

Lance shook Mia. He tried to wake her from the trance. "Mia, Mia," Lance called. "What's happening?"

Lee waved his hands in front of her eyes in hopes of getting a reaction. "Mia, snap out of it," he said.

Mia blinked her eyes and slowly came out of the trance. She didn't remember what happened but she could see the destruction around her and realized she caused it. She saw the look of disbelief on everyone's faces. She wasn't about to explain what happened because she didn't quite understand it herself.

Lance and Lee reassured everyone it was safe to come out. They pulled Mia to the side.

"What just happen, Mia?" Lance whispered.

"All I can tell you is, I have telekinetic powers. I can make things happen with my mind. Sometimes my emotions but I can't always control it." Mia answered.

"Awesome." Lee said wiping dirt from his face.

"Did you have anything to do with the school shaking?" Lance asked. Mia started to answer when the man who brought them to the cave rushed over to them.

"What just happened?" The man asked anxiously.

Mia said, "Don't worry. I'm not going to harm anyone. It's just that sometimes I can't control my powers."

Lance looked closely at the man, whose face was still partially covered. His voice was very familiar. He removed his hood.

"Moody, it's you!" Lance said surprised.

"Yes, Lance, it's me," Moody said, giving him a hug. "I recognized you and your friends in the clearing. I figured I first had to get you away from the Eglipse. One shock was enough. Are you and your friends okay?

"We're good. A little shaken," Lance said. "You look great."

"It's this place. There's nothing here but healthy things to eat and drink. You have no choice but to be healthy."

"How long have you been here?" Lance asked.

"Since the last earthquake. We were in a tunnel when the quake hit. We went into this opening to protect ourselves and were swept down here. That's how we all ended up here. Probably the same thing happened to you and your friends."

"That's just what happened," Lance said.

"Who else was with you?" Mia asked.

The woman stepped forward and pulled her hood back to expose her face. Mia could see it was Marge, but not the same Marge, one who looked young and strong.

"Marge, I haven't seen you in weeks. I was so worried," Mia said, hugging her.

"I'm glad to see you again but not here in this savage place," Marge said, taking Mia's hand. "But we're going to be fine."

"She's right," Moody reassured them. "Together we will survive."

"I don't understand what has happened," Mia said, stressed.

Nadia told them that what happened couldn't be explained. They were in another world, one that didn't evolve over time. "My brother Aman and I have been here for sixty-five days." She looked over at one of the walls with black marks etched on it. The teenagers looked despairingly at the marks.

"I make a mark on the wall to keep track of the days. She turned to them. "Other people have been here," she said.

"What happened to them?" Lee asked, moving closer to Nadia.

"They didn't survive," she said.

"Why were you in the tunnel?" Lance asked.

"We were walking home from the market and took a shortcut through the alley. We heard a dog cry out from the tunnel. It must have heard us talking and was trying to get our attention. We went down into the tunnel and saw the dog with one of its legs trapped under a rock. We removed the rock but the dog was so nervous it wouldn't stand still long enough for us to attend to its injuries. It moved swiftly out of the tunnel, limping. We saw the opening in the tunnel wall a few feet away and went into it just like you did. The force was so great..."

Lee was captivated by Nadia's beauty. He listened intensely to her but was disturbed by the fact that she and her brother had been there for months.

"There is someone else here with us, Dr. Vincent Ram, a geophysicist. He's been here longer than we have. He's very ill."

"I'm familiar with his work," Lance said.

"Yes, I think we all are." Mia said. She looked at Lee. He nodded in agreement.

They followed Nadia to another area in the cave. An elderly, frail man, in his 60s, with long white matted hair, and a beard, lay motionless on a pallet covered with fur skins. His eyes were closed and his face was covered with sweat.

Nadia dipped a rag into a container of water that sat on the floor near Dr. Ram and wiped his face. She explained to them that Dr. Ram was the only survivor from a group of people who were there before she and her brother arrived.

Dr. Ram had been researching the activities of earthquakes in New York that led him to the tunnel. He discovered it was the focal point of the earthquakes. He was examining the opening in the wall of the tunnel and stepped inside.

Dr. Ram saved Nadia and her brother from being killed by a wolf-like creature called a Wolfling that roams the forest at night in search of its prey. When they arrived there it was nighttime so they stopped to sleep.

During the night they were awakened by a loud howling sound made by a giant wolf standing in front of them. They screamed and took off running. Just as the wolf was about to reach out and grab them, Dr. Ram appeared, waving a fiery tree branch. He hollered to them to run down the path to a cave up ahead and threw the flaming branch at the wolf. He ran quickly behind Nadia and Aman.

They made their way into the cave, but not before the Wolfling's claw struck Dr. Ram. It made a large gash on his chest that became infected. Nadia had been pouring coconut milk on it to keep down the infection. She moved close to Dr. Ram. "Can you hear me?" she asked, speaking softly. He opened his eyes and turned toward her.

"Is everything okay? I heard a commotion," he said in a weak voice.

"Everything is fine, Dr. Ram."

He looked over and saw the newcomers. "More people."

"Yes, three," Nadia answered.

Mia leaned over Dr. Ram and felt his hot forehead. She pulled back the cover, exposing the wound on his chest. "We have to get rid of his infection. My grandmother is a great believer in natural cures. What plants are in the forest?"

"Everything you can imagine," Moody said.

"Show me...the sooner I find what I need, the better his chances will be."

"Are you sure you want to go out there, Mia? I should go," Lance said.

"No! I have to go."

"Don't worry, she's in good hands. Moody will take good care of her," Nadia added.

Moody handed Mia a robe. "Put this on. It will protect you from the poisonous snakes in the forest. Besides that, some nights can be very chilly." He grabbed his spear. He told Mia they had to watch out for the large birds, the Eglipses, like the one that followed them through the woods. The birds could see them during the day, but at night, they could only sense their presence.

CHAPTER SIX

Mia and Moody stepped carefully through the dense forest. Mia gathered leaves and plants and stuffed them in a cloth sack. She was amazed at all the colorful berries and fruits. She looked up to see large coconuts hanging from tree branches. Moody pointed out edible plants and those that were poisonous.

"Wow, all these fruits," she said, tasting a few berries. "My grandmother would make a pie out of each one of them."

She looked at Moody, so strong and protective. He was so different from the man she saw leaning against the building by the alley. She could see he wasn't your typical street person. He was very alert. Sam mentioned he read the paper every day. He was looking for something. What? He didn't know.

Lance was probably the only person who really knew him. He looked out for Moody and was very protective of him. Sometimes, when she called Lance, the two of them would be taking a walk through the alley. Lance trusted Moody enough to bring him home, after he convinced his mother he was harmless.

Mia wondered if Moody would share his secret with her. Apologizing for her curiosity, she asked him why he was at that alley almost every day. Moody told Mia to sit down, pointing to a large branch. He began to tell his story.

One day, he was standing in front of the alley near Sam's newsstand talking on his phone. It was so noisy he could barely hear what his client was saying. He walked farther into the alley. He looked up and saw something unbelievable. A reptile-looking creature changed into a human right in front of him. Mia's eyes widened. She was glued to his every word.

He told his friends and family. They felt he was stressed out from working so hard. He went to the police. They put him in a psych ward to be evaluated. They concluded he was paranoid.

In the hospital, he received a visit from a government agent. He questioned him at great length about what he had seen. It seemed the agent wasn't surprised by what he told him. He seemed to be confirming what he already knew.

"He wanted me to try to describe in detail what I saw. I told him for the second time. I was in the alley talking on my phone. I saw this green-looking animal similar to a lizard turn into a human. I was so shocked I dropped my phone. I couldn't move. This thing looked directly into my eyes as it walked past me.

"After I regained my composure, I went looking for this thing that had turned into a man. But he had disappeared in the crowd. I was sure someone would have seen him. He was unusually awkward looking. His ears seemed a little distorted and his head seemed too large for his body. I went into all the shops. I asked everyone but no one had seen anyone fitting the description. I found myself on that corner every day. I was hoping to see him again. I had to convince myself I wasn't crazy, but no luck.

"I became obsessed. Now I am beginning to wonder if my eyes were playing tricks on me. I told Lance what I had seen. Surprisingly, he didn't think I was nuts. He believed I saw something. We just couldn't figure out what it was, or where it came from. We searched the Internet for strange occurrences and asked people in the area if they had heard or seen anything unusual—nothing. Maybe it was all in my mind."

If Lance had shared this story with Mia a week ago, she probably wouldn't have believed it either. But after ending up in that place she knew anything was possible. A peculiar sound attracted Mia's attention. "What was that?" She looked over in the direction the sound came from.

"Probably some animal," Moody whispered to her.

They heard the sound again. Mia pointed. "It came from over there." She started walking toward the sound. Moody pushed her behind him. He told her to be very quiet. They moved closer to the sound. They saw what appeared to be the back of some small fury animal lying face-down on the ground.

"What is it?" Mia asked, moving slowly over to the animal.

"I don't know ...don't get any closer. It could be dangerous." Moody picked up a stick from the ground and gave the animal a little nudge. It didn't move. He nudged the animal again, only harder this time.

"Would you mind not jabbing me with that stick? I am in enough pain already," said the small furry creature with a very proper British dialect.

Moody and Mia looked at each other. They were astonished to hear this black furry bird talk.

"Don't just stand there... turn me over," said the small creature in a demanding tone. Moody and Mia knelt down next to the bird and turned it over. It was an owl.

Mia rubbed the owl. Its eyes opened wide, reacting to the soothing feeling. Mia helped him stand up, but one of his legs was injured. He fell to the ground after several attempts to stand. Mia picked him up and sat him on her shoulder, holding onto him tightly. "Don't worry. You'll be safe with us."

The owl said, "That's what you think. Those terrifying birds are all around us. They were chasing me, and I flew right into a tree. I must have knocked myself out. When I woke up and heard something coming toward me, I dared not move. Then I saw you and for some unknown reason, you chose to jab me with a stick."

"So you can see from the back of your head," Moody said.

"Brilliant deduction, but not accurate," the owl said. "I can turn my head around."

Moody and Mia, with the owl on her shoulder, carrying a sack of herbs, moved rapidly through the forest with the birds hovering over their heads.

A week passed. Dr. Ram had recovered from his infection thanks to Mia's mixture of herbs. Aman, with his long, black silky hair pulled back from his face, had returned from fishing. He held a pole with several fish tied to it. Marge and Nadia cleaned the fish and cooked them over an open fire in the cave. They all sat on the floor of the cave around a fire eating fruits and fish.

"Not bad," Lee voiced.

"It's not a burger," Lance said.

"Just use your imagination," Mia said. "Pretend you're at the restaurant."

"You'll get used to it," Moody said, enjoying his fish.

Mia named the owl Ivor because he had a British accent like her classmate. He was perched on a rock near them.

"Tell us, Dr. Ram, what you have learned about this world?" Lee asked, fiddling with his phone to see if he could get a signal.

"I'm not sure what caused the world to split. Maybe a major earthquake." Dr. Ram explained. He told them what he knew about the world. There was a cruel man who lived there named Oman. He ruled a colony of people that lived in a place called Citadel, on the other side of the river. Oman's army guards his temple. No one was allowed in without his permission.

"He makes the men in the colony carry heavy stones and wood to his temple. There, they work from sun up to sun down. The women work in the field picking fruit and attending to his garden. Their hands were raw from digging up potatoes.

"The food is taken to his Temple to feed himself and his men. The leftovers are taken to the Marketplace and shared with the people in the colony. Anyone caught trying to escape is banished—left in the forest to fend for himself against the creatures."

One of the men who attempted to make the trip with him through the wild forest was from the colony. He had been banished by Oman. He told them about a key that unlocked the door to a machine that would take them back to their world. The machine was hidden in a cave near the colony. The key to the machine was in a room in Oman's temple, inside a box. The box sat on an altar guarded by two Eglipses.

"During our journey through the woods, Oman appeared, riding on the back of one of his birds. He said we would have to tell him where the machine was hidden if we wanted the key. He would go back to our world with us. That would be the agreement.

"We didn't trust him. We knew he would turn on us. We told him we didn't know where the machine was hidden. He laughed and said we would never survive in the forest without him. The beasts would devour us. Our only choice would be to join his colony. We told him we would take our chances in the forest rather than become one of his slaves.

"I was fortunate; everyone else in my party did become victims, one way or another, to the creatures in the forest. It was like Oman knew our every move—maybe his birds were tracking us."

Over the next two weeks, the teenagers and the people with them planned their journey. They had to make their way through the forest, cross the river, find a way into Citadel and retrieve the key. Next, they would have to find the cave where the machine was hidden. It wouldn't be easy but they had no choice if they wanted to return to their world. Dr. Ram mapped out the path. Aman, Lance, Lee, and Moody sharpened sticks for arrows and tree branches for spears.

Ivor could fly again, but he couldn't see very well. He usually missed his target. He flew over to perch himself on Mia's shoulder and ended up on her head. "Oh!" Mia shouted. She pushed Ivor off her head. He fell on the ground.

"You don't have to be so rough," Ivor said, his feelings apparently hurt.

Everyone was amused by the incident. Mia picked up Ivor and hugged him. "Sorry Ivor, you caught me off guard." *Do all owls have poor vision?* She wondered. It was not a scientific fact. Well, regardless, Ivor was a very unique little furry bird. How many owls can talk?

Later that evening. Nadia and Lee looked out through an opening in the cave. Nadia was amazed by the clear sky. It looked like a painting to her. "It's so beautiful out there," she said gazing at the sky.

"It's really clear. At home, I see nothing but towering buildings," Lee said. His heart fluttered; he was feeling nervous around a girl for the first time in his life.

"You have to want to see more," Nadia said.

"I want to learn more about you. What's your favorite movie? What kind of music do you listen to?"

Nadia turned to Lee and started to speak but was interrupted by Lance and Mia.

"It's just a matter of time before we're home again," Lance said.

Aman rushed over to them. He put his arms around his sister. "Is everyone ready?" he asked.

"More than ready," Mia answered.

Ivor flew toward them. Mia caught him just before he went through the opening in the cave. She placed him on her shoulder.

The forest was still, silent and misty, with a slight chill in the air. The shadows of the small party of determined people walking single file are seen in the moonlight. They moved silently down a narrow path through the forest with the Eglipses circling above them.

Dr. Ram stopped abruptly. He raised his hand. An Eglipse, twenty feet or more with its long sharp claws, had positioned itself on the path ahead. The bird moved toward them. Moody picked up a rock and threw it into the woods. The bird followed the sound of the rock into the bushes.

Dr. Ram waved his hand. Everyone moved quickly. But Lance and Lee didn't make it past the Eglipse before it returned to the path, cutting them off from the others. They stood still as the bird moved slowly around them, its claws barely missing them. Their hands were on their spears, prepared to fend it off.

Suddenly, a strong gust of wind blew through the forest. Tree branches flew through the air. The Eglipse could barely move its wings as it struggled to fly away. Lance and Lee took cover behind a tree to keep from being blown away.

"What's happening?" Lance shouted.

"Look," Lee said, shielding his face from the flying branches. He pointed to Mia. "She's using her powers."

Mia stared straight ahead, using her energy to stir the wind. It blew forcefully, then weakened. The bird flew away. Mia came out of her trance. Everyone gathered around her.

"The bird was too close to you. There was no way you could have fought it off," Mia said. "But I was worried you might be blown into something."

"She's right," Dr. Ram said. "One of you may have escaped, but not both of you."

"They are very strong. It's a good thing it's not daytime," Moody said.

"Remind me to treat you to lunch when we get back home," Lee said, smiling.

They continued on. Lee looked at Lance and Mia holding hands walking down the path. It confirmed what he already knew. Mia and Lance's feelings for one another were more than just friendship.

Later that night, they all sat around a fire eating. They were in disbelief that the bird appeared on their trail before daylight. How did it know they were there? Dr. Ram explained that the birds were controlled by Oman. He must have received word that there were people in the forest and sent his birds to find us. Ivor flew off Mia's shoulder. "My sentiments exactly," Ivor said.

"It's hard to believe someone could control those wild birds," Moody said. "How did he gain power over them?" he asked.

"I don't know," Dr. Ram answered, shaking his head.

"There are so many things that can't be explained. Who would believe an owl could talk?" Marge said, looking at Ivor. "No offense, my furry friend."

"None taken," Ivor said.

"Why haven't Oman and his army attacked us?" Lance asked.

Dr. Ram explained, "Because he wants to go to our world. He's hoping we will lead him to the machine."

"We have to stay a step ahead of him," Mia said.

Ivor walked in circles. His head moved from one side to the other. "I've got it. I've got it. There's only one way to find out what he's planning. I'll go to Citadel. They won't be suspicious of an owl."

Mia grabbed Ivor. "Stop Ivor, you're making me dizzy. But you're right. You're the only one that can find out what he's up to."

"Then I'm off. Cheerio." Ivor took off, barely missing a few trees. His furry little body ascended above the trees until only a speck of black was seen in the air.

***

The Citadel

High wooden poles enclosed a colony located in the middle of rolling green hills, surrounded by trees and bushes. A river flowed nearby where animals ran freely and playfully but were cautious of the predators. A winding narrow path led through the colony where families lived in small stone structures. At the end of the winding path was Oman's Temple. It was a big four-level structure surrounded by an army of fierce men carrying spears and holding shields.

Oman, in his early sixties, with long brown, graying hair, stood tall in his long robe, held tightly together with a rusty belt covered with shiny jewels. His presence cast an evil allure in a large room lit by flames shooting out from iron pots. Standing next to him was Advar, short, stocky, with a stringy beard—the enforcer of his devious deeds.

They both stared at a large rusty key enclosed in a small transparent box on an altar in the middle of the room. The box was guarded by two restless Eglipses, one on each side. The birds were chained by one leg to the floor. They would attack anyone but, Oman, who attempted to remove the box.

The birds were hungry. Advar pulled a cord, creating a loud bang that summoned two of his men wearing short robes with swords were attached to their waists. They carried containers of raw meat to the hungry beasts and rushed off.

Ivor flew to an opening in the temple but instead of landing on the ledge, his small body hit the temple wall. "Ouch," said Ivor. "They could have made the hole a bit bigger."

The Eglipses stopped eating and looked up to see him perched on the ledge. Oman and Advar glanced up to see what they believed was just harmless bird. Advar told Oman the intruders weren't far away.

"They have come to steal the key. But they will never get it until they tell me where the machine is hidden," Oman said with a mean look on his face. "You mean you would give the intruders the key?" Advar said. "Don't be foolish, Advar. When I find out where the machine is, I will capture them."

"Good," Advar said with a devious smile.

CHAPTER SEVEN

Everyone was exhausted from the events of the day. They were eager to turn in for the night. They took turns watching over the camp. Lance and Mia lay near each other. The sky seemed darker than usual. Lance thought it was because there were only a few stars in the sky. He turned toward Mia **to see** a sad look on her face.

"Don't worry Mia. We'll get back home. I promise you."

Mia looked over at Lance. "That's a big promise, Lance. But just in case I don't make it back, check on my grandmother for me."

"Your grandmother is going to be fine. You'll be there to take care of her."

"I hope you're right. My mother and father left suddenly and never returned. I can only imagine what she's feeling."

"Once she sees you, she'll be fine."

Lance shared his feelings with Mia. He told her he missed his mother and hoped she got the part in the Broadway show. Even in this bizarre world with its strange creatures, being close to Mia somehow made things less frightening for him.

He remembered when he first saw her in Dr. Bloom's waiting room. Now he knew she was not only cute, but also smart, funny and unusual. "Mia," Lance said, "I really like you. I hope you feel the same way about me." There was no response. Mia was asleep. He wondered if she heard anything he said, because it would be awhile before he got the courage say it again.

Moody and Marge watched over the campsite while the others slept. Moody could see how much Marge had changed. She was smiling, even laughing from time to time. He first saw Marge, coming out of her office building on Wall St. The next time was on the street, pushing a shopping cart. She was homeless. He had heard she lost her daughter.

No one on the streets discussed their past. It was the code of silence. You know not to ask. Moody convinced Marge the streets at night were no place for a woman. He took her to a shelter so she could have a safe place to sleep at night.

Moody walked quietly throughout the campsite over to Marge. "Listen," Moody said.

"Listen to what? I don't hear anything," Marge said.

"That's just it. The animals are gone. I don't like it—scary." Moody looked around the forest. There were no signs of movement. Something was out there. Before Moody could say another word, a loud, howling cry startled them.

"What was that?" Marge asked.

"It came from over there," Moody said, pointing to an opening the woods. He held his spear tightly with both hands, ready to launch it. Marge followed him through the bushes. She whispered, "I see something moving over there."

Everyone in the camp was awakened by the loud cry. They rushed over to Marge and Moody.

"What's out there?" Lance asked.

"I don't know but it's moving closer to us," Marge said.

"It's a Wolfling," Dr. Ram spoke softly.

"Yes, a Wolfling," Nadia said shaking. She couldn't help but think back to the night it almost captured her and Aman. Once again they will have to face this menacing animal. "We have to get out of here."

Everyone gathered around Dr. Ram. "We have no place to go. It will track us down." He said. "It's a wolf during the day. At night it turns into a large beast. It can destroy us before it changes back into a wolf."

"It sounds like something out of a horror movie." Mia said, holding her spear tightly.

"Hold on, you want us to believe there's something roaming around out there like a werewolf? That's a little hard to believe," Lee said.

Another loud, howling cry was heard, made by a gigantic, reddish-brown wolf at least ten feet tall, with large red eyes. The Wolfling jumped out the bushes and then turned its head slowly. He looked at them as if deciding who would be his first victim. Lee aimed his spear at the enormous wolf. He turned to Dr. Ram. "I believe you now."

Lance aimed his spear at the Wolfling. He watched the wolf's movement. Lee moved over to Lance. "We need a plan… now!" Lee said, keeping his eyes on the animal.

Moody and Aman aimed their spears at the Wolfling. They moved slowly over to Lance and Lee. Everything was happening so fast. Mia wanted to use her powers but Dr. Ram said, no. She couldn't kill it that way. The wolf lashed out at them. Everyone was ready to take action.

"Not so quick," Dr. Ram said. "You have to strike the Wolfling in its heart to kill it. You have to get closer to it and that would be too dangerous. It's best to keep it busy until daybreak. It will change back into a wolf—about thirty minutes."

"Then we'll keep it busy," Lance said. "Mia…take Dr. Ram, Nadia and Marge into the woods and hide."

Mia led Marge, Nadia and Dr. Ram into the woods. "Hurry," she said to them. They hid behind a tree. The men shot their arrows at the Wolfling to stall for time. Mia looked back at Lance, Lee, Moody and Aman. There was no way she was going to let them fight the Wolfling without her. She told Dr. Ram and the women to stay hidden. She had to go back.

Mia joined the men. They continued to shoot their arrows at the Wolfling. But they only had a few arrows left. It was obvious they would be completely out before the Wolfling changed back into a wolf.

"We can't hold it off much longer," Lee shouted. "This is my last arrow."

"We're all out," Moody said, looking at the others. "Run to the closest tree and climb as high as you can."

They all ran to the nearest tree, with the Wolfling close behind. Moody paused to give the others more time to get up the tree. He turned to the Wolfling. "Come on...Get me," he shouted, running around the giant wolf until it made its move toward him.

Moody ran to the tree. He climbed a few feet up it but lost his balance and fell. The Wolfling lashed out at Moody but missed him. It raised its sharp claws again. Lance jumped from the tree onto the beast's back. He held on tightly to the Wolfling's neck as it twisted and turned, trying to shake him off.

The creature slung Lance off its back onto the ground. His spear fell out of his reach. The Wolfling turned toward him, bent over with its mouth wide open. Mia, Aman and Lee jumped from the tree to help Lance. They threw stones at the Wolfling attracting his attention to give Lance time to grab his spear. The creature's sharp claw reached out for Lance. He aimed his spear at the creature and with great force he launched it sending it into its heart. Its huge body plunged to the ground and disintegrated. Everyone ran to Lance and embraced him.

"We better move on," Dr. Ram said.

"I agree. The sooner the better. I have no desire to crash here another night," Lee said.

***

Oman's Temple

From outside an opening in the temple's wall Ivor saw Oman seated at a big wooden table with bowls of fruits and berries piled on it. Across from him was Advar, his mouth stuffed with grapes.

Oman drank from an oversized metal cup. Half of the drink flowed out of his mouth down his chin and onto his clothes. A servant moved quietly into the room, carrying a tray with an abundance of food.

Advar said, "I'm amazed the intruders made it to the river."

"Let's see if they make it across before the Sea Monster devours them... I will send my birds to rescue them if they agree to tell me where the machine is."

"Maybe it's time you made an appearance," Advar said. He smiled and wiped his mouth with his hand.

Hearing this, Ivor quickly flew off.

CHAPTER EIGHT

The teenagers and their persistent friends made their way through the forest. They looked up to see, someone riding on a bird flying towards them. Dr. Ram recognized it was Oman.

"It's Oman. Let's hear what he has to say," Dr. Ram said.

The bird carrying Oman stopped close to them. "Don't be afraid, I wish you no harm. I am Oman, ruler of Citadel."

"I know who you are," Dr. Ram spoke out.

"It surprises me you're still alive. I thought you had taken your last breath like the others." Oman said, looking at Dr. Ram and slightly grinning.

"It'll be one surprise among many you have yet to experience." Dr. Ram shouted, shielding his eyes from the glare of the sun shining through the mist.

"All you had to do was tell me where the machine was hidden. Besides, it's no good to you without the key. There is no reason why we all can't go to your world together," Oman said.

"Do you really think we would tell you where the machine is hidden?" Dr. Ram said angrily. "We might as well put our hands in a pit of rattlesnakes."

"Those people lost their lives because they made a bad choice. I hope these people are wiser," Oman said.

"We know you will never turn the key over to us. We'd rather take our chances out here. We won't allow you to make slaves out of us. We'll build a colony of our own. Maybe your people will join us."

"I take care of my people," Oman said with a mean look on his face.

"If you didn't have those birds, your people would have left you long ago," Dr. Ram said. "Because you control those vicious birds, they could never live in peace. But we will fight them, you and your army"

"I know what you're planning... A word to all. There will be death bestowed on anyone who attempts to steal the key."

"Let's capture him now," Lance whispered.

"I'm afraid that would only alert his guards," Dr. Ram said, "and they would move the key. We would never find it."

Mia looked up. Several Eglipses circled above them. "He's not alone," she said.

"You must ask yourselves why you are here. Was it a freak of nature, some mishap, or perhaps it was your destiny?" Oman said.

Lance shouted, "Whatever brought us here is nothing compared to our determination to leave."

"We will conquer your forest and creatures... We will return home," Lee shouted.

"Yes," they all shouted.

In an intimidating voice Oman said, "The choice is yours and may I add your time is running out... you haven't crossed the river yet." Oman climbed back on his bird and laughed as the bird carried him away.

They rested there for the night. Dr. Ram told the others the only way to cross the river was to make their way farther down the riverbank and cross over the bridge. Early the next morning, before daybreak, they made their way to the river. Dr. Ram warned them the river looked peaceful but it was the home of a deadly Sea Monster.

Lance walked to the bridge, followed by the men. He checked the worn ropes that supported the bridge. He felt if they moved lightly it should support their weight. Moody suggested they redo the ropes to strengthen them.

Several oversized gators entered the water near them. Lance and the other men worked on the bridge. One of the gators stopped and looked over in their direction.

"Let's speed this up before we become their dinner," Moody told the others.

"Good idea," Aman said, looking at the gator's large teeth.

"Agreed," Dr. Ram said.

Nadia, Marge and Mia stopped along the riverbank. They dunked their faces in the water. Nadia looked around the riverbank for anything threatening. They removed their long robes. Their undergarments clung to them from the sweat generated from their bodies. Nadia was an excellent swimmer and decided to swim out into the water to cool off. "I am going to take a quick swim. Anyone else coming?"

"I'm with you," Mia said, eager to cool off.

"Be careful. Make it quick," Marge said to Mia and Nadia. She felt uneasy about them going into the river.

Nadia and Mia leaped into the water. They swam a short distance and playfully splashed water on each other. Nadia dove under the water. She came back up holding her face. She screamed out. Her face, arms and chest were covered with leeches. Mia swam over and helped her out of the water. She laid her down on the river bank. Everyone ran over to them. Lee held her up while Dr. Ram looked closely at the leeches on her body. "Don't worry, Nadia. You're going to be fine," Dr. Ram said. He looked closely at the leeches on her body. "I'm going to remove the leeches. It's going to sting a little?"

Aman held her hand tightly. She flinched as Dr. Ram pulled the leeches off her body. Mia grabbed her backpack lying on the side of the riverbank and took out ointment. She rubbed it on Nadia's wounds. Suddenly, the earth shook beneath them. Everyone looked toward the forest, where tree branches flew into the air as something powerful made its way to the lake.

"Everyone take cover in the bushes," Lance said.

They waited anxiously in the tall bushes. Aman and Lee held onto Nadia. "Everything is going to be okay, "Aman said reassuringly to her.

"Quiet, everyone. Don't make sound," Lance said.

A huge dinosaur, with a long neck protruding from its massive body, moved out of the forest. Its heavy legs pounded the earth as it made its way to the river and immersed its face in the water. Suddenly, the Sea Monster, a gigantic snake with a large oversized head, sharp teeth and long glistening body, appeared from the river, face to face with the Dinosaur. Neither of the two deadly creatures made a move.

The loud, disturbing noises made by them were heard throughout the forest. The Sea Monster and the dinosaur engaged in a terrifying battle. Dr. Ram knew this might be their only chance to make it across the bridge. He told everyone to move quickly to the bridge.

Lance, Moody and Aman rushed ahead of the others to the bridge. They tried not to draw attention to themselves from the gators that had situated themselves along the riverbank. They stood on the weak, wobbly wooden bridge to see if it would support them.

They realized it would only hold one person at a time. With any luck, they would all make it across before the fight of the two vicious monsters ended and the winner turned to them. Lance went first, so he could secure the rope on the other side. He walked slowly and cautiously across the bridge. A few loose planks fell into the river. He made it to the other side and held the rope tightly. He looked over to see the Sea Monster struggling to wrap itself around the dinosaur's neck.

He signaled the others to cross the bridge. Mia, Marge and Nadia went first. Lee would be last. Marge stepped on a loose plank. Her leg fell through the opening. She was stuck. Moody told Mia and Nadia to keep moving. He moved carefully to Marge and tried to untangle her leg from the rope.

Everything went silent. The fight between the Sea Monster and dinosaur had ended with the Sea Monster wrapping its endless body around the dinosaur squeezing the life out of it. Now the snake turned its attention to the bridge. Its long, sleek body moved in and out of the water toward the bridge, displaying its large head and sharp fangs.

Dr. Ram and Aman stepped onto the bridge. They walked cautiously to Moody and Marge. One of the worn ropes holding the bridge began to separate. Mia, Lance and Nadia feared the worst.

"Hurry, hurry," they shouted from the riverbank. The rope gave way. The bridge dangled, with Moody, Marge, Dr. Ram, Aman and Lee holding on tightly.

Everyone hollered. The Sea Monster opened its mouth, ready to scoop them up. They let go of the rope. Suddenly, five graceful golden birds flew swiftly to them. Each one of the birds caught one of them. The Sea Monster, angered, stretched its long body out of the water. He watched the birds carry off his prey.

The golden birds carried them to the other side of the river to join Lance, Mia and Nadia. They hugged each other.

"Where did those golden birds come from?" Mia asked, astonished by what happened.

"I don't know where they came from but their timing couldn't been better," Lee said. Ivor flew over to them.

"How did you find us?" Mia asked.

Ivor explained, "I was on my way back from Oman's temple and I flew into my friends. They saw you on the river where the Sea Monster lives. We knew that couldn't be good so we headed to the bridge."

"And not a minute too soon. Thanks Ivor," Moody said, patting him on his furry little head.

"Yes, thanks Ivor," everyone said. "You saved us from the Sea Monster."

"You are a wise owl," Marge said.

They all sat around in a circle and listened to Ivor tell them what he found out at Citadel. He turned to Dr. Ram. "You were right, Dr. Ram. Oman is not a man of his word. He has no intention of taking anyone to your world but himself and possibly his vulgar servant. We'd better continue on with our plans. The sooner we get there, the better."

They moved quickly toward Citadel. The chatter of the animals was heard all around them. Mia talked to Ivor. "The forest is very alive."

"They're spreading the word that you are here. They don't know if you are a threat to them."

Dr. Ram spoke out, "Let's rest here tonight. We don't have much farther to go before we reach Citadel. We'll leave before daybreak; it will be safer to approach the colony at night. There is a stream up ahead. We can wash and fill our containers with water."

"That makes sense. Oman's birds won't see us," Moody said, nodding his head in agreement.

Herds of antelopes, zebras, elephants and horses passed briskly by them. Mia watched the wild horses. She looked at Lance and Lee. "Anyone up for a horseback ride?"

"Can you ride a horse, Mia?" Lance asked.

"I don't know," Mia answered. "It couldn't be difficult."

"You know, Mia... you're from Manhattan, not Texas. The only thing you've ever ridden is the subway," Lance said.

"Well, I say we go for it," Lee said eagerly.

"Okay, let's do it," Lance said hesitantly.

They took off running behind the horses until they got close enough to leap on their backs. The horses carried them swiftly amidst the herd of wild animals through the open field. What a ride they thought, until suddenly their horses made a turn down a very dense path of thickly entwined branches.

The horses reared back on their hind legs to keep from running into the cluster of tree branches. The three teenagers were thrown off their horses. Lance looked over at Mia. "Any more ideas?"

"You have to admit, it was fun while it lasted," Mia said. She looked over at Lee, who was looking toward the bushes. "What is it, Lee?"

"Listen," Lee said. They moved close to the bushes. They could hear the whimpering sounds of animals coming from the other side of the thick branches. The teenagers pulled the branches apart and followed the sounds.

Mia whispered, "It sounds like animals."

"Maybe it's one of Oman's traps," Lee said.

They pushed through the thick branches. They saw animals trapped in the branches that surrounded several large bird eggs.

"This isn't good," Mia said, looking up to see the wings of a large Eglipse circling above them.

"We're in a nest," Lance said. "Let's get out of here."

"First, let's free the animals," Mia insisted.

The teenagers ran quickly to free the horses, birds, zebras, rabbits and other trapped animals. The Eglipse flew down, hovering over its eggs. It turned to see the animals had escaped.

She saw the teenagers and let out a loud anger cry. Mia and Lee followed Lance out of the nest.

The three made their way out of the cave where the three horses waited. They moved at a rapid speed on the horses across the field. The teenagers looked back to see the Eglipse flying toward them.

Mia looked over at her friends and shouted, "I don't think we can outrun it."

"What do you have in mind?" Lee asked.

They stopped. Lance looked back to see the bird gaining on them. Mia stood up and balanced herself on the back of her horse. Lance handed her his bow and arrow. The bird's claw reached down for Mia. She inserted the arrow in the bow and released it, striking the bird, which fell to the ground.

Mia really wished she hadn't had to kill the bird. She wondered what would happen to its babies when they hatched.

"I know what you're thinking," Lance said, "Don't worry; birds have a strong sense of survival."

Maybe they won't be like the ones under Oman's control," Lee said.

"You're right; he probably doesn't know they exist," Mia said, hoping the baby birds would be safe.

CHAPTER NINE

The teenagers returned to the campsite. Everyone asked if they enjoyed their horseback ride. The teenagers looked at each other, knowing this would just be another wild, unbelievable story if they told them. So they decided to keep the events to themselves for now.

"It was wild," Lee said to everyone.

"Moody and I will watch over the camp tonight," Aman said. Mia carried a container of water to Nadia, who rested under a tree. Her face and shoulders were sore from her leech bites. Lee joined them. He looked closely at Nadia's wounds.

"How do you feel?" Lee asked.

"I feel much better; the ointment has taken away most of the pain. The sores should be healed soon."

"You know, there was a time when people only used plants," Mia said.

"Many people in my country still use them," Aman explained.

Lee turned to Aman. "I've watched you practice yoga exercises at sunrise."

"You should try it. You will have greater control of your mental and physical self," Aman said.

"Will it help me kick my opponent's butt in my Karate competitions?" Lee asked.

Aman laughed. "That too."

The night was very quiet—no loud animal sounds, especially howls made by the Wolflings. They gathered around the small fire in the middle of the camp, reassuring themselves everything was going according to plan. Lance, Moody, Marge and Mia continued talking while the others prepared an area to rest for the night.

Lee placed his backpack under Nadia's head to make her comfortable. He began to make a place for himself when he heard a hissing noise. He turned around and saw a snake slithering toward Nadia. "Shush, don't make a move," he mouthed. Lee reached for his spear, resting against a tree. Nadia's eyes opened wide when she saw the snake moving toward her. Her heart began to race. She took a deep breath.

Lee moved fast, landing his spear in the snake's neck. Nadia stood up. She saw more snakes coming out of the forest.

"Snakes! Snakes!" she called out loudly.

Everyone clutched their spears and formed a circle. They stabbed the snakes moving rapidly toward them. Mia lit a tree branch. She used the flaming branch to burn the snakes. Lance and Lee joined her. The others continued to fend them off from the circle. The remaining snakes headed back into the forest to escape the hot flames.

Lee shouted, "Let's surround our camp with fire to keep them away."

"Good idea," Lance said.

They placed fiery branches around the campsite to keep the snakes out. Mia, Lance, Marge and Moody sat together in the middle of the campsite while the others slept.

"I thought what you saw was strange, Moody. But after seeing the things we've seen here in this world, it doesn't seem weird at all," Lance said in a low voice.

"I was beginning to have doubts," Moody said.

"What happened?" Marge asked. "What did you see?"

Moody answered, "I saw something abnormal in the alley near Sam's newsstand. It must have come out of the tunnel."

"What was it?" Marge asked.

"That's something I'm still trying to figure out," Moody said. "All I know is whatever it was, it changed from this lizard-like animal to a strange-looking man."

"Have you seen something weird too?" Mia asked Marge. She could see the concerned expression on her face. What Moody said triggered something inside her.

"No, I haven't seen anything. But I remember hearing something very odd."

Marge said she had overheard a bizarre conversation between two awkward-looking men. The men were slumped over as if they had some type of back problem. She was sitting on the steps of the convenience store near the alley. Her eyes were closed. They probably thought she was asleep. What they were saying didn't make any sense. One of the men told the other one the signal to their lifeline was getting low. They had to come up with a way to strengthen it.

The other man said, "They are working on it every day. They are trying to get the government to fund a project to produce stronger satellite signals." But even more important, they were able to stop the government's top agents from revealing their secret. They were holding them captive in their facility.

"You see, it makes no sense."

Moody said, "No, it doesn't but when you put it all together, it could mean something. I wish I could have seen those men."

"It's still hard to believe our government can't detect foreign elements in our world," Mia said, "especially an alien."

Lance turned to Mia. "Remember the unknown elements we found in the laboratory."

"There could be some connection. But what?" Moody asked.

Dr. Ram joined them. He looked up at the sky. "Look, the moon has traveled in front of the sun, causing a total lunar eclipse."

They were amazed by the sight. They wondered if it could be seen in their world—if it was only one sky. All of a sudden, a flash of light revealed an unusual creature. He was more animal than human. His face was human, his ears pointed. His head, arms and back were covered with fur. He stood on two furry legs with hoofed feet. A tail was attached to his lower back.

They were astonished by the sight of the creature. Ivor knew who this unusual-looking animal was and that he only appeared in times of danger. He told everyone to listen to Orka. He was the overseer of the animals in the forest. He had been there since the beginning of time.

Orka spoke out. "You will be faced with a great challenge and you will have to make a choice. The choice will be whether or not to defeat the most deadly creatures on earth. If you fail they will conquer not just this world but yours as well. Make no mistake, the world's existence is in your hands, your strength and your wisdom... good luck."

The vision of Orka faded away.

They discussed the message from the odd creature, Orka. "Is it possible the beasts Orka talked about could be more deadly than those we've already come in contact with?" Lance asked.

"That's hard to believe," Lee said.

"I think he's referring to something more dangerous. Something very scary," Marge said.

Mia said, "Let's just wait until we are confronted with these creatures. Right now, we don't have a clue."

Everyone agreed with Mia. However, Ivor was deeply concerned. His feathers ruffled. He recalled the frightening stories about the beasts that once hunted the animals in the forest. Luckily, the birds like himself were able to fly out of their reach. He realized this would be a very dangerous encounter for Mia and her friends.

They slept through the night and continued their journey in the early morning before daylight. They stopped to sip water from their containers. Citadel was a short distance ahead. Dr. Ram passed the word to the others to proceed with caution because Oman's men could be in the area. They approached a grassy field outside of Citadel.

They heard loud screams and ducked quickly behind the bushes. They saw two men, a woman, and a girl being chased by several of Oman's Eglipses. They were trying to make their way to the forest.

Mia, Lance, Lee, Aman and Dr. Ram ran to the field to help them. They shot their arrows at the birds. One of them flew away with an arrow embedded in its body. A few fell to the ground.

Moody released his arrow, hitting one of them that was attacking Dr. Ram and one of the men. Mia saw one of the birds hovering over the scared young girl. The Eglipse grabbed the girl with its sharp claws but dropped her on the ground. It tried again but Mia ran over and jabbed its claw with her spear.

The sky darkened. Out of nowhere a forceful wind blew twirling around and around. It sent the birds tumbling over and over until they disappeared. Everyone took cover in a grassy slope until it ended.

The people from Citadel were grateful to the strangers for saving their lives. They all rested on the grassy surface. Quest, in his 20s, muscular, with long dreadlocks, and his wife Sasha, in her mid-twenties with short black curly hair, were anxious to leave Citadel.

They brought Feather with them, a very self-sufficient twelve-year-old girl with two long blond braids and bangs that covered part of her eyes. The other young man from Citadel was Mix. He was Quest's best friend. They grew up together in the colony and shared the belief that one day they would free themselves from the clutches of Oman. This was their first attempt to escape. They didn't anticipate the Eglipses being out before daybreak because of their impaired vision. They now realized Oman sent them to search for the intruders.

"You must move quickly; the Sea Monster is coming," Ivor said hysterically, flying wildly over their heads.

They all jumped up and looked toward the forest. They could see the Sea Monster slithering toward them at a fast pace.

Quest shouted, "Hurry, this way. We have to go back to the Citadel." He took them to a large stone door camouflaged with green foliage. He opened the door leading into a cave. Everyone followed him inside. They piled big rocks against the door to keep the gigantic snake out but it didn't hold.

The Sea Monster's giant head pushed through the door of the cave. Its head shifted from one side to the other, with its opened mouth exposing its sharp teeth. Fearful the Sea Monster would catch them, they ran through the cave.

Mia stopped and turned toward the large snake. She yelled to the others to keep moving. Lance ran back to her. "What are you doing, Mia?"

"I'm the only one that can stop this monster. There's no way we can outrun it."

The Sea Monster slithered closer to them. Lee joined them. "Come on, guys, get out of here. Now!" he said. "Mia, I know what you're planning but there isn't enough time for you to use your power; this thing is right on us."

"He's right," Lance said. "Mia, let's get out of here now."

"We won't make it," Mia said.

"We're out of time," Lance said.

The snake was so close they could smell its offensive odor. Mia stared at the snake; it stared at her. She clutched her fists. Her body trembled. She tried several times to release her powers but it wasn't happening. "I don't know why... I can't do this," she whispered to Lance and Lee.

"Just relax, maybe you're trying too hard," Lance said.

Mia inhaled. Her eyes became fixed. She stared at the giant snake, with her forceful power preventing it from moving forward. Suddenly,the cave gave way, big stones overhead pounded the snake. Lance shook Mia repeatedly. "Snap out of it," Lance said frantically, "before the whole cave comes down on us."

Mia awakened from her trance and saw the lifeless body of the snake trapped under the large stones.

"Come on, guys, move, move," Lee said. He pushed them out of the way of the falling rocks. They rushed to the others huddled together against a wall where dripping water could be heard falling through the cracks in the cave.

They continued on at a fast pace through the wet tunnel until they found themselves overwhelmed by the maddening sounds of wings flapping. A horde of ghastly bats flew toward them. They fought them off with their hands.

Dr. Ram had fallen behind the others. He coughed repeatedly, struggling to keep up. Aman stopped to help him. "How much farther?" Aman called out.

Everyone stopped and looked back at Dr. Ram. The journey had taken a toll on him. Quest walked back to Dr. Ram and Aman. He looked at Dr. Ram, weak and tired. He asked, "Are you well enough to go on? We could rest for a moment."

"Keep moving. I'll be okay," Dr. Ram said, coughing.

Lance and Aman held onto him as they walked slowly behind the others. Finally, they reached the end of the cave. Quest pushed the stone door slightly open. He wiped his wet face from the rain that blew in from the outside. He peeped out to see if any of Oman's guards were in the area. He held the door open and told them all to hurry but beware if they saw any of Oman's guards. He knew his people would be severely punished if discovered. "Hurry! Hurry!" Quest said.

They exited the opening one by one out into the rain. Lee was the last one. He glanced over and saw another cave entrance.

"Where does that lead?" Lee asked Quest.

"It will take you to the machine that will carry you back to your world."

"Yes!" Lee said happily.

"Only a few of us know the machine is here. Oman has been searching for many years to find it," Quest said. "We know if he left, he would turn his vicious birds on us. He would never allow us to live in peace."

"If he did make it to our world, he'd get his butt kicked. No one there would put up with his madness," Lee said.

They all followed Quest down the wet, narrow path behind the structures. They saw one of Oman's guards up ahead on the path and ducked down behind one of the structures. The guard glanced in their direction. He rushed toward them but he was distracted by a barking dog. He bent down and stroked the dog's head and walked back up the path followed by the dog.

Quest signaled everyone to wait. He walked cautiously to one of the structures. He knocked lightly on the door. Hemp, an oversized man in his early sixties, leaning on a large stick, opened the door.

"Is it safe for us to come in?"   Quest asked. "I have other people with me."

Hemp looked around to make sure no one was watching. "Hurry," he said. "We were worried about you."

Quest waved to the others to come quickly. The teenagers and the others from their world followed the people from Citadel into the small dwelling.

"We're glad you weren't harmed by the Eglipses," Nola said, a middle-aged woman with salt and pepper hair standing next to Hemp. They embraced Feather. They were happy to see her but disappointed that she and the others weren't able to escape. They wanted Feather to have a chance to grow up free away from the evil Oman.

Nola looked at Dr. Ram. She could see he was very weak. She led him to a cot and covered him with heavy skins. "I'll get him a warm drink," she said to Mia.

"He's exhausted," Mia said. "Thank you."

"A good night's sleep will do him good," Nola said.

Everyone ate and drank. Nola told them Oman found out some of his people escaped. They were seen in the field but he couldn't figure how they got past the guards.

"It seems some of his birds were destroyed," Hemp said.

"Thanks to the visitors, we're still alive. They attacked us," Mix said.

They continued talking late into the night about their worlds. One thing they all agreed on: Oman had to be removed so they could be free. Feather listened closely. Not in her wildest imagination could she visualize the colony where the visitors came from, called New York City.

The people in the Citadel knew another world existed because over time other visitors had come there. Unfortunately, they were captured by Oman. They still didn't understand how they arrived there. They believed it was magic.

"How far away is New York City?" Feather asked.

"It's a long way," Marge answered. This bright young girl reminded her of Hanna—her smile, her curiosity. Hanna was always asking questions, trying to figure things out. *I know she would have liked Feather,* she thought.

Lee took out his phone. "Look, it's searching for a signal."

"That's amazing," Lance said.

Lee pointed his phone in different directions. "The signal isn't strong enough down here," he said, disappointed.

CHAPTER TEN

*** * ***

Oman's Temple

There was much commotion in the temple. Several of Oman's guards interrupted him while he was eating. "This better be of great magnitude. You come while I eat," Oman shouted at the guards.

One of the guards said, "The intruders are here in Citadel."

Nola dropped a tray of food. "Why must you be so clumsy? Get out, get out," Oman said to Nola. She rushed out of the room and listened from the hallway. Advar walked up behind her. "What are you doing, woman?" he asked harshly.

Surprised by Advar, Nola grabbed her chest and took a deep breath. "Just waiting to clean up a spill," she answered.

"Move on," Advar said nastily. He pushed her aside.

"I'll return later," Nola said.

Advar rushed into the room with Oman and the guards. "What's going on?" he asked.

Oman answered, "It seems I didn't give the intruders enough credit. They're here in our colony. They must possess some kind of magic. Find them and bring them to me. Search every dwelling in Citadel!"

"We'll find them," stuttered Advar. "We will."

"You better," Oman said, knocking a tray of food off the table. Oman's guards stormed the colony. Two of them banged on Hemp's door. Lance and the others moved quickly into the room underneath the floor. Nola and Hemp covered the hole with a a wooden plank that fit tightly over the space.

The guards entered the dwelling. The men shoved the wooden furniture out of their way. Their heavy feet caused debris to fall down into the room below. The people below covered their heads. Dust filled the room. They remained very quiet, trying not to cough or sneeze so the guards wouldn't discover them.

One of the guards noticed the loose plank in the floor that covered the hole. It had apparently loosened from their heavy feet. He leaned over to examine it. Nola rushed over to him hysterically to distract him. She pleaded with him to leave because she had to go to the temple and fix Oman's supper. He would be very upset if his dinner was late and it would be their fault. The guard paused for a moment and walked to the door.

"Let's go," he said to the other guard. "The intruders aren't here."

Being discovered by Oman's guards was the teenagers' greatest fear. They didn't want any harm to come to the people in Citadel. Oman announced he would reward anyone who told him where they were hiding. The person would receive the same rewards as his guards. They would not have to labor in the fields and would receive all of the food they desired. On the other hand, whoever was caught hiding the intruders would be taken to the forest and thrown into one of his traps.

After a few weeks Oman became disgruntled because no one had come forth with news about the intruders. Lance and Lee sat on the floor in the structure with Hemp, sharpening their arrows and spears in case things worsened. Hemp limped over to a pot of boiling water hanging over a small fire. He asked, "Would you two like a warm drink ?" He poured the boiling water over beans similar to a coffee bean.

"Sure," Lance said.

"Count me in too," Lee said. He went over to help Hemp with the drinks. "How did you hurt your leg?"

Hemp sat down with them to tell his story. He broke his leg when he was young like them. He was running in the woods trying to escape from Citadel and fell into one of Oman's animal traps. Fortunately, he said, it was one of the men in the colony who heard his cry and not one of Oman's guards.

"You were lucky," Lance said.

"I was. But I'm afraid...I paid the price of having to work in pain for the next two or three months so the guards wouldn't discover I tried to escape."

A rapid knock on the door interrupted their conversation. Lance and Lee quickly jumped up and headed for the opening in the floor.

"Hold on," Hemp spoke out.

"It's Quest. I know his knock."

Hemp opened the door. Quest was very agitated. He looked around to make sure none of Oman's guards saw him enter the structure.

"You've got to get out of here," he said, walking over to Lance and Lee.

"What's happened," Hemp asked, seeing the disturbed look on Quest's face.

Mia and the others heard the commotion. They climbed up the steps from the room below. "What's going on?" Mia asked.

"Oman has ordered everyone to come to the square. The guards will use the wild dogs to sniff out anyone left behind."

Nola hurried into another room and came out with eight robes. "Here, put these on; many people will be wearing them," Nola said, handing each of them a robe.

"Just keep your hood pulled over your head," Quest added.

They walked unnoticed among the crowd of frightened people to the square outside of Oman's temple. The teenagers spoke softly to each other.

"These people don't deserve to be treated this way," Lance said.

"If he tries to hurt them, we'll have to step up and take our chances," Lee said.

Mia looked over at Dr. Ram. "If anything happens to us, take Marge and Nadia back to the structure and stay hidden."

"Okay, just be careful, Mia. The man's a lunatic," Dr. Ram replied.

The guards grasped the ropes tightly restraining the vicious dogs. People scurried out of their reach as they lunged out at them. Oman stood on a podium between two restless Eglipses.

"It won't be much longer before we find the intruders. And when we do, I will find out who has been harboring them. They will pay the price," Oman shouted.

Oman watched a couple of his guards make their way through the crowd of people. He raised his voice. "Where are the intruders?"

Mia turned to Lance. "This doesn't look good."

"That's an understatement," Lance said, looking around at the frightening scene.

The guards reached Oman's podium. One of them spoke out nervously over the wild barking dogs. He hesitated, as if he didn't want any part of what was going on. Maybe Oman's guards were also afraid of him.

"The intruders are nowhere to be found. We have searched the whole area." Oman was outraged. He hit his fist against the podium. The birds began to cry out. The dogs barked. They jerked their chains. People backed away in fear of what Oman might do. They knew he was mad enough to turn the dogs loose.

"Keep your eye on the guards with the dogs," Lance whispered to Mia and Lee.

Mia walked slowly through the crowd of hysterical people. Feather reached out for her. "Don't go, Mia."

"I'll be okay," Mia said. "Stay here with Nola. If there's trouble get out of here as fast as you can."

Oman shouted, "I'll give you a few seconds to tell me where the intruders are, or I will release the dogs."

Lance and Lee caught up with Mia.

"I think he's bluffing. The last thing he wants to do is lose any of his men. Who would work on his temple?" Lance said.

"I wouldn't put anything past him," Lee said.

"Look around at these people. They're scared to death. We can't take that chance," Mia said.

Moody, Aman, Quest and Mills joined them.

"What's the plan?" Moody asked.

"Get the people out of here. Now! He may be foolish enough to order his guards to release the dogs," Mia answered.

The men shouted to the people to run back to their homes and lock themselves in. Oman looked over at the guards with the dogs. The mean look on his face said it all. He was going to turn those wild dogs on his own people.

Mia stepped closer to the podium. She activated her powers, causing a forceful wind that sent dust rising from the ground. Oman and all those near him were blinded. Oman struggled to get up. He could barely see. He made his way back to the temple. "My eyes, my eyes," he grumbled.

CHAPTER ELEVEN

The next day was peaceful. Oman was in his temple with cold rags on his burning eyes. No one knew what he would do next.

The teenagers, their companions and the people of Citadel made a plan to get the key from Oman's temple. Nola was one of Oman's servants. She prepared his meals. Lance would accompany her to the temple wearing a robe to conceal his identity. He would carry with him a mixture prepared by Mia that would put Oman to sleep.

Ivor would watch from an opening in the temple and alert the others when to move in and overtake the guards. Taking them by surprise would allow them more time to escape before Oman sent his Eglipses after them.

In order to be successful they had to become skilled warriors. It would just be a few of them against Oman's army. They practiced in a remote area near the structures. Ivor, perched on a tree branch, watched for any signs of the guards. Lined up side by side Moody, Marge, Nadia, Aman, Lee, Lance and Mia stood together like soldiers in boot camp.

Feather stood behind them and watched them shoot their arrows. She began to practice with them. They were determined. They realized this might be their only chance to get the key. They released their arrows, one after another, until they could hit a mark carved on a tree.

Nadia had trouble positioning her arrow. Lee rushed over to help her. Nervously, he put his arms around her to steady her aim. "Relax and focus. Hold your bow a little higher."

"Like this?" Nadia asked.

"Yes," Lee said, watching her closely.

She pulled back on the arrow and released it. The arrow landed on the mark. She jumped with joy and gave Lee a high-five. He teased her. "You're almost as good as me," he said.

A few weeks passed. They were all well prepared. It was time to finalize their plan. Transformed into warriors, they stood firm with painted faces made out of red dirt and signs on their arms and body created from thick mud. Bows and arrows hung on their sides and they carried spears in their hands.

Their attention was on Lance. They listened intently to him. "We are now an army... We will fight Oman and his guards and free the people of Citadel."

"We will get the key from Oman and return home," Lee spoke out. "We are warriors."

Mia held up her spear. She repeated the phrase, "We are fierce, fearless and forever together." They all raised their spears to show they were united.

Lance and Nola went to the temple. Lance wore a hooded robe. He kept his head lowered to conceal his face from the guards. He carried a potion made by Mia to put in Oman's food.

Nola and Lance were in a room preparing Oman's food. Nola tried to steady her s h a k y hands. She watched for the guards while Lance mixed the potion into Oman's pottage. She took a deep breath to calm herself and wiped her sweaty hands on her dress. If anything went wrong, Oman would surely make them pay the price. She hesitated for a moment at the door where Oman impatiently sat at his table.

Oman saw Nola standing at the door. He turned to her and said, "Well, woman, don't just stand there; bring me my food."

Nola placed the bowl of pottage in front of him. She spilled a small amount on the table and apologized hoping her behavior didn't raise suspicion. He swallowed a few spoonfuls of the mixture and nodded his head. "Good, good," he said. His eyes slowly closed. His face fell into the bowl. Nola called Lance. They propped him up in his chair to make it look like he was sleeping.

"We'd better hurry," Nola said.

The air was cold and chilly. Mia, Lee and their skilled companions chanted, "We are fierce, fearless, and forever together," as they walked swiftly down the path that led to Oman's temple. They walked past the stone structures. You could hear the doors shut behind them as they went by.

Mia and her companions hid behind a cluster of trees outside the temple so the guards wouldn't see them. They waited for Ivor to alert them.

Inside the temple Nola and Lance walked carefully down the hallway. They looked back to see if any guards were behind them. The sounds of the Eglipses became louder as they got closer to the room.

Suddenly, two guards appeared. They walked toward them. Nola told Lance to keep his head down. The guards approached them. Lance turned his head to the side.

One of the guards asked, "What are you doing here?"

"Showing the new servant around," Nola answered.

"With whose permission?" the guard asked.

"Advar gave permission," Nola said with a firm tone.

"Make it quick," the guard said.

The guards continued down the hallway. One of them glanced back with a bewildered look on his face. Nola and Lance entered the room. They saw Ivor perched on the window ledge above the restless birds. The birds wandered back and forth near the altar. They had to get the birds away from the altar in order to get the key.

Lance slipped out of his robe, exposing his warrior attire. The birds looked at their unfamiliar faces. They pulled hard on their chains to free themselves. Lance used his spear to push the birds back into the corner. They lashed out at him, their sharp claws barely missing him. Nola hurried over to the box on the altar that held the key.

"Get the key. Now! Now!" Lance said. He fought hard to keep both birds from attacking himself and Nola.

Nola struggled to remove the box. She became frustrated. "I can't remove the box."

Lance pointed to a rock on the floor. "Take the rock and break the glass," he said forcefully.

Nola picked up the rock and hit the box, shattering the glass. She grabbed the key. They turned to leave and found themselves face to face with two guards whose swords were pointed at them. Lance was ready to take them on. "All we want is the key," Lance said.

The guards looked at them and laughed. "All he wants is for us to let them walk away with the key," one of the guards said. "A key that doesn't belong to them." He laughed. "I don't think Oman would think kindly of us if we let you take his key."

"I'll tell you what. Come with us and we'll ask him," said the other guard.

The two guards chuckled as they lashed their swords at Lance and Nola. Lance jumped in front of Nola. The birds tried harder to free their feet from the chains attached to the floor.

"I don't think that's going to happen," Lance said. He struck both guards in their hands with his fast moves, causing them to drop their swords on the floor. Nola pulled Lance's arm. She pointed to one of the birds that had freed itself.

The guards unable to escape grabbed their swords to fight the freed bird.

"Let's get out of here," Lance called out. Ivor flew away to tell the others it was time to converge on the temple.

"Just a minute. There's something we must do," Nola said, giving the key to Lance. "The children—we have to get them."

"Where are they?" Lance asked.

"Follow me," Nola said. She led him cautiously down the hall to a room where several children were huddled together. She rushed over to them. "Come quickly, children—hurry." The children ran quickly down the hallway with Lance and Nola.

Lee, Moody, Aman, Nadia, Marge and Mia fought aggressively to overcome the guards. The guards began to back away. Lee's fast movements of his hands and legs knocked several of them to the ground. Mia picked up one of the fallen guards' sword and forcefully moved toward several more of the men. A few of the guards sped off. They realized they were no match for the young warriors.

Nadia and Aman entered the Temple to find Lance and Nola. Two servants ran by them. Nadia and Aman could see Lance, Nola and the children running toward them. Nadia waved to them. "Over here. Hurry!" she said, trying not to attract the attention of the guards shouting for Advar.

The temple was in turmoil. Advar appeared. "What's going on?" he asked the guards in a demanding tone. "We're under attack. The intruders have taken the key," said the guard angrily.

Advar went searching for Oman. He found him sleep in his chair. "Oman, Oman, wake up."

Oman slowly awakened, slightly dizzy and drowsy. He realized something had happened to him. He lashed out at Advar. "Stop shouting you numbskull; can't you see someone put a spell on me?"

"I'm afraid that's not all that has happened. The intruders have taken the key."

Oman was furious at hearing the key had been taken. "Get my key back." he said angrily. "I should have my birds whisk you away. It was your duty to protect me."

"It wasn't my fault...someone betrayed you. Don't worry, the intruders won't get far... the Eglipses will stop them."

"Capture those thieves. They will pay with their lives. If you fail, I will have no choice but to unleash the Spoilers."

"If you free those creatures, they will take revenge on us for letting them stay trapped in the earth."

"I'm not worried. I'll tell them we searched all over for them and it wasn't until the earth opened up that we were able to find them. They'll never know we knew where they were trapped."

Advar sped out of the room to release the birds. He knew Oman would do the unthinkable—release the Spoilers. They would surely come after them. Someone would tell them the truth—most likely someone in Citadel, to get even with Oman. He remembered what Oman told him about the Spoilers and how he came to possess the key.

He was a servant to the Spoiler Titus, the ruler of the world. Titus lived in a large dome. It was big enough to house his large, awkward body. He was surrounded by other animals like himself. The humans were his slaves. Titus put him in charge of the humans and gave him power over the Eglipses to control them.

One day a loud rumbling noise was heard. The earth shook violently. It shifted, and one part began to rise over the other, taking people and animals with it. Trees toppled over. Rivers overflowed. A great hole formed under Titus's dome, swallowing him and a few Spoilers. They were trapped in the earth.

Oman became the ruler in their world. He continued to use the Eglipses to threaten the people in Citadel. He had everything he wanted. It was not until a few years later that he discovered there were intruders among them—people from another world. They had arrived there some mysterious way and were secretly building machines that would carry them back to their world. A world of riches he had heard.

He later learned one of the machines that was hidden in a cave had successfully carried people back to the other world. And somewhere out there was a key that unlocked the door to it. Oman felt someone in Citadel knew the whereabouts of this machine and key. He starved them for weeks, hoping someone would come forth and tell him who had the key and where this magical machine was hidden but no one did.

One day, the people of Citadel decided to carry out a plan to free themselves from Oman. The uprising was swift and brief. The weapons used by the men and women in Citadel were no match for Oman's army of men with sharp swords. They were defeated and taken back to their structures.

While walking through the field after the battle Oman looked down and saw a rather odd-looking key on a chain lying on the dirt. It apparently fell off the neck of one of the men in Citadel. There were no keys in the colony—there was no use for them. Oman realized it had to be the key to the machine. He was very happy to find it. He wanted to go to the other world and share in its wealth but first he had to find out where the machine was hidden.

CHAPTER TWELVE

Lance ran with the others down the narrow path through the structures. He held the key tightly in his hand. The wild birds lashed their vicious claws out to capture them. They shot their arrows to fend them off, but there were too many. Nadia and Nola ran with the children to keep them out of the reach of the birds.

The men from Citadel rushed out of their structures to help them. With their spears in their hands they joined the fight. The fight was loud and fierce. The birds were defeated. One after another fell to the ground.

"We did it," they all shouted and embraced each other.

It was a battle fought gallantly by all. Their plan was successful. They had the key. Even Ivor received a pat on the head. They made their way to Nola and Hemp's structure. They were happy no one was badly injured. Hemp was worried the guards would capture Nola. He hugged her tightly.

They celebrated with food and beverages—joy and laughter filled the room.

"I don't think we have to worry about Oman. He knows he's been defeated. We wiped out his army and most of his birds," Lee said jovially, holding a cup of ale.

"Oman is somewhere in the temple with Advar," Quest said.

"We'll find him and see that he gets the punishment he deserves," Hemp said firmly.

"We'll banish him," Mix said, smiling.

The Citadel people clapped their hands. They were happy to be free for the first time. A loud knock on the door interrupted their celebration. Everyone watched Nola open the door. A man stood uneasily in the doorway, looking around. He handed Nola a piece of paper and swiftly took off. Nola recognized him as one of Oman's guards. Nola opened the paper.

"It's from Oman."

"What does it say?" Mia asked, showing deep concern, along with the others in the room.

Nola's voice trembled as she read the message out loud. "If the intruders don't come forth and return the key, I will set free the most frightening and terrifying beasts that ever roamed the earth... the Spoilers... your time is running out."

"I'm afraid the worst is still in front of us," Dr. Ram said, angrily hitting his fist against the table.

Lance questioned Dr. Ram. "What are the Spoilers?"

"From what I've heard, they are beasts that have been trapped in the earth for a long time," Dr. Ram answered.

"All we know is the Spoilers are trapped beneath the earth in the forest. But apparently Oman knows where." Quest said. "Before the earth divided these animals ruled the world. If Oman releases them they will rule again."

"It will be worse than living under Oman's rule," Mix said.

Dr. Ram looked at Mia, Lance and Lee. "You have to make a choice," Dr. Ram told the teenagers. "You can stay here and try to defeat the Spoilers or leave now. Keep in mind this may be your only chance to return home."

"Whatever you decide, we will help you. We are grateful to you and understand if you want to return to your world," Quest said.

Everyone shook their head in agreement. Feather walked slowly over to them. "It's okay for you to go home," she said sadly.

"And leave you with those wild beasts out there? I don't think so," Lee said to Feather, looking down at her watery eyes.

"How can we stop them?" Lance asked.

"I don't know," Hemp said.

"First we have to find them," Mia said.

Ivor tumbled to the ground. "Besides Oman, there is only one other person who would know where to find them—Orka."

"Where can we find him?" Mia asked.

"Take the path west through the woods," Ivor said. "It will lead you to a soaring mountain. You will find Orka on the mountaintop."

Lee turned to Mia and Lance. "We can do this," he said.

They nodded their heads in agreement. They placed their bow and arrows on their shoulders and picked up their spears.

Mia looked around at everyone. "I guess we've made our choice."

Lee could see the worried look on Nadia's face. "I hope you understand our decision," he murmured to her.

"I wouldn't expect anything less," Nadia said, taking off her colorful bracelet. She placed it on Lee's wrist.

"You're giving me your bracelet...I've never seen you without it," Lee said, puzzled by her actions. He knew the bracelet was special to her.

"It will protect you if you believe in it," she said.

"Thanks," Lee said.

The three young warriors left the dwelling and headed west down the path through the woods. They wondered how they would be received by Orka — after all, they were strangers to him. Mia felt anxious, her heart raced, and beads of sweat trickled down her face. Her telekinetic powers were surfacing. She stopped and raised her hands to her head. Lance put his arms around her.

"Look at me, Mia. You can control this feeling."

"I'll try," Mia said, looking up into Lance's eyes.

"You can control this feeling," Lance insisted.

Mia took a few deep breaths, and the feeling slowly passed over. "Let's go... we don't have much time," she said with a sense of urgency.

The three teenagers moved rapidly through the forest. They shoved tree branches out of the way to keep them from scratching their faces. They heard the distressing sounds of animals in the forest. The heavy mist rising from the ground made it hard for the teenagers to see them. They moved closer to the creepy sounds. They saw frail animals roaming among carcasses.

Some of them lay on the ground, barely breathing. Some of the stronger ones hovered over the frail and dying ones: dinosaurs, big cats, antelopes, horses, birds, dragons and other animals they couldn't identify.

The animals didn't move. Their eyes followed them. The teenagers watched in disbelief.

"Wow, this is too real," Lee said.

"It's an animal cemetery," Lance said.

Ghostly images from the animals lying on the ground rose and faded away. Mia tried hard to understand what was going on. "Could those scary images be spirits?" she asked.

"That's what it looks like," Lee answered. "The only person that would possibly have an explanation for this would be my grandfather."

"Think about it—this place is near Orka's domain," Mia said. "He is the overseer of the forest, which makes him also the overseer of the animals that live here."

"They come here to make their transition to the spiritual world and they do it together in peace," Lee added.

They slowly passed the animal cemetery. They looked back at the animals. It seemed they had gone back to attending to their own. Once again the three teenagers traveled rapidly through the forest making up for the time they lost.

Asteroids shot down from the sky. The rocky objects' impacts were so strong they caused explosions when they hit the earth. They left deep craters in the ground. The sky lit up bright gold and orange. Animals stampeded by them. The teenagers ducked and dodged a big hot rock rolling toward them. "Asteroid," Mia yelled.

"The last major one was 65 million years ago," Lance yelled above the loud noise of the rocks hitting the earth. The stampedes of the wild animals left a trail of thick of dust behind them.

Lee called, "Look! That colossal dinosaur is heading in our direction."

"It's a Tyrannosaurus rex," Lance said.

"No, it's an Allosaurus—its head is too small to be a T- rex," Mia argued.

Lee couldn't believe his friends were arguing. "Really guys, could we focus on the fact this three-ton dinosaur is only a few feet away from us?"

Mia glanced at a big hollow tree trunk. "Come on! Hurry! Get into the tree trunk. He can't reach us in there."

The three quickly removed their bows and arrows and climbed into the tree trunk. Mia was in the middle. "Push the trunk backward with your spears," Mia said.

They used all their force to move the trunk. It slid – but stopped.

"Push harder. Keep it moving. It's right on us," Lance said, struggling.

The enormous dinosaur continued to follow them. It knocked trees out of its way to reach the teenagers. Its large foot stepped on the spot where just moments before the tree trunk stood. The trunk was only a short distance away from a rocky embankment overlooking a river. The dinosaur stopped and turned back. It must have sensed the danger.

The teenagers pressed their spears hard on the ground to stop it from sliding. It stopped for a moment but continued to slide toward the embankment.

"Trade places with me," Mia said frantically to Lance. The embankment was only a short distance away. She saw a tree standing near it.

"What are you thinking?" Lance asked.

"We can't jump out of it while it's moving," Lee said.

"Press the spear hard against the ground. Keep the trunk still as long as you can—enough time for me to use my powers to make that tree fall across the path," Mia said, "then get ready for a large bump."

Lance and Lee pressed their spears against the hard ground. The trunk stopped sliding. Mia stuck her head out of the trunk. She stared at the tree. It broke in half, falling on their path. Lance and Lee struggled to keep the trunk from moving. It was too heavy. It started to slide again. They braced themselves as the trunk hit the tree, causing it to flip over landing on the edge of the embankment.

"Climb out slowly. We're on the edge," Lee said, hoping they would make it out of the trunk before it plunged downward into the river. They moved slowly. Mia was last. Just as her body cleared the trunk, it dived downward into the murky water. They watched it float away.

"That was close," Lance said.

"Too close," Mia said.

They walked back to the path, gathered up their bows and arrows and continued on their way. Lance and Mia resumed their debate on the dinosaur.

"I see the mountain. We don't have much farther to go. If we hurry, we can make it before dark," Lee said.

CHAPTER THIRTEEN

At last, they reached the mountain. They placed their feet on the jagged rocks and climbed. They gave each other a reassuring look. It was just a matter of time before they would reach the top. Mia thought back to her rock climbing class she took at the YMCA. She wasn't really crazy about climbing that wall either but at least she had a belt on. This was a totally different experience for her. One slip and she would find herself at the bottom.

Lance and Lee were side by side a few feet a head of her. Halfway up, Lee stopped and looked over at the vast forest. "What a fantastic view. Incredible."

"Unbelievable," Lance said. "I wish I could take a picture and send it to my mother."

"That would be cool," Lee said.

"I was never one for heights. I'll check it out once I get my feet on the ground," Mia said.

Sweat trickled down their faces. It was a long climb but they did it. Mia was the last one to place her feet on the mountaintop. In front of them stood Orka's dwelling. It was a wide area separated by walls of rocks. Orka's furry back and tail faced them. The teenagers walked slowly to him.

Orka turned to them. "I see you made your choice?"

"Yes, we have. We need your help to find the Spoilers." Mia said. She glanced around his unique dwelling.

"Oman is going to release the Spoilers," Lee said. "We can't let that happen."

"We have to stop him," Lance said.

"The people in Citadel will never be free as long as Oman uses these creatures to threaten them," Mia explained, moving closer to Orka.

"What makes you think you can defeat the Spoilers? Many have tried and failed," Orka explained. "The Spoilers were among the first to roam the earth. One day something unexplainable happened. Light faded into darkness every day but one day darkness stayed. Evil spirits came out of the earth and attached themselves to these animals, causing them to be vengeful.

"Neither man nor our strongest animals could defeat them. They controlled the world and destroyed everyone who disobeyed their command. No one was spared—frightened animals ran through the forest, fearful they would be captured by them. I provided a safe place to protect them from the Spoilers.

The most shocking thing Orka revealed was that when the earth divided, all the Spoilers didn't get trapped in the earth—only a few. The others that weren't destroyed ended up on their part of the earth in their world, which meant they live among them. A lifeline keeps them alive, allowing them to change into human form. The lifeline was hidden in their world.

"Beware of them," Orka stated.

The teenagers were stunned to hear the Spoilers were in their world. Mia looked at Lance and Lee. "It's unbelievable that none of our greatest scientists were aware of these creatures—or maybe they were, and couldn't prove it."

"Remember as you grow and learn, everything can't be explained. Just because you can't prove something doesn't mean it didn't happen," Orka said.

"No one in our world would believe this anyway," Lee said. "I'm still trying to wrap my head around it."

"Follow the owl. I will show him the way to the Spoilers. It will take you too long by foot. When daylight comes, my fastest moving four-legged animals will take you through the forest back to Citadel."

Being on top of a soaring mountain with a unique mystical creature that commanded respect from all those who inhabited his forest was by far the teenagers' most unthinkable experience. They were captivated by the many fossils displayed in Orka's living quarters.

"Wow, look at all these animal skeletons. They're everywhere," Lee said. He walked slowly through the spacious room, followed by Mia and Lance. Mia looked at an enormous dinosaur skeleton hanging from a rock next to two other skeletons, a large bird and some unidentifiable animal. Orka shuffled over to them.

"These are the undefeatable ones, the strongest of them all," he said. He looked admiringly at the skeletons.

"The champions," Lee said. "The strongest do survive."

"I guess that's how your world would see them," Orka said. He looked down at the teenagers. His tail shifted from one side to the other. Mia thought, *Orka may be scary looking but he is very gentle, completely opposite from Oman.* Mia looked up into his eyes. "I know you have the ability to know things others don't. I have something to ask you. I hope you have the answer."Orka extended his furry hand to Mia. She reached out and placed her hand in his. His hand felt like her grandmother's old fur coat. It was very soothing and warm. He led her to the edge of the mountaintop that overlooked the endless green forest.

"Mia trusts Orka," Lee whispered.

"She doesn't even seem to be nervous standing on the edge of the mountain," Lance said, watching the two of them.

"I hope she gets the answer to her question," Lee said. *What an odd-looking pair? He thought.*

Mia looked up at Orka. She felt safe with him, her small hand enclosed in his large, furry one. She understood why he was the overseer of the forest. He looked over the forest with such pride.

"I was a little girl when my mother and father disappeared. My mother had certain powers, just like me."

"I'm aware of your powers."

"So you know something about my parents... I want to know if they are still alive."

"I feel their presence. I don't know whether it comes through you, or if it comes from them. What I do know is that you will find the answer."

Just knowing her parents could still be alive gave Mia a warm feeling inside. Maybe one day her grandmother would have a chance to see her mother again. That was her greatest wish. "Thank you, that's the best news I've had since I've been in this world."

The next morning, they made their way down the mountainside. Mia repeated over and over to herself, "Not much further to go." She paused and wiped the sweat from her face. It must have been at least 100 degrees.

To take her mind off her fear, she smiled, thinking back to a conversation she had with her grandmother about friends. She should have brought Daily home. Her colorful hair and hard rock music would have certainly made her grandmother think twice about her making any more friends at school.

They all felt it would be a good idea for Mia to be in the middle, just in case her fear of heights set off her powers that could cause the whole mountain to collapse. They reached the bottom of the mountain, where three horses waited—the same three horses that took them to the bird's nest.

They mounted the horses. With great speed they traveled through the forest. They returned to Citadel to find people rushing around preparing to leave. They were frantic because they didn't know if Oman had freed the Spoilers. No one had seen or heard from him. They had to go far away to escape the creatures. Ivor went to Oman's Temple to find out if he had gone to the forest to carry out his plan.

Feather, Lance, Mia, Nadia and Lee hurried down the path through the colony to the Marketplace. People had gathered there in hopes of hearing some news of their fate. Feather had attached herself to the teenagers like a sister would to her big brother or big sister. Her mother and father died from a sickness that spread through the colony six years ago. Her father became ill first with a high fever and died. Shortly afterward her mother became ill. Nola helped Feather take care of her mother until she met the same fate.

They had to keep it a secret. If Oman found out, he would have sent the guards to fetch Feather. She would be another one of his slave children. It was another one of his controlling rules— any child without parents became his possession. All births in his colony were recorded so he would know who the children belonged to.

Several people risked their lives to help the children but they weren't able to save them all. One of Nola's duties was to supervise the homeless children. She would take them treats at night and when they became older she would help them escape from the temple before Oman realized they were gone.

At the risk of their own lives Nola and Hemp decided they would not allow Feather to become one of his children. Hemp prepared a room underneath their structure.

After her mother passed word spread among the guards that there was an orphan girl somewhere in the colony. Hearing this, Oman ordered his men to search everywhere for the missing girl.

The guards entered Hemp and Nola's home, where Feather waited quietly in the room below. She could hear the guard's loud, abrasive voices demanding to know where she was. She remembered what Nola and Hemp told her—regardless of what happened to stay hidden.

The guards were finally convinced she had run off into the woods. She was fortunate to be taken in by Hemp and Nola. The slave children spent the days working with the women in the field.

Feather watched a few frightened girls and boys with dirty faces and tattered clothes run through the colony, seeking refuge. They had no place to go but into the deadly forest. Anyone found helping them would be severely punished. Feather thought, if Oman wasn't the Ruler of the colony good people like Nola and Hemp would take care of the children.

Nola and Hemp gave her love. They showed her how to take care of herself, what berries to eat to survive in the forest, and how to make clothes from skins. Nola taught her to read. She was taught by visitors who came to the colony.

Feather considered Mia, Lance and Lee her family too. She knew one day they would return to their world. But she would never forget them. One important thing she had learned from them was to listen closely to her inner thoughts and follow her heart.

They opened up a new world to her, one she could never have imagined. Lee taught her how to use a computer and a cell phone. Lance passed on to her what his father taught him – how to face fear. She never knew girls could be strong warriors like men until she met Mia and saw her in action. She believed Mia must be a goddess because of her powers, and a talking owl was magic. She wondered if all the people outside Citadel were as nice as them.

They entered the Marketplace where people had gathered. The people nodded their heads as they passed by them. There were all kinds of foods—fruits, berries, green leafy plants and potatoes. Necklaces made of colorful jewels and bright sparking colored stones hung from hooks.

Mia and Nadia admired the beautiful necklaces. One of the women in the store placed one around each of their necks.

"Thank you, but we have nothing to give you," Mia said to the woman.

"You don't have to give them anything. It's a sign of friendship. If you break the friendship you are expected to return the necklace. It's just the way things work around here," Feather told them.

Another woman held a tray with a cup containing a warm drink. They each took a cup. Mia took a sip. "This is good," she said, placing her hand on her chest. The warm drink trickled down her throat.

"It tastes like warm ginger ale," Lance said.

Lee finished drinking his tea. "This is awesome; it tastes just like the tea my grandfather made for my family."

Nadia looked at Lee. "It's made out of ginger. It's my favorite."

"You see? We have something in common," Lee whispered to her.

Lance overheard Lee talking to Nadia. He moved over to Lee. "Ginger, that's what you have in common. You're supposed to be the expert on girls. You'd better step up your game," he said, chuckling.

"That was pretty weak. But it's all I got."

Hemp and Quest entered the Marketplace, followed by Moody, Aman, Marge and Dr. Ram. Mills joined them. They stood in front of the agitated crowd. Hemp called the people together. He said, "It's just a matter of time before we are free and Oman is removed."

"How can you be sure Oman won't release the Spoilers?" someone shouted.

Lance said, "Because we are going to stop him."

They left the Marketplace. They realized the future of the people in Citadel rested on them. They couldn't let them down. Their friend Feather would never know freedom. They knew it might take this world some time to catch up with theirs, but in some ways they were more advanced.

The people in Citadel had learned to get along with one another, something that hadn't been achieved in their modern world. In the modern world, people looked at the differences in each other, not what they had in common. Oman could have made a difference but he chose, like some leaders in their world, to let his ego become the driving force, rather than the well-being of his people. He became obsessed with power.

Lee turned to Lance. "Man, you know Oman is wicked. He could be on his way to free those creatures as we speak."

Ivor watched Advar approach Oman in a room in the temple. Advar questioned his decision to release the Spoilers. "Are you sure you want to release the Spoilers? They will kill us."

"It's the only weapon I have left. Let's go—their time has run out. They will never leave this world. The Spoilers will destroy them and the people in Citadel."

Ivor waited at the temple until Oman and Advar left. He headed to Hemp's and Nola's structure. He was eager to tell everyone what he found out. He flew right into their door, making a loud thumping noise. Everyone was startled by the loud noise, except for Mia. She announced, "Ivor is back."

Mia rushed to open the door. She found her furry friend lying on his back. She picked him up. "You made it," she said.

"Yes, just give me a minute. My head is whirling," Ivor said.

"What did you find out?" Lee asked.

Ivor answered, "We don't have much time. Oman and Advar are on their way to free the Spoilers. I will show you the way. My friends will fly you there."

"Be careful," Moody said.

"We will," Lance replied.

"Remember, luck is on your side," Nadia said to Lee.

Mia saw the worried look on Marge's face. She tried to reassure her everything would be okay. "Don't worry," she said, "after all, you survived the streets of New York City. I'm sure I can survive a few ancient creatures."

CHAPTER FOURTEEN

The teenagers cling tightly to the golden birds as they carried them away, twisting and turning like a rollercoaster. The three students from an elite academy, now warriors, might have to confront the most horrifying animals that ever roamed the earth to save a colony of people in another world. Who would believe this?

Lance looked over at Mia and Lee. "If only our classmates could see us now," he shouted.

"They would totally freak out," Lee hollered.

"My grandmother says everything happens for a reason," Mia said as her bird took the lead.

"There must be a good reason why I met you," Lance called out.

"Perhaps," Mia yelled, looking back and smiling.

"This is cool, man," Lee shouted.

Lance turned to Lee. "I want you to repeat that when we're on the ground."

The birds slowed down to make a landing in a clearing encircled by leafless trees. They seemed to understand what was going on. Nothing stirred, not even a tree branch. It could have been the end of the world, where all mankind had been whisked away and nothing was left but silence and solitude.

The three followed Ivor on foot through the forest. A powerful wind blew so forcefully they had to shield their eyes from the blinding sand. They held on tightly to each other. It took all of Ivor's strength to stay in the air. Luckily, he could turn his head to keep the sand out of his eyes.

Lance was in the front. Mia's arms were around his waist and Lee's hands were around hers. Lee was thinking something or someone was trying to keep them from moving forward. Maybe it was Orka's way of telling them there was danger ahead. Whatever it meant, there was no turning back now. They made the right decision—the most important decision they had ever made. It made the other things they use to worry about seem so meaningless.

The teenagers moved quickly behind a large tree to protect themselves from the harsh storm. The three were covered with sand from head to toe. Finally, the storm subsided. They brushed the sand off their face and out of their hair. Not far ahead of them was Ivor. He called out to them, "I can see Oman and Advar."

The two men were struggling to remove a huge tree trunk that concealed a strong wooden cover placed over a hole in the ground. The hole led to the Spoilers trapped beneath the earth. Oman and Advar pushed the trunk with all their strength. Oman was frustrated. "Push harder" he said breathlessly.

"I'm trying, I'm trying," Advar said, falling to the ground.

"Get up! You're useless!" Oman said.

They tried again and were successful. The trunk slowly rolled off the cover. "Finally," Oman said to Advar, grabbing his chest and taking deep breaths.

"How will the Spoilers know they have been freed?" Advar asked.

"They will know... the wind will blow through the earth. The light will shine through showing them the way out," Oman answered.

The teenagers ducked down as they made their way cautiously through the bushes and snuck up behind Oman and Advar.

"You're not going to free the Spoilers," Lance said in a sharp voice.

Oman and Advar were surprised when they turned around and saw the teenagers standing in front of them with their spears aimed at them.

"They will destroy your people," Mia said angrily. "We're not about to let that happen."

"You're twisted. You would sacrifice your own people over a key." Lee pushed his spear against Oman's chest.

"I suppose I would," Oman said angrily. "But don't blame me. It was you who stole the key. Now it seems the people in Citadel will pay the price. However, if you have the key with you, I may be willing to reconsider."

"Not in this lifetime," Mia said.

"Back up," Lee stated firmly.

"We have to hurry and move the tree trunk back over the cover," Lance said anxiously.

Advar pulled his sword, pointing it at them. Slightly amused, the teenagers looked at his hand shaking. "Really?" they responded.

Mia pointed her spear at Advar. "You don't want to do that," she said.

Fearful, Advar stepped back. Suddenly, several Eglipses flew toward them. Oman laughed and said, "You didn't think I'd come without protection. You see some of my birds are still alive. I suggest you surrender to me while you still have time."

"That's never going to happen," Lee said in a sharp voice.

Ivor excitedly flew to a tree branch. He jumped up and down, shouting to his friends to move fast. The Eglipses swooped down to attack the teenagers. Mia used her powers to push them back as they flew toward them. But she was only able to hold them back for a short period of time. After regaining their strength they continued to attack.

Lance moved to Oman, his spear aimed at his chest. "If you don't stop them, you've taken your last breath," Lance said.

Mia was struggling with one of the Eglipses. She used her gymnastic skills and jumped high into the air. She stabbed the bird but it continued to lash out at her. Lance ran over to help her. He launched his spear into the creature. They watched it tumble to the ground. They turned to see Lee shooting his arrows into one of the birds.

"I'm almost out of arrows," Lee hollered.

Lance threw his bag of arrows to Lee. "Here, use these."

The Golden Birds appeared and attacked the Eglipses. Ivor watched in disbelief. The Golden Birds weren't warrior birds. They were no match for the fierce Eglipses but somehow, they had become fearless with super strength.

While the birds fought, the teenagers went quickly over to the tree trunk. Mia stared at the trunk, causing it to roll back on the cover. Unexpectedly, from beneath the earth where the Spoilers were trapped came a loud rumbling sound, similar to the noise made by the rush of cattle.

The earth shook forcefully, causing the tree trunk and cover to fly off a hole in the ground. They all scrambled to safety.

Only a couple of Oman's birds survived the fight. Oman signaled them to come to him making a loud whistling sound but the birds ignored his command. He and Advar waved their hands frantically in the air to get their attention. The birds flew away without them. They took off into the woods to escape the massive eruption.

The teenagers knelt down together and covered their faces to avoid the dirt that shot out of the hole like a volcano erupting.

The earth moved beneath them. They glanced over at the gaping hole in the earth to see if the Spoilers would make an appearance. Whatever happened, they were ready to face them.

"We have to get to the other side," Mia said. "The earth underneath us is sinking. We have to move. Now! "

Lance and Lee both agreed with Mia. The crack in the earth continued to widen. They had to quickly get to the other side. Mia said to Lance and Lee, "Take a few steps backward and then run and jump."

Lee pointed, "Let's cross over there. It's the narrowest point."

They decided to jump one by one. Lee went first. He took a few steps backward and ran fast kicking his legs high in the air, and twisting his body. He landed on the other side. The crack in the earth continued to widen. Lance insisted Mia go next but she refused because she could jump farther.

Reluctantly, Lance positioned himself. He made the jump but fell a few inches short. He landed on the edge of the hole. Lee rushed over and pulled him up. They shouted to Mia to jump. She remembered what Miss Wilson would tell her before she would go out to compete. "Make the jump in your mind first. If it works for you there, you can do it." Mia looked at the wide crack in the ground. She thought, *I've never jumped that distance before.* She pictured the jump in her mind to determine the distance she needed to run to make it to the other side. She dashed into the forest. Lance and Lee watched her run in the opposite direction.

Lee cried out to Lance, "She's running the wrong way. I can't see her."

"Knowing Mia, she has a plan," Lance said, staring anxiously at the woods.

"Look! Here she comes," Lee yelled.

Mia ran from the forest. She touched down on the edge of the earth and thrust her body like a wheel, rolling over and over landing on the other side next to them. "Wow," they said.

***

New York City

The earthquake was so powerful it could be felt in the modern world. New York City suffered damaging impacts. Buildings shook and windows shattered, sending glass onto the streets. Streets buckled, sending cars crashing into each other and into shops and restaurants.

People rushed through the streets, bumping into one another. They held onto buildings and posts. They tried to avoid being hit by the sharp glass falling from the towering buildings. Beneath their feet, they could feel an unusual sensation. Several people took shelter in the restaurant where Irene worked. They huddled together under tables to protect themselves from flying objects. Irene and another waitress were under one of them.

Irene wiped her hair out of her face with her hands. She was frustrated because she couldn't reach Lance. Her phone kept losing its signal. She attempted several more times. She hoped he was safe at home. They had made an agreement that they would meet at home if anything dangerous were to happen in the city. "I'm worried about Lance. I know he can take care of himself but this earthquake is lasting longer than usual. There's something different about it," Irene said to the waitress.

"Lance is a smart kid. He knows how to protect himself. Don't worry. He's going to be just fine," the waitress said reassuringly.

"I know you're right. He's probably at home with his friend, Moody. He has such a big heart," Irene said to the waitress.

The waitress said, "Let's just hope this madness ends soon."

In the mist of all the commotion, a small white terrier jumped through the opening in the door. Irene dodged falling plaster from the ceiling and rushed over to the frightened dog. She picked up the dog and rushed back under the table with it.

She held the fluffy dog tightly, rubbing his back to calm him down. He licked her a few times on her cheek, as if to thank her for coming to his rescue.

It appeared the earthquake had not only been felt in New York—its effects were felt around the world leaving a path of destruction. Lee's mother and father sat on their sofa in a back area of their restaurant where they lived watching television but the picture faded in and out. Every channel was consumed with reports from all over the world. Scientists weren't able to confirm what was behind this extraordinary earthquake.

The earthquake lasted longer than usual. A strange movement in the ground was felt. Some geologist described it as the earth spinning. It was causing worldwide destruction, concrete structures gave way and some areas were experiencing severe flooding.

Lee's sister Kim sat on the floor worried because Lee hadn't returned from school. She would never let him know how much she loved him. She would brag about him to her friends telling them her brother might be a nerd but he was a genius.

"What's happening?" Lee's mother asked. "This earthquake won't go away. No one knows what's going on."

Lee's grandfather Ling walked slowly into the room carrying an old leather-bound book. His father read stories to him from the book when he was a little boy. He knew the mysterious earthquake was similar to an event that was recorded in ancient China. It also caused strange movements in the ground. The story was in the book. He flipped the worn pages.

"What are you looking for, Grandfather?" Kim asked, watching the intense look on his face.

"Father, those stories in that book were written many, many years ago. They're myths, legends. What makes you think there's any truth to it?" his son asked.

"Don't waste your time," Lee's mother said to Ling. "The only thing your son believes in is his restaurant."

"There's no other reasonable explanation...listen," Ling said.

Ling read from the old book, carefully turning the faded pages. In ancient China an unusual earthquake occurred that caused a spinning movement in the ground. People who lived in a remote village could not understand what was causing this occurrence.

Several frightened people covered with dirt ran into their village. Everyone stared at them wondering where they came from. The only way anyone could reach their village was by the sea and there were no boats on the water. The people in the village asked the strangers where they came from. They said from beneath the earth. They were trapped there until a powerful force in the earth created a passage for them to escape. However, they were not alone. They were fleeing from the treacherous animals called the Spoilers who were also trapped there. They told the villagers to leave quickly or they would be destroyed by the creatures.

The villagers wanted to know how to keep them from entering their world. The strangers told them they must destroy them in the earth. So the mightiest warriors in the village were sent into the earth to battle them.

The warriors were given special powers to conquer them. They fought bravely and were able to keep the Spoilers from escaping the but unfortunately the earth collapsed sealing them beneath the earth, as well.

"What you saying, Father? There are creatures living beneath the earth trying to free themselves. That's what causing this earthquake?"

"Do you have a better explanation, son?"

"I think we should leave it to the scientists."

Kim turned to her grandfather. "I think something weird is happening too...I hope Lee gets home soon."

"Don't worry about Lee; he can take care of himself. I see something special in him. He possesses great courage and will overcome all obstacles in his path."

"Well, Grandfather, all I see is a nerdy geek."

Beverly sat on her bed, next to a table cluttered with family pictures, in her small, cramped bedroom. She'd never experienced anything like this before. She got up and walked slowly into the living room. She could feel the building slightly shaking. She leaned against a chair and glanced out the window, looking for Mia. She tried to reach the school but the lines were down. Mia's cell phone wasn't ringing, either.

Beverly was pretty sure the dean told her if there was an emergency the students would be kept in a safe place. She couldn't bear losing Mia too. She couldn't go through the pain again. She never let Mia know whenever she was late those feelings returned.

Occasionally, she would still look out the window to see if Erica was out there somewhere. She hadn't given up hope that one day her daughter and her husband would return home and see how their daughter had grown up to be a beautiful young lady—so compassionate and caring. Mia left a school, where all of her friends attended to go to a school across town because of her wishes. And like her mother, she would help anyone in need.

She hoped everything would settle down soon and the people in the neighborhood were safe inside out of the way of the commotion. There was going to be a lot of cleaning up to do. Mr. Sanchez' fruits had rolled all over the street. A fallen light pole lay in the middle of the street. *What a mess,* she thought. Someone knocked repeatedly on her door. "Hold on, I'm coming," she hollered. She opened the door. It was Mr. Mason, her neighbor from across the hall.

"Just checking on you," Mr. Mason said, holding onto the door. "This earthquake is pretty bad. It's lasting forever."

"Yes, it is," Beverly said.

"Listen, why don't you come over and stay with my family?" Mr. Mason asked.

"Thanks, but I have to be here when Mia comes home." Beverly closed the door and made her way back to her bedroom. She lay on her bed and covered herself with a blanket.

CHAPTER FIFTEEN

The three teenagers saw someone sitting on a golden bird flying rapidly toward them. It was Dr. Ram. "Over here, over here," they shouted.

The bird landed. Dr. Ram slid off the bird's back. "Just a second," he called out and moved cautiously over to the wide hole in the ground. He paused, and looked around at the huge formation that had occurred in the earth. He then knelt down to listen for the Spoilers. "Come quickly. We don't have much time," Dr. Ram yelled to his young friends. They hurried over to him and knelt down beside him. Ivor flew close to them.

"How much time do we have?" Mia asked, staring into the earth.

"There's no time. I'm afraid we have another problem. I have concluded the movements of the Spoilers are causing the two worlds to merge. You have to go now and stop them before it's too late."

"You're right, Dr. Ram. We have to fight them down there. We can't risk them getting away," Lance said.

"It's now or never," Mia said. "We won't have to wonder about them much longer. We'll soon be face to face with them."

"I'll go back to Citadel and let the people know what's happening," Dr. Ram said. He climbed onto the bird and flew away.

Mia looked at her two friends. "Let's do this."

"Maybe I should accompany you," Ivor said. "It will be quite dangerous. I can be your eyes and ears."

"You have to stay here. If the Spoilers escape, you have to fly back to Citadel and warn the people."

Lee climbed into the earth first, followed by Lance then Mia. They used the protruding rocks to manipulate themselves down the bumpy surface. Lee stepped his foot down on the hard ground. He saw big red ants actively running around on the bottom of the cave. "Be careful," he said, "there are hundreds ants on the ground."

Mia and Lance joined Lee walking carefully around the ants further into the cave. The sounds of the Spoilers became louder as they neared the area where they were trapped. The three stopped and looked around the cave. They could see how close the Spoilers were to freeing themselves from the earth.

"We're getting close to them. They sound as if they're talking to each other," Lance whispered, stepping lightly.

"I hope they aren't as hideous as they sound," Mia said. She followed close behind Lance.

"We'll know soon," Lee said.

Several oversized red beetles flew aggressively toward them. The teenagers released their arrows, hitting the insects. They fell to the ground.

"Let's get our arrows. We'll need them," Mia said.

They pulled their arrows out of the hard shells of the insects and continued to make their way through the cave. They walked cautiously over to the area in the ground where the muffled sounds came from and tried to figure out how many of them were down below. They decided it would be better to wait for them to show themselves.

This truly would be the ultimate test of their skills. Not knowing what to expect weighed heavy on their minds if they failed, the Spoilers would take control of the world. Civilization would cease to exist. Mia rested her head on Lance's shoulder. Lee quietly paced back and forth.

"Sometimes I think this isn't really happening," Mia said.

"Think about it," Lance said. "We're trapped in another world. A world no one knows exists. It is like something out of a science fiction movie."

"I will never watch another one of those movies again," Mia said, shaking her head.

Strong movements were made by the Spoilers. Lance and Mia jumped up. It was apparent they were making their way up. Not knowing what would appear; they gave each other a reassuring nod and positioned themselves out of sight behind a large stone.

From an opening in the ground emerged four huge green scaly creatures, with oval shaped heads, and big pointed ears. Their eyes were extremely wide, and their long mouths held many sharp, pointed teeth. The animals had a long flexible tail, two short front legs, and two long legs. When standing upright, they were more than seven feet tall.

"Look at those hideous things," Lee whispered.

Lance whispered back, "They look like they could be related to Godzilla."

"We should be so lucky. Godzilla was on the screen. These monsters are here, in front of us," Lee whispered.

"At least we know what we're up against," Mia said, speaking softly. "Listen... the big one is speaking."

"Finally our time has come. We're going to be free. Out of the earth forever."

His piercing eyes were expressionless. His demeanor was cold, calculating. Another one in a high-pitched voice spoke out.

"You will lead us again, Titus."

"Yes, Pervious," Titus cried out.

"Don't forget about Oman! He betrayed us! We gave him the power over the Eglipses and he left us trapped in the earth!" Pervious said angrily.

"Don't worry, I'll take care of him," Titus said, balling up his crusty hand, expressing his anger.

The Spoilers nodded their heads in agreement. One of them looked in the direction of the teenagers. He seemed to sense their presence. His eyes focused on the stone shielding them. The teenagers slumped down.

"We have to keep them from going any farther," whispered Lance.

"We have to get them back in that hole and seal it. We can't let them escape," Mia said.

"Take a look at them. Our spears will barely penetrate their tough, leathery skin. Plus, there are four of those dudes and three of us," Lee stated.

"If I use my powers the whole cave could collapse," Mia said, looking up.

"And that really wouldn't be cool," Lee added.

"I've got it," Mia said. "Why didn't I think of this before?"

"What is it, Mia?" Lance asked.

"One thing all animals are afraid of is fire," Mia said. "We'll use it to lure them back into the hole and seal it with rocks."

"Don't forget they're spirits. We don't know for sure, if they are afraid of fire," added Lance.

"I guess we'll find out," Lee said.

"Let's go before they discover we're here," Mia said. "We have to make a fire."

The three made their way back through the cave and gathered sticks that could be used to start a fire. They piled dried stems and dead leaves together in a pile. Lance and Lee rubbed the sticks together to produce enough friction to ignite their nest. Mia ripped off parts of her clothing and wrapped them around their spears. They lit them.

Lee looked at Mia and Lance. "Come on. We have to move now."

Flames from their spears lit up the cave. Lance turned to them and said, "Now!"

Their shadowy figures carrying the fiery spears were reflected on the cave's wall. The teenagers hesitated for a second, glanced at each other, and nodded. They burst into the room, taking the Spoilers by surprise.

Lucky for them the Spoilers were afraid of fire. They moved backward, away from the hot flames. Titus lashed out at the teenagers. "You can't destroy us. We're not human."

"We may not be able to kill you. But we'll keep you from getting out of the earth," Lee said firmly, not blinking an eye.

"You won't be able to hurt anyone down here. But believe me when I say this—your time will run out." Mia added.

"Apparently what you don't know is things have changed. If you try to take over our world, we'll blow you away," Lance said, looking directly into Titus's eyes.

With a fierce look on their faces, the unruly beasts lashed out at them. Their mouths opened, exposing their sharp pointed teeth, capable of tearing them apart. Their tails swayed back and forth. They tried to dodge the fiery flames.

The teenagers surrounded them. They found it hard keep them moving backward because they were outnumbered. Titus used his tail fiercely and deadly. Mia jumped over it to get closer to him. He tried to knock her down. She pushed her fiery spear in his face. He moved backwards and fell back into the opening in the ground.

Lance used his spear to manipulate two of the Spoilers. One struck him across his chest, causing him to lose his balance. Mia stormed over to him. She used her fiery spear to keep him from attacking Lance.

Lance jumped to his feet. He pierced the Spoiler with his spear. The creature tumbled into the open space. Mia and Lance both waved their fiery spears at the other Spoiler, sending him back into the ground below.

Lee threw his spear to the ground. He jumped into the air, giving the Spoiler he battled a powerful kick. He repeated the jump, kicking him again and again. The force of his kick sent the Spoiler back into the ground with the others.

Mia threw her fiery spear into the opening, followed by Lee and Lance. They hoped the fire would hold them back, giving them more time. The Spoilers cried out from below. The teenagers placed large rocks over the opening to keep them from getting out.

They headed back to the entrance of the cave. Mia stopped and looked back. She saw the charred hand of one of the Spoilers trying to push through the rocks. She thought, *if they make it out of there. They might make it out of the earth.*

Lance and Lee yelled to her to keep moving. She glanced back at them and shouted, "Go ahead... I have to go back." She went back and saw Titus's charred body was halfway out. Lance and Lee followed her. "What now?" Lee asked.

They watched Titus pull the rest of his disfigured body out of the ground. "I told you. You don't have the power to kill us. It's just a matter of time before we gain our strength back. I see you have no weapons and your fire has gone out. I'm afraid you're going to be the ones trapped down here," Titus said in a weak voice. He could barely stand.

Another Spoiler's hand reached up. Mia stared at Titus as he staggered toward them. His big mouth opened wide. But the force of Mia's powers sent him forcefully into the wall of the cave. The impact caused the earth to give away, burying the Spoilers. The whole cave began to collapse. Lance grabbed Mia. "Let's get out of here now!" he said.

The three ran from the dirt hurtling toward them like a tsunami roaring onto a beach. They were happy to see light from the outside shining on the protruding rocks ahead. Mia climbed up first, followed by Lance. Lee was the last one. He was stuck in the rising dirt. He looked up at Lance and Mia. "Keep going. I'll be okay."

Nevertheless, it was obvious to Mia and Lance he wasn't going to be okay. The dirt was up to his waist. Lee twisted his body. He tried to free himself. Lance and Mia climbed back down the rocks to Lee.

"Give me your hand. I'll pull you up," Lance said, leaning over him, holding onto a rock with his other hand. Mia watched intently. She took a few steps down to Lance. Lee looked at the bracelet on his wrist. He remembered what Nadia said; *the bracelet would bring him good luck.* At that moment, he decided not to give up. He extended his hand to Lance with the bracelet on it and with unusual ease Lance pulled him out of the dirt.

Mia climbed up the rocks and out of the cave. Lance and Lee were behind her. Dirt completely filled the hole. Breathing rapidly, they collapsed onto the ground. They were exhausted.

"Even this world looks good to me," Mia said. She closed her eyes. They all fell asleep. Ivor was relieved to see they made it back safely. He flew over Mia and snuggled close to her. He watched her sleep. After a few hours, he nudged his beak against her cheek to awaken her. "Wake up, wake up."

Mia's eyes were slightly open. "Is that you, Ivor?" she asked.

"Yes," he said joyfully, jumping up and down. "You kept the Spoilers from escaping but we must leave here now. Not a moment to waste."

Lance and Lee woke up. They heard Ivor and Mia. Lee realized they made it out of the hole. He threw his arm up. "We made it."

"Yes," Lance shouted. "We did."

"And the Spoilers are once again buried deep underneath the earth," Mia said, hugging Ivor. "We stopped them."

"I'm afraid there's another problem. One that can stand in the way of you returning to your world. A vision came to me," Ivor said.

"What was it?" Lee asked.

"Tell us what you saw, Ivor," Lance asked.

"The cave to your world is falling. You don't have much time."

"Let's go then," Lance said.

"The birds are waiting in the forest," Ivor said, flying away.

CHAPTER SIXTEEN

The early morning sun beamed down on a temporary shelter supported by wooden beams, covered with thick tree branches. Several people lived in the shelter, including Feather, Nola and Hemp.

Feather finished lacing up her shoes and braiding her long hair. She rushed outside to Nola. She watched her flip fish in a pan over an open fire. She knew Nola would need water soon. She headed to the river.

Nola felt uncomfortable about Feather going to the river, even though she had done it many times. "Be careful, Feather," Nola said. "I don't have a good feeling about you going off alone. Some of Oman's birds could still be out there."

"Don't worry, I shouldn't be long," Feather said, walking away carrying a large orange clay container. Her bow was slung over her shoulders and a pouch with arrows was attached to her waist. She practiced shooting her arrows every day. She wanted to be able to fight like the men in the colony.

Oman forbade anyone other than his guards to have weapons. He would have their structures searched from time to time to make no one had them. Now the men had armed themselves and were free to go into the woods.

Feather reached the river. She knelt down and splashed water on her face. She then filled her container with water. She saw a frog and played with it. She laughed, dipping it in and out of the water. She was startled by a man's voice. "So you like to play with frogs." Feather jumped up. She turned around to see the Oman. She reached for her bow and arrow.

"I wouldn't try that," he said, looking around at his restless bird a short distance away from them. He snatched Feather up and pulled her into the woods.

"Where are you taking me?" Feather asked, trying not to show fear. "My friends will find you and punish you for all the wicked things you've done."

"Don't worry, I intend to let your friends know exactly where they can find me," said Oman, grinning.

He took Feather into the woods, to one of his traps in the ground, where the tigers roam. He signaled his bird to chase the four-legged animals away and threw Feather into the underground trap where she landed on a pile of leaves.

"You'll get what you deserve," Feather called out to Oman. She stood up and tried to climb out of the trap but stopped when she heard the roar of the tigers. They had returned. Feather looked up. She could see their shadows. She knew they were aware of her presence but smart enough to stay away from the opening in the ground.

Mia, Lance and Lee returned to Citadel to find the colony almost completely in ruins. Only a few structures remained standing. The rest were destroyed by the earthquake. They walked through the ruins to the shattered Marketplace, where people applauded them, showing their gratitude for saving them from the Spoilers.

Nadia moved through the crowd to Lee. She hugged him tightly and gave him a kiss. "I felt you were in great danger," Nadia said, clinging tightly to Lee.

"I was, but the bracelet you gave me saved my life," Lee said rubbing the bracelet.

"What happened that made you feel the bracelet saved your life?" Nadia asked, looking up into Lee's eyes. She raised her hand and brushed the dirt out of his hair.

"I was stuck in dirt. It was already up to my waist and it continued to rise. I told Mia and Lance I was okay. I wanted them to make it out of the hole but they came back to help me. Lance grabbed my wrist, with the bracelet on it. It was like something pushed me upward."

"I gave you the bracelet for good luck," Nadia said. "Your belief in it gave you the power to pull yourself out. It also brings people closer together." She smiled.

Advar walked nervously into the Marketplace. The men were mad. They yelled out. "Capture him...capture him ...make him tell us what Oman is planning to do next!"

The men knew Advar was Oman's faithful servant. They wanted to capture him but Quest stopped them. "Let him be...

He's more of a victim of Oman's cruelty than we are. Imagine doing his bidding all these years and living in that temple with his wild birds."

"Thank you, merciful one," Advar said. "I don't mean any of you harm."

"Say what you have come to say," Quest said.

Advar said, "I have a message for you from Oman." Everyone looked at each other. The room was silent. They knew a message from Oman couldn't be good. Mia, Lance and Lee walked over to Advar. They wondered what Oman could possibly do now. His army had been defeated and only a couple of his vicious birds remained.

"What is the message?" Hemp asked Advar.

"Out with it," Quest said.

"You must return the key and tell him where the machine is hidden if you want to see the girl again," Advar said in a low voice. He didn't want to arouse the crowd.

"He's taken Feather," Nola cried out.

Lance rushed over to Advar. "Where is he?"

"He said to meet him at the lake when the sun rises," Advar said nervously, looking around at the angry looks on the people's faces. He turned and hurried out of the Marketplace.

"Oman still hasn't given up," Lee said. "He'll stop at nothing to get what he wants."

"We'll get her back," Lance said to Nola. "Don't worry... I promise you."

"We need the key," Mia said anxiously.

"I hid it before the earthquake. Come with me," Quest said.

They rushed out of the Marketplace. Quest led them to a rock; underneath was the key inside a pouch. The next morning, Ivor and the three teenagers with the key in their possession waited behind a rock at the lake for Oman to appear with Feather.

"What if he doesn't have Feather with him? He could be setting us up," Lee said.

"We don't have a choice. There's no other way. We don't know where he has taken her," Mia sighed. "We'll play him like he's trying to play us."

"He wants this key more than anything else. It's the only power he has left," Lance said.

"He won't harm Feather. He has nothing else to bargain with," Mia said.

Lee looked up. "There's Oman. He's by himself."

"Not surprising," Mia said.

"He must have hidden Feather in the woods," Lance said, watching Oman. He knew he was not to be trusted and once they got Feather back, he would make sure he didn't harm anyone else. He would turn him over to his people.

"Oman has many underground traps in the woods," Ivor said. "He must have her hidden in one of them."

"Take Lee and me into the woods. We'll search his traps while Lance keeps him distracted," Mia said to Ivor.

"Our time is running out. Feather could be in danger out there," Lee said.

"Follow me," Ivor said.

Lee and Mia crept through the bushes so Oman didn't see them going into the woods. Oman left his bird and continued to the lake.

"I'm over here," Lance said. He stepped out from behind a large rock.

"Are you here to save the girl?" asked Oman.

"Where's Feather?" Lance demanded. He didn't want Oman to become suspicious in case Lee and Mia didn't find her.

"Don't worry, the girl is safe ...for now," Oman answered.

"If you hurt her..." Lance said.

"Don't be so hasty, young man. All in due time," Oman said, smiling and wiping the sweat from his forehead. "Hand over the key and tell me in which cave the machine is hidden. It's as simple as that. Then...I'll tell you where the girl is," Oman said.

"You'll get everything you asked for when you return Feather," Lance said, stalling for time.

Mia and Lee dashed through the woods with Ivor flying overhead. They ducked and dodged overturned trees. A young dinosaur with a long tail and small head jumped on the path. They ducked behind a tree. Lee looked up at it. "It looks like a Hipsiophodon. I do remember that much from class," he whispered.

"You mean you actually stayed awake in Mrs. Flower's science class? I'm impressed. I thought all you were interested in was computers."

"You know, I'm more than just a computer geek. Some people actually find me charming," Lee said, smiling.

"Do me a favor. See if you can charm this dinosaur, because it's coming right toward us," Mia said, reaching for her spear.

"You know, you do have powers. You could keep us from being ripped apart."

"If I used my powers, I could cause the trees to tumble. Feather could get hurt."

"Got it," Lee said.

Mia and Lee inserted their arrows in their bows, preparing to shoot the dinosaur.

"Let's hope he's friendly," Mia said. "He's sort of cute in a scary way."

"I hope our arrows will slow it down," Lee said.

"Look Lee, Ivor is talking to the dinosaur."

Mia and Lee watched Ivor and the dinosaur talk. "He won't harm you. He's trying to figure out what kind of animals you are. He thinks you're rather odd-looking," Ivor said. He asked the dinosaur, "Have you seen any unusual animal in the forest that looks like them –only smaller?"

The dinosaur slowly responded. "No but a strange cry is heard."

Ivor asked the dinosaur where the cry came from. The dinosaur explained, "The cry came from under the ground where the fast, four-legged fast animals wander." Ivor flew back to Mia and Lee. He told them Feather was hidden in one of the traps. "It's not far away." They picked up their speed again. Feather leaned against the wall of the open pit, out of the reach of the tigers' big paws. Her biggest fear was one of them might fall in. The two teenagers and Ivor arrived at the open pit in the ground. They watched from behind a tree – two large saber-tooth tigers lashing their paws in and out of the trap.

"Somehow, we've got to get those tigers away from there," Lee whispered.

Mia turned to Lee. "I'll lead them away while you get Feather out of the trap."

"Are you sure?" Lee asked.

"Yes," Mia whispered.

Mia jumped from behind the tree, waving her hands in the air and making loud noises to get the tigers' attention. She ran down the path through the woods. The tigers chased after her. They made long strides at a rapid speed. Ivor flew overhead, watching the tigers as they moved close to Mia.

Lee knelt at the trap. "Feather, Feather, can you hear me?"

"I'm here," she said, trembling from the coldness in the ground. Lee leaned over the trap, extending his hand. But her arms were too short to reach his hand. He looked around for a tree branch long enough to reach her. He looked around to make sure there were no tigers nearby.

"Grab onto the branch, Feather. I'll pull you out," he said. Feather held on tightly to the branch. Lee pulled her out of the trap. She was relieved. Her face was smudged with dirt and her clothes were torn. Yet she managed a wide smile. She was fearful of the tigers and looked around to see where they were.

"You're safe?" Lee said. He could see she was frightened. There was no way she could have freed herself with the tigers circling above the trap.

"I knew you would find me." She gave Lee a hug.

"Let's go. We have to move fast. Mia's being chased by the tigers," Lee said.

Mia continued to run from the tigers. She could see Lance and Oman up ahead. She hollered, "Lance, watch out for the tigers." Lance looked around and saw the tigers chasing her. Mia grabbed onto a tree branch and flipped herself on it. Lance drew an arrow from his pouch and placed it in his bow.

"Slay them! Slay them!" Oman screamed, running off toward the woods. One of the furious tigers chased after him. The other raced directly toward Lance. He aimed his arrow at the tiger only a few feet from him. He released it, piercing the tiger. It fell to the ground, rolling over and over.

Lance rushed over to Mia sitting on the tree branch. He stretched his arms out. "Jump, I'll catch you," he said to her.

"Are you sure?" Mia asked, smiling.

"Yes," Lance said.

Mia jumped from the tree branch into Lance's arms. He stood her up. Their eyes met, their faces came together, and they kissed. Lee and Feather watched from a distance.

Lee said, "I don't believe it. They finally hooked up."

"What do you mean by hooked up?" Feather asked.

"It's just a saying we use when two people get together," Lee explained.

"Oh," Feather said, smiling.

The four headed back to Citadel. They wondered if Oman got away from the tiger. One thing was for sure; if he showed up at Citadel, he would answer to his people.

CHAPTER SEVENTEEN

People shouted with joy at seeing the teens return with Feather. They embraced them. Nola and Hemp hugged Feather. They expressed their happiness for her safe return.

"Listen," Hemp said anxiously, looking at Mia, Lance and Lee. "We have to get to the cave right away. We're clearing the dirt out as fast as it falls. It's just a matter of time before the whole cave gives away."

Eager and anxious, everyone hurried to the cave. The grubby faces of people in soiled clothes were seen clearing piles of dirt out of the cave. Like an assembly line, they passed containers of rubble from one person to another.

Dr. Ram stood out in front of the cave giving directions. He turned to see the teenagers and Feather approaching the cave. He moved quickly over to them. Smiling, he hugged them. "A job well done," he said.

"Citadel can now be rebuilt without the threat of Oman," Mia spoke out.

"Yes... and I will stay and help the people build a new colony. You must go now," Dr. Ram said, glancing at the young heroes.

Nadia stepped out of the cave covered with dirt. She went to Lee and embraced him. People gathered around them to say goodbye. Quest hugged each of them. "We are sad to see you leave," he said. "You gave us our freedom. We no longer have to live under the fear of Oman. He's gone forever." The teenagers were eager to hear what happened to him. Quest explained to them that one of their people was in the woods and saw a tiger chasing Oman. An Eglipse few down and lifted him up. He thought this bird was saving him. But it turned out to be one of the birds he kept chained in his temple—the one that escaped. Oman begged for his life. He was heard screaming from the clutches of the bird's sharp claws as it carried him away. "Please! Please! I took care of you. I fed you."

Lee grinned. He said, "Man, what a story—you couldn't make that up. Oman finally got what he deserved."

Mia glanced around at the people. She could see the sadness on their faces. *How little they have?* She thought. Not once had she heard them complain. The only thing they wanted was to be free of Oman.

There were people of all mixtures, resulting from the many people who ended up there from different places. They were one people, with different looks. They would finally have a chance to be happy. She spoke out, "We hope one day you will come to our world, and we will welcome you like you welcomed us."

Mia, Lance and Lee went to Feather. She had gathered their backpacks that contained their clothes and tech devices. Mia took the necklace from around her neck and placed it around Feather's neck.

"You are my best friend forever. Be strong and remember you are a warrior girl," Mia said, giving Feather a hug. Feather handed them their backpacks filled with their clothes and electronics. Lee unzipped his and took out his laptop. He told her to keep it nearby because one day the signal might be strong enough for them to communicate. Feather smiled at him. "I won't forget."

Lee reached for Nadia's hand. "We'd better be going now," he said.

"I can't go with you. Not now," Nadia said sadly. She held Lee tightly. "My brother and I have decided to stay and help the people rebuild Citadel. The children need me... I can teach them."

Disappointed, Lee pulled her close to him. "I'll miss you...my life won't be the same without you."

"Our paths will cross again. I promise you," Nadia said. She went to her brother, wiping the tears from her eyes.

"Remember to meditate," Aman hollered to Lee. He raised his fingers making the peace sign.

Lee smiled at Aman and acknowledged him as he made the peace sign too.

Moody and Marge approached Lance, Mia, and Lee. "We're going to stay here too," Moody said. "This world needs our help."

"Why am I not surprised?" Lance said, embracing Moody. "You and Marge have become so much a part of this world. Promise me when the opportunity comes again, you will return to the City."

"You've got yourself a deal." Moody said smiling. He walked a few steps away and stopped. He turned around. "Oh, by the way, my real name is Sean Blakely. You never asked. I just thought. I'd tell you anyway." He waved good-bye to Lance and joined the other people.

Marge told Mia she had been given a second chance for happiness. She could now move on with her life, something she couldn't do at home. "We've all changed. Look at you...the once bubbly teenager is now a fierce warrior. I have a feeling this is just the beginning for you and your friends," Marge said with tears in her eyes. Mia held her tightly. "I'm going to miss you," Mia said, "but if you're happier here, this is where you belong."

Marge said, "I'm going to miss you too. Just remember, if it hadn't been for you, I wouldn't have survived our world."

Dr. Ram walked to the cave with the teenagers. "There's something you need know."

The teenagers could see by the worried look on his face it must be serious.

"What is it?" Lee asked.

Dr. Ram said he didn't want to alarm the people there, but once the cave gives way, the entrance to their world would be sealed. He also said the earthquake left an opening in the earth. This opening could be a passage between the two worlds. But it would take a considerable amount of time to make a way through it, at least a year or two. Whether they could clear it before the world there was extinguished. He couldn't say.

"What do you mean, Dr. Ram?" Mia asked. "What's going to happen to this world?"

"This part of the earth has suffered severe damage from the earthquakes. The crust on this part of the earth is thin. Unlike our part of earth that has three layers, this part has only one. It probably happened when the earth shifted into two parts. Another major earthquake will demolish this world. I have been monitoring the seismic waves. It will take place within the next year or close to it. Our world is the only place these people can go."

"Do our people know about this?" Lee asked.

"Yes. I told them. They chose to stay."

"What can we do?" Lance asked.

"The only thing you can do is monitor the earthquakes. They will become stronger and more frequent."

"I'll watch closely," Mia said. "Hopefully, one day soon, we will be able to communicate with you."

"Meanwhile, enjoy your lives," Dr. Ram said, squeezing each of them. "Just remember, whatever happens, you saved the people here in this world."

Mia, Lance and Lee entered the cave. They turned and waved goodbye to their friends, the people whom they had gotten to know so well. They felt sad because they were leaving their friends behind with the uncertainty of the future. But they were excited that only a few feet ahead of them was a machine that would carry them back to New York City, where they would be with their families again.

They moved cautiously through the cave where e**a**ch step they made caused parts of the cave to fall down on them. Their hands covered their heads from falling chunks of dirt and stone. Just a few feet ahead of them, was an old, worn door with a large keyhole.

Lance's hands slightly trembled as he tried to insert the key into the keyhole. He turned it up, then down, took it out and put it in again. He dropped it in the dirt. Mia picked it up and made several attempts. The key was very rusty. Finally, she succeeded. They pushed the door open. What stood in front of them was a round contraption. Above it was a dark open space that led upward through the earth. They stepped into the machine, sat down in one of the several seats and fastened their seat belts. In front of them was a handle attached to a board. They hoped the old machine still worked.

"Push the handle, Mia. You have the golden touch," Lee said.

"Do it," Lance said.

Mia reached over and pulled the handle down. The machine sounded like a flooded car. Then all of a sudden, with great force, it launched upward like a spaceship. The teenagers held on tightly to their seats until they passed out.

After a couple of hours, the machine slowed down and came to an abrupt stop—they awakened. They took several deep breaths and stood up. They changed into their school uniforms.

"Well, this is it," Mia said.

"The end of our journey," Lee said.

They pushed the door open. Not sure if they had arrived in New York City, they hesitated before they stepped out of the machine. Holding each other's hands, they walked out of the machine into a partially-built tunnel. They looked back at the machine and smiled. The area ahead of them was boarded up. They peered through an opening and saw one of the boards on the ground. They looked at each other and smiled. They recognized the board was the one that was nailed across the entranceway of the tunnel that connected to their school. They pulled off the rest of the boards. They were back home.

"Which way should we go?" Lance asked, looking both ways. "One way will take us back to the school. I'm not sure where the other one leads to."

"We can't go back to the school. We've probably been reported missing," Mia said.

"Mia's right, we don't have our story together," Lee said.

"Then let's go the other way," Lance said, pointing to the opposite direction.

Hand in hand, they rushed through the cold, damp tunnel until they saw daylight shining in from the outside. They walked out onto a busy street. A street sign read, *Broadway St.* Excited, they threw their hands up in the air and yelled, "We're home! We're home!"

They were stunned to see the devastation caused by the earthquake. They stepped around broken glass that covered the ground. The pavement was destroyed from large cracks in the earth. Storeowners were busy sweeping up pieces of glass in front of their shops. Loud sounds radiated from car horns by impatient drivers. They continued to walk down Broadway Street until they reached Sam's newsstand. He was picking up magazines and newspapers scattered all over the sidewalk.

"Hey, I'm glad to see you guys. I saw you turn into the alley. Some quake, huh?" Sam said, stressed out.

"Really bad," Lance said. He picked up a few magazines scattered on the ground.

Lee asked, "What day is this?"

"It's Friday, November 8," Sam answered.

The teenagers were puzzled and confused. They looked at each other. How could that be? It was the same day they were swept away. It was the same earthquake. Lee pored through the papers scattered on the ground. He picked up yesterday's paper. "Look," he said to Mia and Lance pointing to the date, November 7. "Time stood still while we were in the other world. The world below revolves slower than this world. Their hours are equivalent to our minutes and their minutes are equivalent to our seconds. This caused a lapse in time."

Sam shook his head. "Teenagers," he mumbled.

"We'd better go and check on our families," Mia said.

"You know some of the subways aren't working—a lot of damage underground," Sam said.

The earthquake was so powerful the effects were felt all over the world. It seemed the earth shifted. Scientist couldn't figure out the cause. A lot of people felt it was Armageddon. The three agreed for now they would keep their journey to themselves. After all, who would believe them anyway?

They wondered how many Spoilers had invaded their world. It would be up to the three of them to protect the world from the creatures—if they were a threat. They waved goodbye to each other and went their separate ways.

CHAPTER EIGHTEEN

Lee walked into his family's restaurant. He saw tables and chairs scattered throughout the room. He went quickly to the back room of the restaurant. He was relieved to see his family was safe. His sister was snuggled next to his mother and father on the couch. Her face lit up when she saw him standing in the doorway.

"Lee," she called out, quickly jumping up from the couch. She went over to him and threw her arms around. "You're okay."

His mother and father also embraced him. Lee's mother said, "We were worried about you, son." She gave him a kiss.

"She was worried about you. I knew you could take care of yourself," his father said, trying to cover his true feelings.

Lee's mother looked at his father and shook her head.

Lee said, "I'm glad to see you guys are safe. Man, what a day."

"Where were you when the quake hit?" Kim asked.

"With friends," Lee answered.

"You were probably in your little cozy world with your high society friends," Kim said with a smirk on her face.

Lee answered. "Right...another world maybe, but not one you could imagine."

Ling entered the room with the old book in his hand. He stepped fast and almost stumbled. Lee caught him. "Be careful, Grandfather," Lee said, still holding onto him tightly.

"I'm glad to see you, Lee," Ling said. "So much going on with this earthquake.

I've never seen anything like this before."

They turned their attention to the television. News reporters were reporting the damage caused by the strange earthquake.

In a low voice, Lee said, "Grandfather, do you believe another world could exist outside of ours?"

"What do you believe?" Ling asked, looking at Lee, as if a light bulb went off in his head. Kim overheard their conversation and interrupted them. "Grandfather thinks there are creatures trying to enter our world. It tells all about them in his book. Show Lee the book, Grandfather."

Ling opened the book to the chapter about the Spoilers and showed it to Lee. "The stories in this book were recorded by our ancestors," Ling said. "It's up to you to decide whether or not they are true. But I feel, grandson, you already know the answer."

"I'd like to read the book, Grandfather."

Ling handed Lee the book. He put it in his backpack. "You never know." Lee said. "There could be some truth to it."

"Oh, you didn't answer my question," Ling said.

"It was just a thought, Grandfather."

Ling knew something was weighing heavily on Lee's mind and hoped one day he would share it with him.

Lee went back into the restaurant and started placing the chairs and tables back where they belonged. His back faced the door. He heard someone entering the room and turned to see an attractive girl with long black flowing hair who displayed a striking resemblance to Nadia. Speechless, his heart raced. *Could this be Nadia?* He asked himself. Then he realized it was a ridiculous thought.

"Sorry to bother you. Do you have a phone I can use?"

"Hold on, mine is charging. Let me get my sister's phone," Lee said. "Do you live around here?"

"Not far," the girl said. "I was in the bookstore down the street when the earthquake hit. Something very weird happened, really odd."

Lee grabbed a chair for her to sit on and one for himself. "Tell me what happened," Lee said, eager to hear the story.

"I was in the back room of the bookstore with three other people. We were waiting for the earthquake to end. The owner didn't really want us there; in fact, when the earthquake started he told us to get out. He told us to find shelter someplace else but it was too late. The building began to shake; books were flying all over. So we ran into the back room of the store with him."

"I know who you're talking about -- the tall dude. He has a closed sign on the door most of the time," Lee said." I don't know when he sells any books."

"He was acting really odd," the girl said.

"Odd like how?" Lee asked.

"While we were in the room his body started twitching. He ran out of the room, covering his head from pieces of the falling ceiling. He must have gone into the basement. After things calmed down, we called him to make sure he was okay. We tried to open the basement door but it was locked."

"That was weird," Lee said, staring at the girl. He thought, *she could be Nadia's twin.*

"My name is Patina," the girl said.

"I'm Lee; let me get you the phone."

Lee left the room. He went into the back room of the restaurant, where his family was watching television. They were looking at images of the destruction caused by the earthquake. Kim sat on the floor, chatting on her cell phone.

Lee signaled Kim with his hand to get her attention. He mouthed to her to hang up.

"Hold on, it's my nerdy brother," Kim said.

"Hang up ...please, this is important," Lee said.

"I'll call you right back," Kim said, frustrated that she had to hang up. "There must be a fire somewhere."

"I need to use your phone for a minute...please, it's important," Lee said, reaching for her phone. She held out the phone and pulled it back when he reached for it. She laughed. Their mother nudged their father and said, "Look at your kids-- see how they act. It's your fault."

Lee's father glanced over at Kim and Lee tussling over the phone. He raised his voice. "Kim, let Lee use your phone. Please!"

Lee took the phone out of Kim's hand. "Thank you," he said.

He slicked his hair back with his hands, gained his composure and returned to Patina. He gave her the phone. "Sorry I took so long. I have a crazy sister."

Patina smiled at the remark Lee made. She called her mother to make sure ever-thing was okay. Lee noticed Patina wrist. She was wearing a bracelet like the one Nadia gave him. He thought, *it's just a coincidence.*

"Is your family okay?" Lee asked Patina.

"Yes, everyone is fine," she said, handing the phone back to Lee. "I better leave now."

"Listen," Lee said, "it's getting dark. If you don't mind, I'd like to hang out with you. Make sure you get home okay."

"Are you sure? Patina asked.

Lee said, "I wouldn't have it any other way."

Kim came into the room. She walked over to Lee and stuck out her hand. Lee gave her the phone. "Thanks for letting me use your phone," Patina said.

"No problem," Kim said, looking back at Lee and smiling as she walked out of the room. Lee was glad she left without making any smart comments.

Lee and Patina left the restaurant. They chatted, walking away down the dark street.

Lance peered through an opening in the window at the restaurant where his mother worked. He saw her and another waitress picking up broken dishes. Her face glowed when she looked up and saw him. She waved at him. He rushed inside and gave her a hug. The little white dog barked at him.

"I was worried about you," Irene said. "I couldn't get you on your phone."

"My phone was dead," Lance explained.

"Where were you when the earthquake hit?" Irene asked.

"Mom, I don't think you would believe me if I told you," Lance answered.

Irene didn't question him. "You're safe; that's all that matters. Let's go home," Irene said, picking up the dog.

"Where did he come from?" Lance asked, petting the dog on its head.

"He got lost in all the commotion," Irene said. "He'll be staying with us tonight. Will your friend Moody be sleeping on the couch tonight?"

"No Mom, Moody has a place of his own."

"That's good," Irene said. "I hope it's nice."

"It's out of this world," Lance said, happily.

Mia climbed up the stairs of her apartment building passing several people coming down the steps. The power was out. The elevator wasn't working but that's how it was most of the time.

Mrs. Mason held her son's hand as they walked down the long flight of stairs. She stopped Mia.

"My husband checked on your grandmother. She's just fine," Mrs. Mason said.

"Thanks a lot," Mia said, watching her son playing with his action figures. The little boy looked up at Mia.

"Look," the boy said, holding up one of his action figures. "The hero has destroyed the monsters."

"He has such an imagination," Mrs. Mason said.

Mia wondered if it was really his imagination, or if he was able to see something that no one else could. Maybe, people should really listen to what children said. She continued up the stairs to the apartment and unlocked the door with her key.

"Where are you, Grandmother?" she called, dropping her backpack on the floor.

"I'm here. In the bedroom," Beverly called out. She was happy to hear Mia's voice.

Mia moved briskly over to her. She kissed her. "I was so worried about you, Grandmother."

"No need to worry. I'm fine. I am glad you're home. I knew the school would take good care of you."

"Yes, Grandmother. They took good care of me."

Mia and her grandmother watched a special news report. The reporter was interviewing a geologist. She asked him if there was any explanation for what had taken place. He said, "Not at this time but what we do know is the earth made a drastic shift. We won't know the effects for some time."

"That's strange," Beverly said. "If I didn't know better, I might have thought you had something to do with this peculiar earthquake."

Mia hugged her grandmother. "You know I don't have that much power."

Later that night, Beverly peeked into Mia's room. She could see the window curtains blowing from the wind. She also heard an unusual sound coming from outside her window. Mia woke up and asked. "What is it, Grandmother?"

Beverly said, "It's turning cool outside. I'd better close your window. What is that noise?"

Mia answered, "Probably an owl."

Beverly looked out to see an owl perched on a tree branch. "It's a noisy little creature." She shut the window and walked out of the room. Mia looked toward the window. She whispered to herself, "He can talk too." She closed her eyes.

CHAPTER NINETEEN

THE RETURN

The world was peaceful over the past year except for a few minor earthquakes. But that was soon to change. Recently, the earthquakes had become more frequent and more powerful. The teenagers often thought about their friends in the world below. They knew at some point in time they would connect with them again, hopefully before the major earthquake hit. But for now they had comfort knowing the Spoilers no longer posed a threat to them.

Mia, Lance and Lee were excited because in a few weeks they would be graduating from Charlton Academy. Dr. Bloom appointed himself their advisor. He had personally taken charge of their academic careers. He also appointed them a mentor to assist them with their research project.

They had been taking classes at the university since their junior year. The university was very happy to have these three brilliant students join their institution. The teenagers had their own rooms on campus where they spent most of their nights. Even before this opportunity, the three teenagers had decided to complete their education in New York. They wanted to stay near the area where the strange events had occurred. Even the focal point of the earthquakes was in the tunnel near Manhattan, according to Dr. Ram.

Dr. Bloom was very much a part of their lives. The Board of Directors was considering him f o r the new Headmaster of Charlton Academy position. To his credit, he did select the three gifted teenagers, and for the first time Charlton Academy was known for its academic achievements, not just social status. The families were very appreciative of Dr. Bloom's guidance and support, however, the three teenagers felt he was too controlling.

They kept a close watch on the activities at Charlton Academy because they knew the school was somehow connected to some of the past unexplainable events. It was no coincidence the machine they arrived in was connected to a tunnel leading into their school. They had no proof, but Mia remembered what Orka told them: just because you can't prove something doesn't mean it's not true.

After the earthquake, the tunnel was completely repaired. The hole in the tunnel wall no longer exist, it was sealed with concrete—a good thing.

The three teenagers met every Friday at 1:00 at the popular coffee house, 1322 Broadway Café, a very retro shop near the theater. It was frequented by actors who came in for a drink or sandwich between rehearsals. Pictures on the walls showed the two brothers, owners of the café, with famous actors. The coffee house was in walking distance from their school. It was also a hangout for some of their teachers.

Mia had matured into a very stylish girl. Contacts replaced her glasses and she loved to plop one of her many hats on top of her curly locks which had become her signature look.

She spent a lot of time thinking about her mother and father. She went to Washington, D.C. to gather information about them. She searched records and questioned a few people in the State Department but no one seemed to have any information on them. Their file had been expunged. She was discouraged but vowed never to stop looking for them. She wanted her grandmother to have peace.

Lance wore an old rusty key around his neck, the one that opened the door to the machine that brought them back from the other world. He had grown a couple of inches but was still lanky. He shortened his hair because Dr. Bloom felt he needed to look more conservative when he went in front of the Board to interview for his research grant.

Mia teased him. She told him he looked like a young version of Dr. Bloom, especially when he wore the suit Dr. Bloom gave him. "All you have to do," Mia said, "is walk with your shoulders hunched over." Lance reassured her he would never wear the suit again.

Lance and Mia's relationship had blossomed, but it wasn't the usual teenage romance. Instead of going to the movies and hanging out at the mall, the two spent their time together working in the lab with their mentor Mr. Eldermeyer. They wondered why Dr. Bloom chose him when he had nothing to contribute. All he did was watch them, take notes, and report to Dr. Bloom.

Mr. Eldermeyer was a very unusual-looking man. He was in his forties, one side of his body was lighter than the other and his red, faded, frizzy hair was streaked with greenish highlights. He had a tendency to be cold all the time. Mia and Lance wondered if he had some type of illness. He told them his blood was just thin.

Lee also worked with them. Together, they created a device called the Enhancer, a small three-inch metal electronic piece that had the capacity of increasing a satellite's signal ninety-nine percent of its current capacity. Imagine what the world could do with that small device. It would give countries a significant advantage to know when they are under threat. The teenagers felt this was the reason Dr. Bloom was so secretive about their project and wouldn't allow them to discuss it with anyone.

Because Lee was computer savvy, he spent half of his time in Washington, D.C. at the International Rocket Center. There, he developed the software for the Enhancer. Lee was very protective of the device if it fell into the wrong hands it could be disastrous. He was the same computer geek, with a unique since of humor and urban lingo that set him apart from his friends. He took the story in the book his grandfather gave him to read serious.

He knew there was truth surrounding the events that took place in ancient China, it confirmed what he and his friends already knew about the Spoilers.

His grandfather was a wise man. It wouldn't surprise him if he had already figured out what took place during the earthquake. In Lee's words he was right on. He would soon tell his grandfather about the world beneath them and the confrontation with the Spoilers.

Mia and Lance sat at a table sipping on lattes waiting for Lee. Mia looked at the time on her phone. "Lee is fifteen minutes late," she said, glancing out the coffee shop's window.

"He probably got held up," Lance said.

"Do you think he's over Nadia?" Mia asked. "He really liked her."

"It's hard to say," Lance said. "He spends a lot of time with Patina. It's amazing how much they look alike. They could pass for twins. He says they have a connection but I don't think it's a romantic one."

Lee strolled into the coffee shop pulling his bag on wheels. He stopped at the front counter to place an order. "Order time," Lee said to Seam, who hurried over to take his order.

Seam was an unusual looking girl—definitely into Goth. She was dressed in a long black vintage dress. Her face was heavily made up. Her short black hair was streaked with purple highlights and her eyes were lined with thick black eyeliner. She wore black lipstick that matched her black nail polish and had several body piercings.

She smiled at Lee. "The same?" she asked.

"Hit me with an extra shot of espresso. It's going to be one those days," Lee said.

"You need to chill. You seem stressed out. I'm out of here in a couple of hours. Maybe you'd like to hang out with me. I'm going to visit a friend of mind. He's an artist. In fact, you may find his paintings very fascinating. "

"That's pretty cool but maybe another time. I'm hanging out with my friends today."

"I'm going to hold you to that," Seam said. "Make it sooner than later."

Lee watched her prepare his coffee. He had seen her a few months ago with a group of her Goth friends walking down Broadway St. He felt, *Goths get a bad rep because they dress in dark clothes and tend to see the world opposite from everyone else. But one thing is for sure, Seam's got her own thing going on. I've seen enough of the gloomy—the unearthly.*

Lee paid for his coffee and joined Mia and Lance. He sat his cup on the table and slipped his bag underneath.

"What's up?" Lee asked. "Why are you both smiling? Oh Seam... she flirts with everyone."

"She doesn't flirt with me," Lance said.

"That's because she knows you're with, Mia." Lee said.

"You know, you've always had that special something with the ladies. I just haven't figured out what it is," Lance said, grinning,

"It's my allure," Lee responded jokingly. He slicked his hair back with his hands. The three burst out laughing, attracting attention from people sitting at tables near them.

Suddenly, the room shook, everyone reached for the closest immovable object. The teenagers took cover under their table during the impact that lasted about ten seconds. Everyone in the coffee shop seemed to be a little shaken, some of their cups with coffee had spilled onto the floor. One of the clerks immediately announced free coffee for everyone.

Lee turned to Mia and Lance. "This could have been the major one."

"Yeah, the one Dr. Ram warned us about," Lance said.

Mia opened her computer and traced the damage caused by the earthquake. She could see the physical changes that occurred beneath the earth were similar to the changes that took place before the past major earthquake. She was convinced the next major earthquake wasn't far off—a matter of days. Not only would it demolish the world below, but their world would also suffer.

"We don't have much time. Check this out," she whispered.

Lance and Lee looked closely at the computer screen. "This doesn't look good," Lee replied.

"Especially for the people in Citadel." Lance said. He did some quick statistical analysis in his head. "You're right, Mia."

"We have to get word to Dr. Ram right away." Mia looked around at the people seated at the tables near them to make sure no one was listening. "I have the Enhancer with me. Hopefully, when I attach it to the computer, the signal will be strong enough to make contact. It's our only chance"

"Let's go to my grandmother's apartment. It's just a few blocks away," Mia said. "We won't be disturbed."

The three grabbed their things and headed for the door. Seam winked at Lee as he walked out of the café.

Beverly was very surprised to see Mia with her two friends at the door. "Is everything okay?" She asked.

"Everything is fine, Grandmother," Mia said, embracing her.

Lance and Lee gave her a hug, too. "I'm happy to see you guys," Beverly said. "Don't be such strangers. So, to what do I owe this pleasure?"

"We have an important project to work on, Grandmother. We're going to work on it here so we won't be interrupted if it's okay with you."

"As long as you don't blow up the building," Beverly said jokingly. She looked at all of Lee's electronic equipment protruding from his backpack.

"We haven't eaten, either, Grandmother," Mia said.

"Don't give it a second thought. Dinner will be ready in an hour. Before you say anything else, yes, I'll make your favorite—spaghetti with turkey meatballs," Beverly said.

"Thanks, Grandmother," Mia said.

Lance and Lee followed Mia into her bedroom. Lee attached the Enhancer to his computer. The computer screen resembled one used by an Air Traffic Controller.

He explained to Mia and Lance what he was doing. "I'm highlighting the area of the tunnel where we arrived in the other world. We know that's the area where Citadel is located."

"That's fascinating," Mia said, looking over Lee's shoulder.

"How will you know if the signal reached them?" Lance asked Lee.

"Watch the screen; follow the red signal as it moves downward. When it reaches the bottom it will flash. Hopefully someone down there will see it."

"What if they don't?" Mia asked

"We'll give them a few hours," Lee answered.

"What if this doesn't work?" Lance asked.

"Let's just hope it does," Lee said. "I haven't thought that far ahead."

"It has to work. We don't have a clue how to reach them," Mia said, sitting down on her bed. She took off her hat that covered her curly locks and tossed it on top of a pile of hats in a corner of the room.

On the computer screen the red ball made its way slowly downward. But something happened; it stopped, flashed and faded away.

"Seriously?" Lee said, closely watching the activity on the screen. "This isn't going to work here." Frustrated, he rubbed his fingers through his hair.

"What happening, Lee?" Lance asked, leaning over his shoulder.

"Man...there's just too much activity between us and the surface of the earth. We have to go where there's less interference."

"Let's go to the school...set it up in the basement. No one's there at night," Mia suggested.

"I overheard Mr. Eldermeyer talking to Dr. Bloom. There's going to be a meeting at the school tomorrow evening. The door will be unlocked. We can get in."

Beverly called them to come and eat. They walked quietly into the dining room, looking very serious. Beverly knew something was up by the looks on their faces. "You three look like the cat that swallowed the canary. I've never seen you this quiet before. Your project must be very important."

"It is, Grandmother," Mia said. "Our future is at stake."

"Well, if you three can't solve the problem, I don't know who can," Beverly said.

CHAPTER TWENTY

Chilled by the cool night air, Lance shivered in his hooded sweat shirt waiting for Mia and Lee in a dimly lit area by the side of the school building. He watched Dr. Bloom and Miss Finney with two other people walk toward the school, chatting among themselves.

Unbelievable, Lance spoke to himself, that's *the weirdest group of people I've ever seen. Maybe it's just the way they walk—a little hunched over.* A man moved swiftly to catch up with them. Lance recognized the man. He was a State Senator but he couldn't remember his name.

Lee, Mia, and Ivor hurried over to him. Mia and Lee also wore hooded jackets pulled over their heads so they wouldn't be recognized. Lee's duffle bag was slung across his shoulders.

Lance pointed to Dr. Bloom and the others going up the school steps. "Look," he said, "they're heading into the school now."

Mia looked hard at one of the men. "The man who just entered the building is Senator Miller. He used to be the representative in our district, always promising things that never happened. This must be a pretty important meeting."

"Oh, Senator Miller...I couldn't think of his name. I've seen him on TV," Lance said, looking at Mia. "You're right, something must be up."

"There doesn't seem to be anyone else coming. "Let's go," Lee said anxiously.

They quickly climbed up the steps and entered the school to the stairs leading to the basement. They stepped softly down the hallway past several rooms.

They opened the door to the lab and locked it behind themselves.

Lee attached the Enhancer to his computer. Now they just had to wait until the red ball moved downward and flashed. How long it would take? They didn't know. Mia browsed around the room. She discovered the jars that contained the green substance were missing. "The jars are gone. Someone's been in here."

"Maybe the maintenance man," Lance said.

"I doubt if it was him," Mia said. "He wouldn't be interested in anything in this lab but where he stashed his bottle." She opened the drawer, where the maintenance man kept his liquor bottle. She took the bottle out and shook it. "It's empty."

"Yeah, he's been here," Lance said, looking at Mia.

"We might as well get comfortable. It's going to be a long night," Lee said, watching the red signal move slowly down the computer screen.

"I think I'll check out that meeting upstairs." Lance said.

"Watch your back," Lee said.

Ivor flew over to Lance. "I'll accompany you."

"Be careful," Mia urged.

Lance left the room. He cautiously made his way up the steps to Dr. Bloom's office. Ivor flew ahead of him. The door to the reception room was slightly opened. The only light in Dr. Bloom's office came from one nightlight plugged into the wall.

"That's odd," Lance said. "Why meet in the dark?"

"Perhaps it's because they don't want anybody to see them," Ivor said. He flew over to Lance, landing on his head.

"Do you mind?" Lance said, pushing Ivor off his head.

Ivor lost his balance and landed on his back with his small claws sticking straight up once again.

"You could have asked. You know, you people are so rude."

"Okay, okay ... I'm sorry, Ivor," Lance said. He lifted him up. "Now can we get back to this?"

They were too far from Dr. Bloom's office to hear what the people inside were saying. Ivor flew to the top of Dr. Bloom's door and looked into the room. His eyes opened wide. He was startled by the images before him and flew quickly back to Lance. "Brace yourself... it's them... the Spoilers. They look just as you described them."

"What do you mean it's the Spoilers? That's impossible," Lance said, moving slowly over to the office. He gazed into the room. He could barely contain himself. "Incredible," he whispered. He watched the five scaly green creatures—Spoilers in his school.

Even though Lance was warned by Orka to be aware of the Spoilers in their world, it was still hard for him to believe the creatures had actually invaded their world, especially their school. He thought about the frightening thing Moody saw coming out of the alley. It could have been a Spoiler—maybe one of them.

One thing was for sure, the Spoilers were more terrifying out of the earth. At least in the earth they were contained but watching them move around freely was scary. No one would ever believe the outstanding people meeting in the school were animals.

"We've got to find a way to destroy them. Let's see if we can hear what they are saying," Lance said, looking up at Ivor. He moved closer to the door. The Spoilers talked about their lifeline hidden in a facility outside D.C. Lance couldn't make out which Spoiler was who but felt the one with the high-pitched voice and green eyes was a female—Miss Finney. Her green eyes shined through the wide sockets in her crusty head.

Lance felt it was only logical that the one speaking, encircled by the other four was Dr. Bloom. He seemed to be in control. When in human form, they seem taller than most individuals. If you looked closely at them, their shoulders were slightly hunched over. They had odd-looking ears, similar to an elf's, and their skin had a faint greenish tone to it. At least that's the way Dr. Bloom appeared to be. Whether or not they all possessed these characteristics remain to be seen.

The Spoiler presumed to be Dr. Bloom spoke. "You know our lifeline is failing; the signal from the satellite is not strong enough to keep it powered. But the good news is my brilliant young students have invented a device called the Enhancer. It will be attached to a new satellite, making the signal so powerful our lifeline will exist forever. We will live forever!"

"It's all coming together," another Spoiler said. "I sit on the President's Defense Committee. We control all military weapons. When the time comes for us to rule, we will use those weapons to destroy other countries. They won't know what hit them, only that this country betrayed them."

"We're going to have to work fast. They've infiltrated the government," Lance said, crawling out of the room.

In the laboratory the red signal flashed. They had successfully reached the location of the people in the other world. Lee and Mia nervously watched the computer screen hoping someone in the world below would see the signal.

Lance and Ivor abruptly entered the lab eager to tell Mia and Lee what they saw. "You aren't going to believe this," Lance said, breathing hard, his heart pounding.

"Don't tell me. Let me guess. You saw a Spoiler coming out of one of the rooms," Lee said jokingly, smiling.

"Not quite," Lance said.

"But... you're on the right track," Ivor said, flying around them.

"They're all Spoilers—Dr. Bloom, Miss Finney, the Senator and the other two men. I saw them in their natural form. I know it's hard to believe. I saw it and I still don't believe it," Lance said excitedly.

"So, we were right," Mia said anxiously, looking at Lance. "We knew somehow this school was tied to the other world. The Spoilers have been in our school for a long time. Remember the photos in the album. They have also established themselves among the elite."

"Man, I was just joking. The last thing I would have thought was there were Spoilers in our school," Lee said.

The teenagers wondered if the Spoilers destroyed the machine and boarded up the tunnel when they discovered humans were coming here from the other world. They would love to see the look on their faces when they discover another machine is there.

"We have to stop them," Lance said. "Their lifeline is hidden in a facility somewhere outside of D.C. You see, it was all a plan— recruiting us into Charlton Academy. The government would never monitor the research of teenagers. Remember, Dr. Bloom insisted we work on a project that would enhance the capabilities of satellites. The Enhancer will keep them alive."

"So they used us," Lee said. "Just remember what they say about payback."

"They'll get what they deserve. But for now, we'll just let them go on thinking their species will be saved," Mia said, pacing back and forth.

"What do you have in mind?" Lee asked.

"After they leave, we'll search Dr. Bloom's office... there must be something in there about their facility and where it's located," Mia said.

"Are you sure Miss Finney is one of them? She's strange enough as a human," Lee said. He thought about all the times he'd seen her and never suspected anything. She was attractive. Never much to say but always looking at herself in the mirror.

Lance answered, "Trust me, there's no mistaking those green eyes. The only difference is they were shining through her reptile body."

Suddenly, a blurred picture showed on the computer screen and a faint voice was heard. The teenagers moved close to the screen. "Hello, hello, this is Mia. Is anyone there? Can you hear me?"

"Yes Mia," Dr. Ram answered. "We can hear you. We can't see. The picture is too fuzzy. I'm here with Moody and Feather."

"We can't see you, either. But the main thing is we can hear each other," Lee said. "I'm glad you saw our signal."

"There's not a day that goes by, Feather doesn't check the computer or cell phone," Moody said. "She saw the signal and ran to get us."

"I knew we would hear from you," Feather said very excitedly. "I knew you wouldn't forget about us."

"Is everyone well?" Lee asked.

"Yes," they all responded.

"Is Nadia there with you?" Lee asked.

"No," Feather answered. "She's with the children."

Lance moved in close to the computer. "It's good to hear your voices and know everyone is well."

Dr. Ram expressed deep concern. He told them they had been hit by several tremors and he believed the major one wasn't far off.

Mia said, "I'm afraid you were right, Dr. Ram."

"You have to get the people out of there right away," Lee said.

"Did you finish digging the path through the earth?" Lance asked with great concern.

"We've been working day and night to clear the passage but we're blocked. There is a mound of dirt cutting us off. It's different from the other dirt. It's hard more like rock. We can't dig through it," Dr. Ram said. "Some of the men think there is something inside the mound. They hear strange sounds and movement."

"It could be the Spoilers," Moody said.

"You're right, Moody," Lance said. "It could be them."

"We have to destroy their lifeline. It's the only way to stop them," Mia said.

"The people here will be trapped in the earth if we can't get past the mound of dirt before the earthquake," Dr. Ram said. His voice trembled.

"Don't worry, Dr. Ram, and tell the people there not to worry. We'll do whatever it takes to keep you and them safe."

"Remember," Mia insisted, "you don't have much time left. Get out of there."

"We'll contact you soon," Lee said. "We have to go now; it's not safe where we are."

The three teenagers watched Dr. Bloom and the other people leave the building. They had transitioned back to human form. "It's still hard for me to believe they're not human," Mia said. "They seem so normal."

"We saw what they wanted us to see. It was all there... right in front of us," Lance said. "Their odd appearance—remember the photos dating back centuries. But most of all, Dr. Bloom's possessiveness."

"We won't make that mistake again," Mia said.

"I'll follow them," Lee said. "I'll keep it low."

"Good idea. Mia and I will search Dr. Bloom's office," Lance said.

Mia and Lance entered Dr. Bloom's office where the scent of the animals lingered in the air. Mia cracked the window.

"This smell is all too familiar," she said, rushing over to join Lance. "Just like the smell down in the hole where they were trapped."

They opened drawers and rambled through papers. "Nothing here," Mia said. "Check the file cabinet."

Lance went over to Dr. Bloom's file cabinet and pulled on the drawer. "It's locked," he said, jerking it. Mia joined him. She stared at the drawer, opening it.

"You know, you could have done that in the first place," Lance said.

"I wanted to give you a fair chance. After all, you're always saying I like to show off." Mia turned to Lance and gave him a kiss on his cheek.

"Right," Lance said, slightly blushing "Let's just see what's in the drawer." They flipped through folders looking for any clue that would lead them to the Spoilers' secret facility.

"Nothing here," Lance said, disappointed. "But we'll find it. We have to."

"Let's get out of here," Mia said.

They walked quietly down the hallway to the school door, cracked it slightly and looked out to make sure it was safe to leave. The night air was cold. They zipped up their jackets and dashed from the school to a tree near the building. Mia instructed her phone to call Lee.

Lee sat at a table in the corner of the coffee shop. His face was hidden behind a menu. He glanced over at the five Spoilers sitting at a table, talking and drinking coffee. His phone vibrated. The Spoilers were too engaged in their conversation to notice him.

"I'm in the coffee shop," he said softly. "It seems to be one of their regular meeting places. Who would have thought the Spoilers have a thing for coffee?"

"This is all too unreal. Can you make out what they're saying?" Mia asked.

"No, I can't, but Seam is cleaning the table next to them. She'll tell me what they're saying. Did you find anything in Dr. Bloom's office?"

"Zero," Mia answered. "Hold on, Lance wants to talk to you."

"Listen, I just thought of something. Dr. Bloom had a briefcase in his hand when he entered the school. Does he have it with him?"

Lee could see Dr. Bloom's briefcase on the floor next to him. "Yes," Lee replied.

"He must keep his important papers in it," Lance said.

"You're probably right. But there's no way I can get to it," Lee said. "If I find out anything. I'll call you back."

"Okay," Lance said. He looked over at Mia. "He's not going to be able to get the briefcase."

Seam came over to Lee's table and sat down across from him. He looked across the room at the Spoilers. He asked, "Could you hear what they were saying?" He sipped on a cup of coffee, trying not to look conspicuous.

"The only thing I could make out is someone is going on a trip."

"A trip where? I really need to know what you heard. It's really important," Lee said impatiently.

"Okay, okay give me a minute... they sort of rambled on and on... not making much sense, about a place not far from D.C, a facility. The stiff dude, the Senator, said it only takes him about a half hour to get there from the Capitol. Sorry, but that's all I got."

"You've been a big help. More than you'll ever know. Thanks a lot. I owe you one."

Seam reached over and pressed her hand on Lee's hand. "Listen," she said. "You can trust me. A lot of strange things have happened. Some better left alone."

Lee had never seen this serious side of Seam before it was like something had spooked her. He wondered, *if she could possibly know about the Spoilers.* "What are you referring to?" Lee asked. He hoped she would confide in him.

"Meet me at the corner under the street light. Give me ten minutes," Seam said.

"Are you for real?" Lee asked.

"Yes...Just be there," Seam said firmly.

"Okay... okay," Lee said.

Lee looked over at the Spoilers. He wanted to make sure they didn't see him and Seam together. The last thing he wanted to do was put h e r in danger.

Lee left the coffee shop. He walked to the corner and waited under the street light. He stood there thinking, *this whole scene is crazy. What else is happening in front of our eyes? Maybe we should go to the feds. What would we say? Oh, we want to report a group of creatures called the Spoilers. They're planning on taking over the world. They came from a world beneath ours...oh, we know this because we've been there—we're screwed.*

Seam walked swiftly over to Lee. Her pale face was partially revealed underneath her faux fur hooded coat. "It's getting cold," she said.

"Where are we going?" Lee asked. He wondered where she was taking him.

"Just trust me."

The two walked a few blocks. Seam stopped in front of a Catholic Church. She looked over at Lee. "Here," she said.

"The church?" he asked.

"Yes," Seam answered.

He followed Seam into the church. A young priest walked vigorously to them. Seam walked ahead to greet him. "Welcome," the priest said. "Oh... that's you, Seam." Lee looked at the flickering lights from the candles on the altar. He felt very peaceful. He knew evil spirits wouldn't be welcomed here. He could see the serious looks on the faces of Seam and the priest. They glanced over in his direction. Finally, they walked back to him.

"Come with us, Lee. There's something you should see," Seam said.

Lee followed them down some narrow steps. They walked into a room where several priests were kneeling down in front of an altar chanting, casting the evil spirits away. Lee watched them. He knew praying was common for priests but this chanting gave off an alarming vibe.

The priest led Seam and Lee into his office. He told Lee what he just saw and heard was not common. That Seam brought him there for a reason. She believed he had discovered something evil and by the look on his face, she was right.

"You know about the creatures... My friends and I felt no one would believe us." Lee exhaled with a sense of relief.

"The Church has been battling these evil beings for some time, but the force is greater now. There are more of them." He told Lee how he became aware of them. "One of the members of my parish, Mrs. Brooks, came to me very upset. She said her kitchen window faced her neighbor's kitchen window. She was washing dishes and looked out the window. Something horrible was in her neighbor's kitchen. A devil, she called it.

"She thought she was having some kind of breakdown. She dropped a dish on the floor and called her husband. She looked out the window again. Her neighbor smiled and waved at her. She really believed this woman was the devil. I told her to invite the neighbor over and I would casually drop by. I didn't want her to live in fear.

"I went to her house later that week. Irene, the neighbor, was there. She looked normal except for an excessive amount of makeup on her face. She was covering up some kind of blemish. She was surprised to see me. I extended my hand to greet her but she backed away. She said she was sick and didn't want to spread her germs.

"I left the room for a moment and removed my cross from around my neck. I held it in my hand so she couldn't see it and made an excuse to leave. I told her it was nice meeting her. I gave her a slight touch on her shoulder with the cross in my hand. She grabbed her shoulder and jumped up from her chair. She said she felt sick and left quickly out of the room. I didn't want to alarm Mrs. Brooks. I told her to keep away from Irene. She might be sick. I also told her I thought her imagination could have gotten the best of her.

"I didn't tell her what I really knew. Irene wasn't what she appeared to be. The creature she saw in her window was Irene, a evil spirit that couldn't endure the touch of the cross."

"That's frightening," Lee said, looking at Seam.

"It is," Seam said. "My friends and I saw one of them. We were coming from a party one night. We thought we were hallucinating. The next day, I came here and told my brother." She peered over at the young priest. "Yes, he's my brother. Far out, huh? We do have something in common. We both wear black."

"Wow." Lee said. He looked at Seam, then her brother. "I see the resemblance. Listen, these animals are dangerous. There's a lot about them you don't know. Be careful." Lee got up to leave when a forceful tremor shook the church. It knocked him onto the floor.

Seam and the priest held on tightly to the desk. Books and papers slid off the desk onto the floor. The light blinked off and on. It lasted only a few minutes but it was powerful.

"That was stronger than the others," Seam said. She picked up some of the books and papers that fell on the floor.

"They're getting stronger and stronger." Lee replied.

The priest left the room. He went to check on the other priests and to see how much damage the tremor caused to the church.

"I'll let you know if I find out anything else," Seam said.

Lee left the church. Luckily, the church didn't suffer much damage. It could have been the major one, he thought.

CHAPTER TWENTY-ONE

The next day, Lance, Lee and Mia met in the school library to discuss their next move. They decided they would have to look in Dr. Bloom's briefcase to see if it contained the location of the Spoilers' secret facility. They would have to come up with a plan soon to extinguish the Spoilers' lifeline. Time was running out for the people in Citadel to make their way safely to their world.

Mia's attention was on the big clock on the library wall. It said twelve forty-five. She knew Miss Finney would be going to lunch in fifteen minutes. Mia said to Lance and Lee, "Wait here. I'm going to Dr. Bloom's office. Maybe I can get a look into his briefcase." She carried her research paper in her hand.

"Are you sure?" Lance asked.

"It's cool," Mia said. "He has no reason to be suspicious of me. If we all show up, he may think we're up to something."

"We'll wait here." Lee said.

"Okay," Mia said in a low voice, rushing away.

Miss Finney was holding a compact, admiring herself in the mirror. She was spreading red lipstick on her lips. Mia stared at her from outside Dr. Bloom's reception room. She had a humorous thought. *Is Miss Finney applying lipstick to her natural or human form? Or maybe she has no reflection in the mirror.*

After all, vampires don't cast a reflection in mirrors. She has come a long way from her scaly body to a human dressed in designer clothes. She should write a book sharing her secrets. What an inspiration she would be to all creature women. It would be number one on the bestselling monsters' list.

Mia went over to Miss. Finney. "Good afternoon, Miss Finney, you look hot... did you change your hairstyle?"

"I just added a few highlights," Miss Finney said. "If you're here to see Dr. Bloom, you'll have to come back later. He's very busy."

"This is very important. It's about my research paper. I need his advice." She showed the paper to Miss Finney. "I'm sure he would want to see it before I turn it in." Mia looked up at the clock. She thought, *Miss Finney, you should be leaving any minute.*

"Okay, okay," Miss Finney said. "Have a seat. You can go in when he finishes. I have an appointment."

"I'll be quiet as a mouse," Mia said.

Miss Finney looked up at Mia. She was puzzled by her remark, comparing herself to a mouse. She shook her head and left the room.

Mia peeped through the crack in Dr. Bloom's door. He was working on the computer. His briefcase lay open on the desk. Mia wanted to get a look at the papers in it. She knocked on his door while opening it.

"Mia, what are you doing here?" he asked.

"I want you to look at my research paper before I turn it in." She sat the paper down on his briefcase.

"I'll be right with you. I have to finish this first."

Dr. Bloom was frustrated. He couldn't get his computer to work. Mia went over to him. She picked up her paper and glanced at the papers underneath. Nothing about a facility. She would have to go through his briefcase, and that would be impossible with him there. "What are you doing?" Mia asked.

"I'm trying to make reservations. I can't seem to get into the site for some reason."

"Here, let me do that for you."

Dr. Bloom gave his seat to Mia. He looked over her shoulders while she typed. "All my information is on the paper next to you. Miss Finney usually takes care of this but she had some appointment – probably shopping. The woman is obsessed."

Dr. Bloom realized he left his briefcase open. He picked up Mia's research paper and shut it quickly. Mia watched him out of the corner of her eye. She smiled.

"Don't worry, Dr. Bloom. This is the least I can do for you. You've done so much for me and my friends."

"I'd better go now and return before the earthquake," Dr. Bloom said, pondering. "For the life of me, I can't figure out how one can predict an earthquake."

"Most geologists can't. But there is a way you can compare the earth's activity prior to an earthquake. Besides, these aren't normal earthquakes. "

"I'll leave that to you scientists... I am curious about something."

"How to destroy mankind?" Mia said jokingly to Dr. Bloom. She knew that was his intention.

Dr. Bloom laughed. "Okay, putting all joking aside," he said. "Will these earthquakes affect our project?"

"No, the satellite will travel way above the earth's surface."

"That's good to know. The airports will probably shut down in a couple of days. I've got to get back here."

"You know rumor has it you're going to be the next headmaster of Charlton Academy," Mia said. "You deserve to get everything that's coming to you."

"Thanks Mia, it's not a done deal yet, but between you and me, it's just a matter of time," Dr. Bloom said, smiling, sticking his chest out and straightening his tie.

"Tell me where you are going?"

Dr. Bloom answered. "To Washington, D.C. this Wednesday. Anytime in the afternoon is fine... Oh, I'll need a car."

"Got you," Mia said in a low voice.

"What did you say, Mia? Got you?" Dr. Bloom asked, bewildered by Mia's response.

"It's just a saying we use."

"Oh, some of that slang."

"Yeah, right."

Mia stopped typing. "Okay, you're all set. Wednesday, one o' clock, Southern Air, and you'll pick up your car at Speedy Car Rental at the airport."

"Great job."

"Oh, I almost forgot, I have to go with my grandmother to her doctor's appointment. I think she's coming down with the flu." Mia left quickly, before Dr. Bloom could respond.

She rushed back to the library, where Lance and Lee were talking with Daily and their other classmates. Everyone was excited. They were discussing what universities they would attend in the fall. They didn't seem very nervous about the earthquake. Their plans after they graduated were all that mattered to them.

Mia pulled Lance and Lee aside. "Dr. Bloom is going to Washington tomorrow."

"We'll beat him there," Lance said. "Let's hope he's going to the secret facility."

"He's got to be going there. He would have told me if he was going to the Rocket Center," Lee said."

They joined their classmates and updated contact info in their phones. The three had become very popular. When they first arrived at the school, their classmates felt they were different because they lived in urban areas and attended schools there. They had no clue what their lives were like.

But once Mia, Lance and Lee achieved high academic awards that drew attention to their school, they were readily accepted by everyone. Some of their classmates took the time to get to know them. Others just wanted to befriend them to enhance their own popularity. They were invited to all the parties but usually declined because of their busy schedules.

They did hang out with Daily. The fact that she came from a very wealthy family didn't faze her one bit. She just wanted to play her guitar to anyone who would listen. She wanted her parents to realize playing music was her destiny.

She would visit Mia and play her guitar. She was pretty funny too, especially when she did her impression of Miss Finney. She would stare into a mirror, open a tube of lipstick and smear it all over her lips, and in a very proper voice, she would say, "Dr. Bloom is very busy. You need to make an appointment." They would laugh to the point of hysteria.

Daily was bubbling over with excitement. She made an announcement. In the fall she would be attending Julliard. Mia knew it was her dream. She applauded her. "Way to go, girl," Mia said. "For sure you're going to be a rock star."

"Listen everyone," Daily said. "I'm having a party tonight if we don't have another earthquake. Please come; it will be my last one for a while. You can all stay over. There's plenty of room."

"We'll be there," Mia said, looking at Lance and Lee. They nodded their heads in agreement.

Lee added, "The only thing that could keep us from your party would be if we were kidnapped by aliens." He turned to Mia and Lance. The three looked at each other and smiled.

CHAPTER TWENTY-TWO

Daily's party was at her family's home in Connecticut. Lance drove the three of them down the highway in their rented van. Nightfall was approaching but they could still see the elegant mansions. They'd only seen these elaborate homes on television and in magazines. The teenagers agreed there could possibly be three worlds, the one they were passing through, where they lived and the world below.

"How much farther?" Mia asked.

Lee looked at the GPS displaying the miles to Devon Road. "Not too much farther... 10 miles," Lee murmured.

"We'll be there soon," Lance said, turning up the radio to hear his favorite song. Mia spotted a quaint-looking restaurant up ahead. It looked like a cottage: brightly lit, green awnings, with antique tables and chairs out front.

"Stop at that restaurant," Mia said. "I want to use the restroom and get something to drink."

"You got it," Lance said, making a sudden turn into the entrance. Mia and Lee braced themselves. Lance swerved into a parking space and stopped abruptly jerking Mia forward. She took off her hat and hit Lance with it. "Really Lance, couldn't you have made the turn a little slower?" she said, regaining her composure and stuffing her hair back under her hat.

"Well, you should have told me sooner. I almost passed it." Lance said, looking at a couple of barking dogs at the side of the restaurant. The three got out of the van. The dogs ran to them, barking as if they were trying to tell them something. Lee reached out and patted one of them on the head. Lance knelt down and stroked the other one. "They seem upset, frightened," Lance said.

"I don't see anything," Mia said, looking around. "I'm going to look around the back. That's where the dogs came from."

"Be careful, it could be a Wolfling," Lee said jokingly. He and Lance chuckled.

Mia stepped slowly. She saw a large fenced-in area. She went back to the front. "Nothing back there," she said. "Maybe they were scared by a snake."

They entered the fifties décor restaurant where the waitress, hair pulled back in a ponytail, dressed in a red skirt and white blouse, greeted them. She seated them at a booth and handed them a menu.

"What can I get you?" asked the waitress, smiling. "I just made some fresh lemonade."

"I'll have a glass," Mia said, looking around at the colorful room. A jukebox sat in the corner of the room. Mia remembered her grandmother telling her about jukeboxes. She would put a quarter in it and play her favorite song.

Lee had been eyeing a couple of pies on the counter. "I think I'd like to have a piece of pie and a glass of lemonade," he said to the waitress. "Apple, please."

"I think I'll have the same," Lance added. He looked at Mia. He knew she loved pies.

"Okay, make it three," Mia said. "It looks delicious, like the kind my grandmother makes."

Mia excused herself and followed a sign in the back of the room pointing to the restroom. She moved down the long narrow hallway until she reached the room. She heard movement and disturbing sounds coming from inside. She knocked on the door. "Are you okay in there?" There was no response. She placed her ear against the door. The waitress came swiftly down the hallway, only this time, she wasn't smiling. She was mad. "Follow me!" she stated in a firm voice.

Mia wondered why she was so upset. She glanced back at the room. She could still hear the unsettling noises. She followed the woman up the stairs to a restroom on the second floor and thanked her. The waitress responded with a grunt.

Mia returned to the table. Lance and Lee were eating their pie.

"What took you so long?" Lance asked.

"I was about to eat your pie," Lee said, smiling.

"Something very odd happened," Mia said, looking over at the counter. The waitress and man were talking. They both glanced over at her. "I'll tell you later." She sipped her lemonade and ate some of her pie. She glanced at the counter again. They were still talking. The man seemed upset. He wiped sweat off his face with a towel.

"You're not eating," Lance said.

"I guess I wasn't hungry," Mia said. She knew something strange was going on. "I guess we'd better go before we miss the party."

Lance picked up the bill. He went to the counter to check out. He handed the woman some cash with the bill. Mia looked at all the pictures of wild animals on the wall. She heard the waitress ask where they were going.

"Not far," Lee answered. "A friend of ours is having a party... Daily."

"Oh," the waitress said, "Dr. Anderson's daughter. A bunch of her friends were here earlier."

The three left the restaurant. They climbed back into their van. Mia felt uneasy. She looked back at the cottage. It seemed very normal—but it wasn't.

"Mia, what happened when you went to the restroom? You looked shaken when you returned," Lee said.

"I'm not really sure. Something strange was happening in the restroom. There was a loud thump against the wall, and weird sounds."

"What kinds of sounds?" Lance asked.

"Sounds like those made by the Spoilers. But then it could have been my imagination."

"Before you came back to the table, the grumpy-looking dude came out from the same area you did. He was sweaty and pale," Lee said. "We thought he was having a heart attack."

"It's sort of hard to believe Spoilers would be in this isolated area," Lance said.

"Think about it," Mia said. "It's the perfect place...it's very remote. Your neighbors are miles away. No one can get on your property without being invited."

"You're right," Lance said.

"I guess we'll never know," Lee said, looking out the window at the wind blowing the cluster of trees. There was a faint resemblance to the forest in the other world. They turned off onto a dirt path. Traveling at slow speed, they reached an open gate. In front of the gate was a sign, the family's name, THE ANDERSONS. A security camera was mounted on a pole next to the gate. The two-story brick mansion was centered in the midst of trees surrounded by thick shrubbery. Lance parked his car behind a long line of cars.

"Amazing," Mia said, looking at the elaborate mansion.

"I don't know if amazing is the word," Lee said. "I would say creepy is more like it."

"There is something mysterious about older homes," Lance said.

"Well, I still say creepy," Lee said.

They stood on the front porch; a bright light shined on them. They rang the doorbell. A woman dressed in a long gray dress with a white collar opened the door.

"Follow the music," the woman said, annoyed. She disappeared into one of the rooms down the long hallway.

Daily's party was in full swing. Patina and a few of her friends were already there. Everyone was welcome. Daily was cool that way. Mia and Lance danced together to the rock music played by Daily and her band. The sound was loud and brassy. They couldn't help but notice Lee dancing with Patina. He kicked his legs up high and made karate motions with his hands. They looked at each other and giggled. "Patina better watch out. Lee may take her out," Mia said, trying to contain herself.

"I knew Lee didn't like to dance. Now I know why," Lance said, smiling and watching his friend, who seemed to have captured an audience. A couple of his classmates tried to imitate his moves.

"Everyone is looking at Lee," Mia said in amusement. "They probably think it's some kind of urban dance."

Mia and Lance moved to the area where Daily and her band were performing. She was backed up by a drummer and a keyboard player.

"She's really good," Lance said to Mia as they moved to the beat of the music.

Lee and Patina left the dance area. They went over to the buffet table and filled their plates with all kinds of foods. They grabbed sodas out of a cooler.

"Having a good time?" Lee asked Patina.

"Yes, it's a great party," answered Patina. "I'm surprised you made it. You're always working."

"Daily is a cool person." Lee said. "I couldn't miss her party. But I do have to go to D.C. tomorrow."

"Be careful. You know we're supposed to have an earthquake, or what some are calling a strange earth phenomenon. It's getting pretty scary." Patina said.

"Just make sure you're in a safe place." Lee responded. He touched her bracelet. "You and I wear the same kind of bracelet. You know it's real."

"It's supposed to bring good luck," Patina said.

"It will if you believe in it," Lee said. He looked over to see Seam entering the room. He invited her to the party. He felt she and Daily would hit it off. They both liked music. Besides that, Daily lived a very sheltered life. She would be on her own in Manhattan, a place he knew wasn't safe. Seam would look out for her.

Lee excused himself and walked over to greet Seam. "You made it," he said. "You came alone. I told you could bring your friends."

"I know, but my friends sort of hang with their own crowd. It's just the way they are."

"That's keeping it real. Come with me. I want to turn you on to some of my friends." He led Seam over to Patina. He introduced the girls to each other. Mia and Lance gathered around them.

"I see you guys with Lee every Friday at the coffee shop," Seam said, looking at Mia and Lance.

"We really like it there. Especially the coffee drinks," Mia said.

"A lot of famous people come there," Seam said.

Daily joined them. She was hardly recognizable. She wore round tinted glasses, a hat on her head, a short denim dress, long boots and several beads around her neck. Lee introduced her. "And this is Daily."

"I heard a lot about you from Lee," Seam said. "You're moving to the city. I'll show you around. Oh, don't let the black scare you. I'm a Goth, not a witch. "

"Didn't give it a second thought," Daily said. "I'll check you guys later... there's a couple more sounds I want to play. I hope you like them."

Daily's music rocked the room. Three guys approached Seam. She couldn't decide which one to choose, so she danced with all three. Lee watched her dancing with his classmates. He gave her a thumbs-up.

Mia and Lance went out into the hallway. A few of their classmates were lounged on the floor, happily engaged in conversation. They stopped and chatted with them. It seemed most of them would be staying over in Daily's guest house. Daily did say there would be enough room for everyone to stay over. That was putting it mildly.

She and Lance continued down the hallway. Original paintings in antique gold frames mounted the walls.

"Check out the painting," Lance said, "it's like a museum in here."

"I can see why Daily can't wait to leave here. It's more like a museum than a home," Mia said, turning into one of the rooms.

"Maybe we should go back. I have an eerie feeling," Lance said, looking around the very organized room. "It looks like this room is staged. Not one thing out of place."

"Just a second," Mia said. She went over to the shiny circular desk where several books, mostly medical, were neatly piled on top. "What kind of doctor is Daily's father?"

Lance read one of the many framed documents on the wall. "He's a surgeon, and he must be pretty good from the looks of all these awards."

Suddenly, the shadow of something passed quickly by the window. They turned to each other. "Did you see that, Mia?"

"You couldn't miss it."

They opened the window to get a closer look. They tried to see which way it went but all they could see was movement as it traveled through the bushes.

"Whatever it was, it's gone," Lance said.

"It looked like..."

Before Mia could finish her sentence, a heavy voice from behind them said, "Shouldn't you be with your friends at the party?"

Lance and Mia quickly turned around to see a man fitting the description of a Spoiler standing in front of them.

"We were just looking at all the paintings...yes...the paintings in the hallway, and ended up here," Lance said, stumbling over his words.

"But you know, you're right. We probably should be getting back. Daily will be looking for us," Mia said, baffled by the fact that a Spoiler was in Daily's home.

"I'm Dr. Anderson," the man said.

"It's nice to meet you," Lance said, looking at Mia.

"I recognize you both... Dr. Bloom speaks highly of you two. He said you are very smart. I was hoping the school would make an impression on my daughter. But it seems she made more of an impression on the school."

"Daily is very talented. You should be very proud of her." Mia said, defending her friend. "You're right. She did make an impression on the school. She took away some of its stuffiness."

Lance snatched Mia's hand. He pulled her toward the door before she could say anything else to Dr. Anderson.

"Well, it was nice meeting you," Lance said, looking at Dr. Anderson.

Mia looked back. She stared at his awards on the wall, causing them to fall onto the floor.

Dr. Anderson was stunned by what happened. He stood at the door, mouth wide open, and watched Mia and Lance disappear down the hallway.

"That was close," Mia said. "I just can't believe Daily's father is a Spoiler."

"Think about it. His tie to the school. All his contributions. It's not so surprising," Lance explained.

"What about Daily? Does that make her one too?" Mia asked. She was upset. She couldn't bear the fact that her friend could be a Spoiler.

"I don't know, Mia. Let's just wait until we know more," Lance said.

Daily came down the hall toward them. "What happened to you guys? I thought you bailed on me," she said, raising her voice.

"No, we were checking out your paintings. We ended up in your father's office," Mia said.

"Don't tell me. Let me guess. You met my charming stepfather, Dr. William Anderson."

"He's your stepfather?" Mia said with sigh of relief.

"Yes," Daily said. "My father is working out of the country. I came here to live with my mother and her new weirdo, disappearing husband."

"I agree with you on weird. But why disappearing?" Lance asked.

"He seems to disappear a lot, especially at night. Lately, he's become obsessed with the earthquakes. He's always in our safe room. He says he's making sure it's well supplied. He even added an underground exit that leads to the outside. One evening, I went to the room looking for him. The door leading to the outside was open. I looked out and saw something running through the garden. It was nighttime. I couldn't make out what it was."

"You know," Lance said, "we saw an animal outside your father's office window. It ran into your garden."

"Shortly afterward your stepfather appeared," Mia said. She didn't want to worry Daily. She just wanted to find out how much she knew about her stepfather.

"Maybe my stepfather has a pet. Who knows?" Daily said. "Anyway, I'm out of here after graduation."

"Stay safe," Lance said.

"We have to leave now," Mia said. She was glad Daily would be moving to the city. The sooner they destroyed the Spoilers, the safer everyone would be.

Lee saw them in the hallway. He rushed over and embraced Daily. "We had a great time, Daily."

"I was hoping you would stay over," Daily said disappointedly.

"We'll get together soon," Mia said. "We have to go to D.C. tomorrow." She gave Daily a hug.

Lance moved close to her. "Stay away from your stepfather. I get bad vibes from him," he said in a serious manner. He couldn't take a chance on telling her the truth. She might let something slip. What if she told her mother? It could be dangerous.

"Just be careful." Mia said.

The three teenagers left Daily's home. They had decided earlier they would wait at the airport for Dr. Bloom to make an appearance, and then follow him to the secret facility.

Mia rested on her bed in the small campus room the university provided for her. She looked over at Ivor, perched on her window sill.

"How was your day, Ivor? Did you meet any other owls?"

"No, things have been rather boring lately. It seems there are no talking animals here, and this is supposed to be the advanced world."

"Just give it some time. There's got to be at least one or two exceptional birds like yourself out there."

"So far, all I've encountered are some annoying little birds that run around eating off the streets," Ivor explained. "No class at all."

Mia turned on her computer to track the earth's movements. She could see the damage taking place beneath the earth's surface. "Ivor, this doesn't look good."

"What are you going to do?" Ivor asked.

"There really isn't anything I can do. I just hope people take the warning seriously."

She closed her eyes and went to sleep.

CHAPTER TWENTY-THREE

The early morning sun beamed between the towering buildings in Manhattan. Shop owners unlocked their doors. In another hour or so, their customers would flock into their establishments. Just getting through the day without another tremor was what most people wished for.

Lee went to see his family. He decided it was time to tell his grandfather about his experience with the Spoilers. They all agreed that someone should know what was going on in case their mission failed.

The restaurant's breakfast crowd was already there. Lee recognized some of the regular customers. His mother waved to him from behind the counter. He went over and gave her a kiss on the cheek. "Hi Mom," he said. "Where's Kim? Have you had her committed?"

"Don't talk about your sister that way. You know you miss her."

"I do miss her but don't tell her. She'll think I like her," Lee said, smiling. He was very protective of his sister. When he left the neighborhood to attend the academy, he asked his friends to watch out for her.

"Kim and your dad left early to go shopping. We worry about the earthquake."

"Well, I'm sure Grandfather has everything under control. Where is he?"

"Your grandfather is in the alley with some of the neighborhood kids."

"Let me guess… he's showing them Karate moves." It hadn't been that long since he was one of them. He couldn't wait until school was over. He knew his grandfather would be waiting in the alley to teach him some new karate move.

"That's what he does most days. He misses you."

"My friends and I have to go to Washington in the morning. I'll just grab a few things, then go see Grandfather." Lee walked to his small, narrow bedroom in the back of the restaurant. His robotic computer greeted him in an automated voice.

"Hello Lee. You're home. You have messages. Do you want me to display them?"

"Yes," Lee said. "Display messages." He was amused by a message from Lance. *Bring food. I already called in the order.* Lee knew what he had ordered. Shrimp-fried rice, two egg rolls. He always ordered the same thing. Even for breakfast.

Lee hurried around the room. He picked up a shirt, a couple of electronic parts, and stuffed them in his backpack. Kim stuck her head in his room. "I thought I heard that freaky robot's voice," she giggled. She walked over to the computer to get a closer look.

"Stranger, stranger. Should I sound an alert?" said the automated voice from the computer.

"A stranger," Kim said, hitting the monitor. "You're a stupid machine."

Lee laughed. "Even the computer knows you're strange."

"Why couldn't you have invented something cool, something fun?" Kim asked. "Instead of a nerdy machine to go with your nerdy self."

"Okay, I will if you stop bugging me," Lee said, "but for now, I want you to listen to me. There's going to be another earthquake. Stronger than the ones before. I want you to stay close to home. Okay?"

"Sure, whatever," Kim said. Lee stopped by the kitchen. His mother was cooking. He looked through the takeout order bags on the counter. He removed the one with Lance's name on it. "I've got this one, Mom." He stuffed it in his backpack.

"Your friend Lance is wacky. Who orders shrimp-fried rice and egg rolls for breakfast?"

Lee shrugged his shoulders. "I don't know, Mom. He's sort of picky when it comes to food."

He went outside to the alley, where his grandfather was showing one of the kids how to kick. Ling looked up and saw Lance. He stopped and rushed over to him. He put his arms around him. "Take off your jacket...join us. Let's see if you are still as good as you used to be."

Lee placed his backpack on the ground. He removed his black leather jacket and threw it to one of the boys. The boy caught it and smiled. He was proud Lee chose him to hold his jacket.

Lee had a reputation in the neighborhood as being undefeated. All the kids looked up to him. He positioned himself. His grandfather stepped forward aggressively to attack him. Lee didn't want to hurt him, so he jumped high, out of his reach, twirled around and landed behind him. His grandfather was stunned to see how good he had become.

"I can see you've been practicing."

"It was a matter of necessity."

Lee took his jacket from the boy and ruffled the boy's hair with his hand. He picked up his backpack. "I want to talk to you, Grandfather."

The two walked a short distance through the alley. They passed dumpsters overflowing with smelly bags of garbage. A few cats ran by them, following the foul scent.

"This must be pretty serious," Ling said. "The last time we made this walk, you wanted to know how to ask a girl out. What was her name?"

"Shelly... I wish this was that simple," Lee said.

"You want to tell me what happened to you and your friends during the earthquake. Your experience with the Spoilers. Well, I have been waiting."

"How did you know, Grandfather?"

"Because the stories in the book are true. Now tell me what happened."

Lee wasn't really surprised his grandfather was aware of his encounter with the creatures. He believed the recordings of his ancestors. He told his grandfather he and his friends weren't able to kill the Spoilers because they were immortal. But they did stop them from getting out of the hole. He went on to explain that the Spoilers were in their world and it was up to him and his friends to destroy them.

"You're right, grandson. You have to stop them."

"Don't worry, Grandfather. My friends and I have discovered a way to eliminate them once and for all."

"Be careful. They are deadly. Let me know if you need my help."

"Okay, I'll keep in touch. Take care of yourself and the family. I'd better go now." Lee continued down the alley. He felt better knowing his grandfather knew what was going on. He could always count on him. He would know what to do if something went wrong.

The teenagers, with Ivor sitting in the back window of the van, headed to Washington. Lance drove them to the Washington Dallas Airport rental car area. They waited there for Dr. Bloom to appear.

"What time is it? He should have come out by now," Lance said. He wondered if somehow they missed him.

"It's two-thirty," Mia said, watching every car leave the rental car lot. "He has to come this way."

"This is the only exit," Lance said.

"Look! Look! That's him! Go! Go!" Mia shouted.

"That's him all right. There's no mistaking his big head," Lee said, watching from the back seat.

Lance sped off to catch up to Dr. Bloom. All of a sudden, Dr. Bloom slowed down. Their van was only a few feet behind his car.

"Do you think he recognizes us?" Lance asked. He pulled his hood farther down over his head.

"No, he's talking on his phone," Mia said, pulling her hat down to hide her face in case Dr. Bloom gazed through his rearview mirror.

"Listen to this," Lee said. He read from his tablet, "Scientists have confirmed there are massive movements of rocks under the earth's surface which will trigger a major quake. They want people to be prepared. This isn't good. We have a lot to do in a short amount of time."

"I agree wholeheartedly," Ivor said. "Time is definitely not on our side."

"Look! Dr. Bloom is turning," Mia said.

"There's a sign up ahead. Can you read it?" Lance asked.

Lee stuck his head out the window to get a closer look at the sign on a post. "It says, 'Government Facility: No Trespassing.' Cool, cool. That's got to be it."

Dr. Bloom continued moving rapidly down the forbidden highway. Lance swerved the van off the highway onto a muddy path through the woods. Snapping sounds were heard as he hit the matted tree branches. The van got stuck in a ditch. He shifted the gear back and forth, causing the tires to spin, splashing mud in every direction

"We have to push," Lee said.

"No need," Mia said, "everyone out." The three teenagers and Ivor exited the van. They followed Mia several feet away from the vehicle. Mia stared at the back of the van. Within minutes, the van launched forward with great force out of the ditch. The teenagers covered their faces to avoid the flying mud. They watched the van barely miss a tree.

"Good job, Mia," Lance said. "But I have to admit, I thought the van was going to crash into the tree."

"Me too," Lee said, looking closely at the distance between the van and the tree.

"After all, we've been through, you don't trust me?" she said.

"We trust you," Lance said hesitantly.

"It's just when you activate your powers," Lee said, "we know all hell can break loose." Ivor nodded his furry head up and down. The three laughed.

"We'd better walk the rest of the way," Lance said. "There could be guards from the facility in the woods."

They picked up their bows and arrows. Lee slung his duffle bag across, his shoulders. They followed a path through the woods. Ivor and Mia led the way. Not far ahead of them was a large single story concrete building nestled among the trees. They hid behind a tree. Two men with weapons in camouflage military clothes guarded the entranceway of the building. A wired metal fence surrounded the back of the building with signs posted on it stating, KEEP OUT GOVERNMENT PROPERTY.

"There it is," Lance said.

"Incredible," Lee said taking in the whole scene. "That's Dr. Bloom's car parked on the side of the building. He's in there. That's for sure," Mia said. She looked through her binoculars at the two men guarding the facility. They were Spoilers. "Take a look," Mia said, handing the binoculars to Lance.

"They're Spoilers disguised in military clothes," Lance said, holding the binoculars close to his eyes. He handed the binoculars to Lee.

"I've seen the lists of government's facilities. This is definitely not one of them," Lee said. "We have to find a way to get past them," Lee said. He adjusted the binoculars to get a closer look.

"I'll go in," Mia said, sounding very confident.

"You have to get past the guards," Lance said, taking the binoculars from Lee. "That won't be easy. We have to create some kind of diversion." He turned to Ivor. "You have to distract the guards, so Mia can get past them."

"Okay," Ivor said, flying up from the ground.

"Hold on," Lee said. He reached into his overloaded duffle bag. He spilled the electronic devices, wires, and screws on the ground.

Mia and Lance bent over and helped him sort the items out. "Really, Lee." Mia said. "You couldn't get a larger bag?"

"I've had this bag forever. I've become attached to it."

"Well, you could organize it," Mia said, frustrated.

"Here it is," Lee said, holding up a small object the size of a hearing aid. He attached the small device to Mia's shirt.

"What is this, Lee?" Mia asked.

"It's a tracking device. We'll be able to follow you on the screen." Mia stuck out her hand. Lee placed his hand on top of hers and Lance placed his hand on top of Lee's hand.

"We can do this," said the three together.

"Be careful," Lance said. He gave her a hug.

"We'll be watching you every second; if anything goes wrong, we're coming in." Lee said.

Mia left her bow and arrow behind. She used the trees to shield herself as she made her way closer to the building.

Ivor flew to the guards. His furry little body hit one of them in the head. The guards raised their arms to capture him. While they were busy trying to catch Ivor. Mia moved quickly to the side of the building without being noticed. She paused for a second and ran past the guards into the building. She stopped and looked back at the scuffle. She hoped Ivor didn't get hurt.

She continued down the hallway. She ducked behind doors to avoid being seen by the Spoilers. Some of them were in human form, some in their natural forms. She didn't want to risk being discovered, especially by Dr. Bloom.

Mia wondered how many of these creatures were in her world. It was obvious they plan to defeat them. They had already started positioning themselves in high power positions. The pictures on Dr. Bloom's walls showed him with important people. It was part of the plan.

CHAPTER TWENTY-FOUR

Ivor flew through the facility to Mia. She patted him on the head. "Good job, Ivor." She wiped sweat from her forehead. The facility was extremely warm, just like the lab where she and Lance worked with Mr. Eldermeyer.

She never would have believed Mr. Eldermeyer was a Spoiler. However, the fact he didn't hold a degree in any field related to their work always puzzled her. Now it made sense. He was just there to spy on them and record their progress.

One day she and Lance walked in on him searching their files. He was most likely trying to find the prototype for their device. Only the three of them knew where it was kept—in a safe in Lee's family's restaurant.

Mia heard the Spoilers' heavy bodies' pound against the floor in a room nearby. She hesitated. She moved into a room across from them. The creatures, with their tails curved around their bulky bodies, were seated on the floor. They seemed to be very restless and agitated. They spoke to each other in their creepy voices.

Lee and Lance tracked Mia on the computer. She wasn't moving. They didn't know if she was in danger because there was no activity.

"What do you think?" Lee asked. "Should we go in?"

Lance didn't want to move too quickly. He knew Mia would use her powers if she was forced to. They couldn't afford to be discovered. Their whole plan would be blown.

"Let's give her a little more time," Lance said.

Dr. Bloom was in his natural form. His voice was still recognizable but somewhat slurred. He stood in front of the Spoilers. He urged them to be patient that everything was going according to plan. "Don't worry. It won't be much longer before the device is installed on our new satellite. I must be careful. I don't want to draw suspicion," he announced.

"Can we trust the three humans to prepare our lifeline for the transition?" asked a Spoiler with a high-pitched voice—a female.

"There's no need to worry about them. They know in order to keep their families safe, they must keep our lifeline alive," Dr. Bloom said.

Mia was amazed—three human scientists. She repeated what the Spoiler said. She had to find them and help them escape. Loud sounds generated from a room nearby. She and Ivor made their way to the room.

Two Spoilers left the noisy room, dragging their tails behind them. They used their short front arms to push their bodies forward. They left the door open wide enough for Mia and Ivor to enter the room without being seen.

Centered in the middle of the large, dimly–lit room was a large container holding a green pulsating substance—apparently alive. The container was attached to a machine with several tubes coming from it, similar to a respirator. A red light, a signal powered by a satellite that could only be seen inside the room, beamed down through the glass in the ceiling. It powered the substance in the container—their lifeline.

Mia was stunned at the whole scene. She saw the three human scientists, one woman and two men, dressed in white jackets. They were surrounded by several Spoilers in their human form. One of the scientists in a white jacket adjusted the machine. He turned it slightly. Mia whispered to Ivor to move in closer and listen to what they were saying. He moved to a table close to the machine and hid behind some boxes. He watched the Spoilers examine their lifeline. One of the Spoilers spoke meanly to the scientists. In an intimidating voice he said. "You better keep our lifeline powered until we replace it."

A male scientist, in his forties, close-shaven head, answered. "We can't control the satellite signal...we told you it was fading."

"In a short period of time, we will have one so powerful it will last us a lifetime. Do whatever it takes to keep this one powered," said another of the Spoilers.

The female scientist, slim with curly brown hair, in her thirties, said, "We kept our part of the bargain for thirteen years."

The older human scientist, with grayish hair, in his late sixties, said angrily, "You kept us captive with the threat of harming our families. We want to be released once your new satellite is launched."

"Then you better make sure everything goes off as planned. Remember, our people in Washington have access to your most powerful weapons, your missiles. We can use them to wipe out the world. All it takes is one phone call," said a Spoiler with a nasty look on his face.

Ivor returned to Mia. "Did you hear that?"

"Yes," Mia said. "We have to talk to the scientists."

Ivor said, "Let's wait for them to come out and follow them."

"Good idea, Ivor," Mia said. She and Ivor waited behind a cart filled with supplies for the scientists to come out of the room. Mia reached for her cell phone. "I'd better check in with Lance and Lee and let them know we're okay."

"Look," Ivor said, "they're coming out of the room."

"Let's go," Mia said, putting her phone back in her pocket. The two followed the three scientists. They tread cautiously down the hallway. They stopped to hide whenever the Spoilers were close by.

The scientists continued until they came to the end of the hall, to a door. The woman pressed a pass against a scanner on a door and it opened. The three of them went through the door, which closed tightly behind them.

"Now what?" Ivor asked.

"Stay here," Mia answered. "Let me know when anyone comes. I'm going to try to get their attention."

Mia moved quickly down the hall. She made sure no one saw her. She knocked softly on the door. She prayed no Spoilers were on the other side. "Please, if you hear me, open the door," Mia said, looking back over her shoulder.

Ivor flew swiftly to her. "They're coming... they're coming... you have to hide," Ivor said.

Mia heard the sounds of Spoilers' voices coming toward them. Lee and Lance saw the images of the Spoilers moving close to her. Lance called Mia on her phone—no answer. He called her again. This time she answered.

"There are two subjects approaching you. We can't see who or what they are but you need to get out of there fast," Lance said, following the images on the screen.

"I know," Mia said. "I may have to use my powers."

Lee snatched the phone out of Lance's hand. "Hold on, Mia. Listen, look down to your right—there 's a vent. Remove the cover and crawl in... it leads through the building, exiting out at the back."

"Okay," Mia said, looking at Ivor. She waved to him to fly away. She yanked hard on the cover but it was nailed shut. She stared at it, using her powers, causing the cover to fall off, making a piercing noise. She crawled into the narrow space and reached for the cover but there wasn't enough time.

She listened to the heavy footsteps of the Spoilers coming down the hall. She sat very still on the cold metal.

"What's going on here?" Dr. Bloom asked.

Mia recognized his voice. He was only a few feet from her. She could see his shoes. She never realized his feet were so big. He was breathing heavily. The other Spoiler, also in human form, bent his inflexible body down to get a closer look at the opening. Lucky for her, he couldn't bend down far enough to look into it.

She slid her body farther away from them. The Spoiler with Dr. Bloom picked up the cover to the vent. He examined it closely.

"It looks like it just fell off. The nails are old and rusty. I'll get someone to fix it," he said.

"Or maybe someone is trying to find a way to escape. Let's see if our humans know anything about this."

Mia had to control her feelings to prevent her powers from activating. She inhaled a couple of times to calm herself down. She was worried Dr. Bloom might think the scientists tried to escape and harm them. She tried to call Lance and let him know what was going on but there was no signal.

Mia had to leave. She didn't want Lance and Lee to think something happened to her. They would come looking for her. She crawled through the winding vent. She stopped abruptly. Loud noises echoed from the room below that contained the lifeline. She looked through the cracks in the vent and watched the Spoilers busily moving around the room.

Lee followed her on the computer. Lance and Ivor waited for her on the other side of the barbed wire fence in the back of facility.

"Over here," hollered Lance.

Mia lifted herself out of the vent. "Be right there," she said. She stepped backward, far enough to give herself enough room to run and jump. She ran to a barrel next to the fence, jumped on it and flipped over the fence.

They moved swiftly through the woods to the van. Ivor flew over their head. They took a minute to catch their breath. Lee handed Mia and Lance each a bottle of water.

"What did you find out, Mia?" Lance asked.

"What's going on in there?" Lee asked.

"Their lifeline is in there. It's this green looking thing in a container. Similar to the green substance in the jars we saw in the lab at school. It's alive. It beats like a heart. There are tubes connected to it. A red light seen from inside the room beams down on it. It must come from their satellite through a window in the ceiling."

"That confirms what we already know. Now we can move on. I know what I have to do," Lee said. "Another thing," Mia said. "There are three humans in there. Most likely they were kidnapped and forced to keep their lifeline alive... We have to get them out of there."

"That's brutal," Lee said.

"What's scary is they threaten the woman and two men. If they fail to keep their lifeline alive, they will use our missiles to destroy us," Mia said anxiously.

"Then it is possible for them to wipe out our world," Lee said.

"Are you sure these scientists aren't Spoilers? They walked among us every day and we didn't know the difference," Lance said.

"I overheard their conversation with the Spoilers. The Spoilers threatened to harm their families if they didn't keep their lifeline alive," Mia said.

"I saw them up close. They're humans. They look peculiar just like you," Ivor said.

"You're right, Mia," Lance said. "We have to get them out of there. There's no telling what they'll do to them."

"I doubt if they plan to set them free. We'll find a way to get them out," Lee said.

CHAPTER TWENTY-FIVE

The van driven by Lance carrying Mia, Lee and Ivor sped down the highway back to New York City. They tuned in to the news. The Mayor was encouraging people to find a safe place to go away from high rise buildings.

Scientists were aware the tremors were unusual. There were no fractures in the rock formations, yet they continued to shift beneath the earth's surface. The seismic waves became longer and more frequent. The major quake would take place soon.

"We better get in touch with Dr. Ram. They need to get out of there ASAP," Mia said to Lance and Lee. They both agreed with her. They headed to the school to contact the people in Citadel. There was still one question they couldn't answer. When they annihilate the Spoilers' lifeline, would the Spoilers trapped in the earth be destroyed at the same time? There was a time difference that could cause a delay, which meant the Spoilers would still be blocking the path, preventing the people in Citadel from making it safely through the earth.

"There're just too many things that can go wrong down there," Lee said.

"Hopefully, the part of the path that is blocked by the Spoilers is in our world," Lance said, "but we can't be sure."

"Look, we just don't have any way of knowing how long the Spoilers will live after we demolish their lifeline," Lee said.

"The only way we can be sure Dr. Ram and the others will be safe is to go back into the earth," Mia said. "If we have to face off with the Spoilers again, we will."

The teenagers arrived in Manhattan. They hurried down into the tunnel. Lee opened his computer and attached the Enhancer to it. They watched the red ball move downward. Now, they just had to wait until someone saw the signal.

"Anyone there?" Lee asked anxiously. "Can anyone hear me?"

A voice on the other end answered, "Yes, Lee I can hear you." It was Dr. Ram.

"Mia and Lance are also here. You have to get the people out of there. Now!"

"We've had several tremors. I know the major is not far off. The birds have flown off. The forest is quiet, no animals in sight. We're preparing to leave at daybreak. The men have gone ahead," Dr. Ram said.

"There is some good news. We found the location of the Spoilers' lifeline," Mia said.

"That is good news," Dr. Ram said.

"We will get rid of them. But there's something you need to know," Lance said.

"What is it?" Dr. Ram asked.

"There is a time difference between the world there and this world, which means after we destroy the Spoilers' lifeline, there is a possibility they may still be alive in the mound of dirt. We're not certain. We don't know how it will play out."

"Don't worry about us. If you kill the Spoilers, you will save our world," Dr. Ram said.

"We're not about to give up on you and the people there," Mia said.

Lee jumped into the conversation. "How far is Citadel from the path in the earth?"

"About three miles east," Dr. Ram said.

Lance pulled up a map of Manhattan. "This should be easy," he said. "There should be an opening in the ground here that leads to that path in the earth." The teenagers looked closely at the map. Mia's eyes lit up. She pushed her hair out of her face. She pointed. "There! The sewer in that tunnel will take us underground to the path."

"We've got it," Lee said to Dr. Ram. "Stay safe. We'll be in touch soon."

The three spent the night in Mia's campus room. Ivor was perched on the window ledge, his favorite spot. Mia stared at the ceiling while Lee and Lance slept on blankets piled on the floor. She couldn't help but think about the three scientists. It seemed to her that someone would have missed them.

She reached for her laptop on a table. She Googled missing government scientists—nothing. She entered, "Washington, DC Missing Scientist." An article appeared with a picture of a man: *Government Scientist working on new satellite project has been missing for three months.*

Mia waved to Ivor. She told him to listen to what the article said about the missing scientist. She read: 'The famous scientist Dr. Jason Ward is missing. He was last seen working in his laboratory. His disappearance could be linked to the project he was working on. The government will not comment on the nature of the project, only that it is classified.' Mia said to Ivor, "This could account for one of the scientists held prisoner by the Spoilers, most likely, the elderly man. But there was nothing mentioned about the other man and woman."

Not able to sleep, Mia left the room, closing the door quietly behind her. She sat on the steps outside the dormitory. She looked up at the sky. She wondered if she would ever have a normal life again. What if things don't go as planned and somehow the Spoilers won the battle. Would it be because they failed?

Lance appeared on the steps. He sat down besides Mia. "You can't sleep either," Lance said.

"Not really," Mia said. "There're too many unanswered questions."

"We may never know the answers to all of them. As scientists our job is to develop a scientific theory, then prove or disprove it."

"You tell me how you go about gathering facts and information about possessed animals that don't exist in our world of reality."

"We'd have to capture one, keep it alive and analyze its composition."

"We both know that's not going to happen."

"What we can't do is to let this occurrence become an obsession. We have to move on with our lives once this is over," Lance said.

"You're right. But this is one mission we can't fail." Mia said.

"We won't." Lance said.

Early the next morning the teenagers watched the news. Scientists warned the public that the activity underground had increased. They expected the earthquake to impact the earth within the next forty-eight hours. People must stay off the streets. All emergency services were on alert.

Ivor was perched on the van. He watched the teenagers place their bows, arrows, spears and backpacks in the van. They placed the box with the Enhancer on the seat.

The van, driven by Lance, carried them swiftly through the streets of New York. People rushed out of buildings carrying bags filled with different items. Long lines were formed outside of grocery stores. Cars lined up at gas pumps. Most of the street vendors had packed up and left.

Lance steered the van over to the curb and stopped. A middle-aged man was selling bottles of water. He rushed over to the van smiling and carrying a few bottles.

"Five dollars apiece," the man said. "All the stores in the area are out. My price may go up. Better get it now."

"Really? Don't you think that's too much money for a bottle of water?" Mia said. She glanced over at all his coolers filled with bottles of water. A woman with several children counted change to purchase water.

Mia felt he was taking advantage of people. She stared at the coolers filled with water, causing them to tumble over. Bottles of water rolled down the sidewalk. People picked up the bottles. Some returned them; some didn't.

The man was stunned. He looked around for a possible answer. There were no heavy winds. No one pushed the coolers over. He looked frightened. "Take the water. No charge," he shouted to the people in line. He shoved a few bottles at Lance.

Lance drove off. "There're always some people who will take advantage of any situation," he said, shaking his head.

"I don't think he'll be one of them," Lee said, looking back at the man handing people bottles of water.

The teenagers were concerned about their families. Mia knew her grandmother wasn't happy about leaving their home. "I don't want my grandmother to be by herself," Mia said.

"We'll take your grandmother and my mother to one of the government bunkers.

Tell her to get ready, then call my mother," Lance said.

"Okay. What about your family, Lee? Shouldn't they come too?"

"My grandfather will take care of them," Lee said. "He built a safe room in our basement."

They arrived at Beverly's apartment building. People were busy placing their belongings in cars. Her grandmother stood in front of the building, "I'll go get her," Mia said. She hurried to her grandmother. She reached for her shopping bag. "What's in this bag, Grandmother? Mia lifted the bag into the van. She peeped in it. There was a picture of her mother and her when she was a baby. Tears filled her eyes. She questioned if she was doing the right thing by leaving her. Nonetheless, she had no choice. She couldn't even tell her what she was doing. She would worry or much worse, think her powers were affecting her mind.

"Things that can't be replaced are in that bag, so be careful," Beverly said. She observed Ivor sitting in the window in the back of the van. She thought, *Mia sure does have a strange pet.*

Irene closed the door to her building and joined them. She carried a blanket, radio and a tote bag stuffed with magazines.

She said to Beverly, "Don't worry. We aren't going to be bored or hungry. I brought sandwiches."

"It won't last long. You'll be safe at the bunker. It's very strong," Lance said, reassuring them.

"Well, if you ask me," Beverly said, "this could be the end of the world."

They arrived at the government bunker. People flashed their passes to the guards standing in front of the building. Because of Lee's work at the International Rocket

Center, he was able to secure passes. They couldn't be turned away.

"You really will be safe here," Mia said, looking at her grandmother. She tried not to let her grandmother see the concerned look on her face. Her grandmother always knew when she was upset about something.

Lance gave his mother a hug. "Mom, I know you don't feel it's necessary for you to be here. But it's not safe to be in an apartment building. In fact, most of the buildings here in the city aren't strong enough to withstand the impact."

"Okay son," Irene said, "but I think you guys should be coming with us."

She's right. But I know that's not going to happen," Beverly said. She embraced Mia and whispered in her ear, "I'm not going to ask you where you are going. All I'm going to say is if you have to use your powers to save yourself or this world, you have my blessings."

"I love you, Grandmother."

Irene and Beverly got in line with the rest of the people. They waved goodbye. The teenagers waved back and followed the signs out of New York to Washington, D.C. Lee dialed his grandfather's phone.

"Hello Lee," Ling said.

"Listen, Grandfather. We're on our way to D.C. to carry out our plan. I'll call you later."

"Okay Lee. Don't worry, I've got everything here under control. Good luck."

CHAPTER TWENTY-SIX

They arrived in Washington, D.C. A convoy of military trucks carrying water, medical equipment and generators passed by them. The street was bumper to bumper with cars. The ones surrounding the capitol area were blocked off. They had to take another route.

Once they arrived at the Rocket Center. Lee used his security code to gain access into the building. People were busily moving throughout the center. He carried the box containing the Enhancer. They had to enter through another security door. Lee handed the box to Lance while he swiped his badge. The door opened.

Dr. Bloom and one of the engineers stood in the hallway chatting. Dr. Bloom saw the teenagers coming toward them. "Right on time," he said, smiling from ear to ear. "Everyone is ready."

The engineer was very excited about the device and what it was capable of doing.

"We're all impressed with your work. It's such a magnificent device," the engineer said to them. "And you're so young."

"We hope it lives up to its reputation," Lee said.

Don't be so modest. I wouldn't expect anything less from you three. I knew you were brilliant," Dr. Bloom said, overjoyed. "I went to great lengths to recruit you three. I followed your achievements. I knew what you were capable of and I came up with a plan to have you accepted into Charlton Academy. I didn't even have to kidnap you. And that silly Miss Finney questioned my judgment."

"The credit belongs to you, Dr. Bloom. You encouraged us to work on this project.

Helped us get grants so we could do our research at the university," Mia said. "If it wasn't for you, we would have never created the Enhancer. All for the sake of advancing mankind. You are truly a hero."

"You give me too much credit, Mia," Dr. Bloom said. He smiled so widely his right ear actually shifted—probably the Spoiler in him.

They followed Dr. Bloom and the engineer to an area near the satellite's launch site. They slowed down behind him.

"Did you have to lay it on so thick, Mia?" Lance asked.

"If I had a bugle, I would have played, *The Battle Hymn of the Republic*," Lee said.

"Okay guys, lighten up. I just wanted to make sure his last thoughts are about us," Mia said.

The teenagers rushed to catch up with Dr. Bloom and the engineer. They walked through a large room filled with engineers. There was no denying some of them were Spoilers. They had cold, expressionless looks on their faces.

"Did you check out the engineer with Dr. Bloom?" Mia whispered.

"Yes, he's definitely one of them," Lance uttered. "The sooner we get this over with, the better."

"The room is filled with them," Lee added. He opened the box and removed the Enhancer. He wiped the sweat from his forehead with his hand and walked with Mia and Lance to the area where the satellite rested on the rocket.

They climbed up the stairs next to the satellite. Lance held the device while Mia handed Lee a tool to open a section on the satellite. Lance gave him the Enhancer. He installed it in the satellite and screwed the cover back on. "It's done," Lee announced. "Now we just have to wait and see what happens."

Mia whispered to Lee, "That's your plan? Wait and see what happens?"

They went back into the building. All eyes were on them. The teenagers could sense the tension. There was no room for failure. So much rested on this moment—the future.

"I hope you have a plan, Lee. There's no turning back now," Lance said.

"Did you see the looks on their faces?" Mia asked. "One thing is for sure. If this rocket doesn't launch these creatures will attack us."

"Don't worry," Lee said.

The three entered a small room with a computer sitting on a desk. Lee gave Dr. Bloom a thumbs-up as he passed by him standing in the hallway with several other men.

Lee sat at the computer to program the device into the satellite's system. Mia and Lance sat next to him. Dr. Bloom was very nervous. He watched Lee input information into the computer. He paced back and forth. "How long will the launch take?" he asked.

Lee said, "Considering where it's going, it could take up to forty-eight hours. The satellite has to reach its destination. It has to rise above the earth's atmosphere then it has to separate completely from its container."

Dr. Bloom's phone rang. He walked away to take the call and returned "Some-thing came up. I have to leave. Keep me posted. If anything changes, call me."

"What do you suppose that was all about?" Mia asked, watching Dr. Bloom walk rapidly away down the hallway.

"I don't know," Lance answered. "But if I were to guess, I would say he's headed to their facility."

The loud, excruciating roar from the rocket sounded as it launched from the space pad. All the engineers stood and applauded. The rocket carrying the satellite made its way up to the blue sky. It left behind a trail of white smoke that blended in with the clouds.

Mia, Lance and Lee stood up. They smiled and threw their hands up in the air. Everyone followed their lead.

"We don't have much time. We've got to bail," Lee said, raising his voice to be heard above the noisy crowd of people.

"So we don't cause too much attention, Mia and I will get the van and pick you up at the front entrance," Lance said.

"I'll be there in ten minutes. I have one more thing to do," Lee said, looking at the computer. He hoped he was as good as everyone believed. Because now he couldn't afford not to be.

"We'll see you out front in ten minutes," Lance said.

Lee looked at his two friends, who were somewhat hesitant. "Everything is going to be okay."

Lance and Mia eased their way out of the building. No one really noticed them. Everyone was watching the satellite on their computer screens.

Mia and Lance didn't know what Lee was planning. On the way to the rocket center, he mentioned blowing the place up but changed his mind because some of the people in the rocket center were humans.

Lee sat back down and typed quickly on the keyboard. He signed off seconds before a group of engineers came over and congratulated him on the successful launch.

Lee excused himself to go to the bathroom. He waited until no one was looking and dashed out of the building. He jumped in front seat of the van next to Lance. "Let's get out of here before they discover I'm missing."

Mia and Ivor watched from the back window of the vehicle. The street behind them was clear—only a trail of fume from their exhaust pipe as they sped away.

"No one is following you. That's a good sign," Mia said, relieved. "I think we made it." She leaned forward, close to Lee. "Okay, tell us what you did."

"Spill it," Lance said eagerly.

"It was easier than I thought. Lee said. He ran his fingers through his hair and smiled broadly.

"So what did you do?" Lance asked.

Lee looked at Mia and Lance. "I changed the course of our satellite with the Enhancer to make it collide with the Spoilers' satellite in space. The change won't appear on the screen until minutes before the impact. "

They all screamed happily. Even Ivor spoke out. "Way to go Lee," in his proper British accent. He bounced up and down. They all laughed at him. They'd never heard the saying spoken so properly before.

CHAPTER TWENTY-SEVEN

They traveled down the highway to the Spoilers' facility to free the three human scientists. After exiting the van in the wooded area, they peered through the bushes and recognized Dr. Bloom's car. He was inside. Several heavy armed guards strolled back and forth in front of the building. Somehow the Spoilers had to be drawn away from the building so the teenagers could enter. All three would go in this time in case they had to fight their way out.

Mia decided to start a fire in the woods in back of the building to draw the Spoilers out. She would risk burning down the woods, something she had no desire to do, but there was no other way.

"I'll start a fire in the woods," Mia said. She looked at an electrical pole standing in the back of the building. It stood near a cluster of trees. She had a plan.

"We'll go with you," Lee said. "We can make the fire quicker together."

"Lee's right," Lance said.

"It's too risky for all of us to go." Mia said. "Don't worry. I've got this. I'll meet you in front of the building."

Mia made her way through the woods to the back of the facility. She stopped and stared at the pole with the electrical wires attached to it. The pole fell into the trees. Sparks from the wires ignited a tree branch. In a matter of seconds bright red flames shot up. The fire spread quickly. She could feel the heat. She heard loud noises but couldn't see anything through the thick smoke. The sounds came from the Spoilers. Mia's eyes burned. She stayed close to the building, out of the way of the Spoilers who trampled by her. Ivor flew into the facility. Lance and Lee waited at the door until Mia joined them.

The teenagers entered the building. Only a few Spoilers remained inside. They traveled cautiously down the hallway toward the door where the scientists lived.

Dr. Bloom and several others Spoilers, including Miss Finney and the Senator, sat at a table. They were in human form. Ivor was hidden in a corner above them. He listened closely to Dr. Bloom assure the other Spoilers the fire in the woods was no threat to their facility. He said to them, "The guards have hoses with water. They will make sure the fire doesn't come close to the building." He told them everything was going according to plan and the satellite was on its way to space. "What a great day for all of us," Dr. Bloom shouted. Applause filled the room.

Miss Finney, in her high-pitched voice, asked, "What about the three humans?"

"They will be disposed of. They know too much," Dr. Bloom answered.

Ivor flew back to the teenagers hidden in a corridor near the area where the scientists stayed. He said in a shaky voice, "They have no intention of freeing the scientists."

"That doesn't surprise me," Lance said, looking up at Ivor. "Their fate was sealed the moment they were captured."

The teenagers checked out the area where the scientists lived to make sure there were no Spoilers in the area. Lee knocked quietly on their door. No one answered. He knocked again. "We're here to help you. Please open the door," he said.

"I'll fly back and keep an eye on the Spoilers. I'll signal you if they come this way," Ivor said.

The door slowly opened. A woman peeped out from a small crack in the door. "Who are you?" she asked in a low voice.

"We're not Spoilers. We're humans. There's not much time. We're going to get you out of here," Mia whispered.

"How did you get past the Spoilers?" the woman asked.

"We'll explain everything. We don't have much time. They will return soon," Lance said.

The woman let them in. They followed her down a hallway to a room. The man in the room, one of the scientists, observed them closely.

"They're not Spoilers," he said, baffled by them. "Wait here," he said. "I'll be right back."

The man left the room abruptly and returned within minutes with an older man. Mia recognized the man from his picture in the paper. "I know who you are," she said. "You're Dr. Jason Ward."

"Yes, I'm Dr. Ward. I was taken from my laboratory by the Spoilers about fourteen years ago. I was working for the government. I was analyzing a green substance they found in a lab. I concluded it was foreign to our world – perhaps from another planet. I was to turn in my findings the next morning. That night two men came to my lab. They forced me to go with them."

"Did the government know about the Spoilers?" Lance asked.

"No," said the younger man. "I was a government agent assigned to follow up leads from people who had seen strange things. Lizards that turned into humans. At that time, I thought it was some kind of conspiracy."

"When did you realize these creatures actually existed?" Lee asked.

They all agreed it wasn't until after they were captured and saw them in their natural form. Over time they learned more about them. When they transformed themselves into human form it required more power from their lifeline.

Dr. Ward explained, their lifeline was developed centuries ago by a brilliant young American scientist who discovered their presence. He was fascinated with them. He performed many experiments where he combined Spoiler DNA with human DNA and a unique chemical. Finally with the correct formula he developed what he called their lifeline. It was a green substance that would keep them alive. But it only generated enough energy to allow them to take human form for a few minutes.

Later, with new satellite technology, a government scientist, a Spoiler discovered the energy from a satellite's signal could power their lifeline allowing them to morph into humans for extended time periods. But now the green substance was weakening. The original formula was most likely destroyed by the scientist who invented it. Perhaps, he uncovered the Spoiler's plan to control the world.

The Spoilers tried to recreate the formula but weren't successful. Recently, they confirmed, a more powerful satellite signal producing more energy, would restore their failing lifeline.

"That's where we came in," Lee said. "We'll explain everything to you, later. Oh, we didn't introduce ourselves. My name is Lee. This is Lance." But before he could introduce Mia, the woman quickly turned to the man standing next to her. She whispered something to him. Joyfully, they went to Mia. "I know who you are. You're Mia," the woman said. "You're fifteen years old and you have telekinetic powers."

"How did you know that?" Mia asked, startled by what the woman said.

"Because there are only a few of us that have telekinetic power. You would be one of them because you are my daughter. I'm Erica, your mother, and this is your father, Aaron." They both embraced her.

"Do you remember us?" Aaron asked. He took Mia's hand.

Mia was startled. She looked closely at her mother and father. "Yes," Mia answered. A vision of the last day she saw them flashed before her. Her mother kissed her. She told her to be a good little girl and do what Grandmother said. Her father seemed to be a lot bigger but she remembered his smile. It was the same big smile that was on his face now.

Mia's search for her parents was over. Her wish had come true. Tears ran down her cheeks. Lance watched them hug. "Unbelievable," Lance said. "Mia thought she would never see you again."

"This is really cool, but our time is running out," Lee said. "We've got to get out of here. The Spoilers will return once they get the fire under control."

Mia held on tightly to her parents. She asked her mother, "How did you know I was your daughter?"

"You look just like me when I was your age," Erica said. "Besides, a mother knows her child."

"We have to get out of here now. We'll explain everything later," Lance said.

"We're more than ready to leave this place," Aaron said. "What about the Spoilers? They're everywhere. They'll track us down."

"Don't worry about them. Their life here is short-lived," Lance said.

"We're faced with another problem... an earthquake," Mia said.

"We know," Erica said. "We heard the Spoilers talking about it."

They all started to move out except for Dr. Ward. "I'm going to stay here. There's a room down below where they store their eggs. I want to make sure they are destroyed. One of our duties was to keep the room at a certain temperature. Besides, nothing would give me greater satisfaction than to watch the Spoilers take their last breath."

"They may hold you responsible," Mia said.

"Don't worry about me. I'll be fine," Dr. Ward said.

Erica and Aaron embraced Dr. Ward. "Be careful," Erica said.

"Let's go," Lance said. He glanced out the door to make sure it was safe to leave. Mia removed the cover to the vent.

"Follow me," she said. "It's narrow but you can make it."

Mia went first, followed by her mother Erica, Aaron, Lee and Lance. The loud, unnerving sounds of the Spoilers could be heard as they traveled through the vent.

"You were here before," Erica whispered.

"Yes," Mia said. "That's when I found out you were here."

They heard a commotion below in the room that contained the Spoilers' lifeline. The Spoilers had discovered Erica and Aaron were missing. They were frantic. One of the Spoilers called out to Dr. Bloom.

"We've looked everywhere. They must have escaped through the vent."

"Uncover the vent in every room. They have to be in there somewhere. Tell the guards to go to the back of the building in case they come out there," Dr. Bloom said in a harsh voice.

Several Spoilers left the room. Dr. Bloom looked up at the vent above them. He ordered the Spoilers to uncover it. Mia and the others picked up their pace.

Lance didn't make it past the opening in the vent before the cover was removed. He waved to the others to keep moving. He leaned back against the wall so the Spoiler wouldn't see him. He held his breath. One cough, one sneeze and they all could be caught. Luckily, it was dark. The Spoiler stuck his oversized head through the opening. He stared a moment at Lance's blurry image. He probably thought it was only a shadow. He left and closed the vent behind him.

Lance joined the others. They could see a light up ahead and smell the heavy aroma of burnt trees. Mia turned to the others. She asked them to wait there. She went to the opening and looked outside. The Spoilers wandered back and forth.

"Here's what we're going to do," Mia explained. "I'm going to jump out and cause a commotion. I'll use my powers to keep them away from you. Go to the van. I'll meet you there."

"Are you sure?" Erica asked in a low voice. "I should come with you."

"No, it's too risky. They might change into animals. I can outrun them. It's the only way."

"Okay," Lee said.

"Be careful, Mia," Lance said.

"It's too dangerous, Mia," Aaron said.

"Don't worry. I'll be fine," Mia insisted. She could hear Ivor making sounds to warn her the Spoilers were close by. She pushed back the cover over the opening. She yelled,

"Here I am! Come get me!" She teased them while the others moved out of the hole to the woods.

The Spoilers were stunned by her actions. They moved slowly to her with their weapons drawn.

She activated her powers, sending a forceful wind that blew them backward. Tree branches whirled around them.

Lance, Lee, Aaron and Erica looked back at Mia. She had come out of her trance. "This isn't good," Lance said anxiously. "They're changing back to animals."

"They can run faster as animals," Erica said.

"I have to go back and get her," Aaron insisted. "We can't lose her again."

"Don't worry. I'll get her," Lance said. "Just follow Lee and be ready to take off."

"Let's go," Lee said anxiously.

Lance watched the Spoilers struggle to stand up. Lance motioned to Mia to come quickly. The two, along with Ivor flying above, raced to the van. The fierce animals were close behind them. Everyone yelled, "Hurry! Hurry! Aaron sat in the driver's seat, ready to take off. Ivor flew into the van, followed by Mia and Lance.

"Step on it," Lance said breathlessly.

"They're gaining on us," Mia said, breathing hard.

Aaron pressed his foot down hard on the accelerator. They sped down the highway. The animals continued to chase them.

"Hold on," Aaron said, looking out the rear view mirror. The van swerved from one side of the road to the other.

"We made it," Lee said, looking back, "They've stopped."

They returned to New York to the tunnel that contained the sewer. Once inside the sewer, they would follow a path leading them through the earth, the same path their friends would be on— and possibly the Spoilers.

"What's next?" Erica asked.

"We have to help our friends. Their world is about to be wiped out by the earthquake. To get here, they have to make their way through the earth. Their path could be blocked by the Spoilers. We have to go back into the earth and help them."

"What other world?" Erica asked.

"I'll tell you everything later, Mom. Stay with Grandmother. We don't know how much damage the earthquake will do."

"Just be careful. All of you," Erica said.

"We will," Mia said.

Lee said to Aaron, "I need your help."

"What do you want me to do?" Aaron asked.

"After you take Erica to the government bunker, pick up my grandfather. Call him. His name is Ling."

"What do you want us to do?" Aaron asked.

"Go to our school. The Spoilers may be there," Lee said. "You'll know if we were successful in eliminating them."

"Okay," Aaron said.

"Look in the glove compartment; there is a government pass to get into the bunker," Lee said. He wrote down his grandfather's telephone number and address and gave it to Aaron.

"We don't have much time," Lee said.

"Ivor will go with you," Mia said. "He'll show you the way." Aaron and Erica waved goodbye and hurried into the van. Ivor took his usual place in the back window. There were a lot of things going on Aaron and Erica didn't understand. One thing they were sure of — Mia had grown up to be a very smart, brave girl. They couldn't be prouder of their daughter.

CHAPTER TWENTY-EIGHT

Once again the three teenagers placed their bows on their shoulders and attached the pouches containing their arrows around their waists. With their backpacks on their backs and spears in hands, they entered the tunnel. Lee entered the tunnel location in his computer to find the location of the sewer.

Lance and Mia gathered around Lee to see what appeared to be the inside of the dark, dewy enclosure. Lee enlarged the picture. "Look," he said, "there's a hatch up ahead. That's got to be it."

"I hope you're right," Lance said.

"There's only one way to find out," Mia said, walking ahead of them to the hatch. She removed the rusty metal cover. Dozens of large rats scurried out of the hole between their feet.

"Rats," the three hollered. They all jumped back, startled by the large size of them.

"Wow," Lance said, "those are the biggest rats, I've ever seen."

"They could take over the city," Mia said, watching them.

"This is crazy," Lee said. "There's hundreds of them. You would think the city could do more to control them."

"Trust me, that's the least of their problems," Mia said, thinking, *they have a state representative who's a Spoiler.*

Lance climbed slowly down the hatch. He used his flashlight to light the way. Lee and Mia stayed close to him.

"What a smell," Lee said, holding his nose.

"I've smelled worse in Chemistry," Lance said.

"I don't think so," Lee said. "Come on. Let's pick up the pace. The farther away from these pipes, the better."

"This section has been closed for a long time. That's why it smells so bad. I left the hatch half open so it will air out," Mia said. "Just keep moving."

The tunnel led them farther down into the earth. A faint mist covered their faces. A wall of crumbled rocks stood in front of them.

"It's a dead end," Lance announced.

"No! It couldn't be," Lee said, looking at his tablet. "This path continues on."

Mia placed her ear against the rocks. "Listen," she said. "I hear water falling."

Lance and Lee pressed their ears against the rocky surface. Lee pulled one of the rocks from the wall. "Remove the rocks," he said. "The path continues on the other side."

The three pulled the rocks down one by one. They created an opening large enough for them to climb through.

Lance turned to Lee. "How much time do we have before the satellite's impact?" he asked.

"About four hours," Lee said, climbing through the opening.

Mia and Lance followed him to a ledge overlooking a giant waterfall of crystal clear water. The water poured down into the river below, making loud splashing sounds.

"The waterfall is so beautiful," Mia said. "I don't think, I've ever seen anything like it. Not even Niagara Falls."

They walked carefully around the waterfall. Flocks of birds flew over their heads.

Mia looked down and turned her head quickly. "I can't believe I'm in this situation again. I'd rather face the Spoilers," she said nervously. "I know—I'll think of something else. It worked for me when I was climbing Orka's mountain.'

"Sounds like a good idea," Lance said.

The only thing Mia could think of was her first frightening experience. She told them the story. Her grandmother took her to Niagara Falls when she was a little girl. She tilted her over so she could get a better look at the falls. She thought she was going to fall into the water and be swept away.

"That's a good reason to be afraid," Lee said.

They reached the end of the narrow passage and continued downward through the rocky earth.

Lee looked at his tablet and followed the rocket on the screen. It moved at a rapid speed toward the Spoilers' satellite.

He hoped it would stay on course. If it failed, he knew the Spoilers would use their existing powers to bring down as many people as they could.

***

New York City

The streets were empty except for police cars. Aaron drove Erica speedily down the street to the bunker. They looked around at the familiar places. It'd been eleven years since they were last there. They both agreed once everything was back to normal they would start over. They passed by people packed in buses going to the shelters. They reached the bunker, where people waited anxiously in line to enter the facility.

"Don't worry about Mia. She's a fighter like you."

"She's much braver. When I was her age, I was afraid someone would find out I had telekinetic powers."

"Remember, there hadn't been much research done in that area when you were her age. At least now there is an acceptance it exists."

"There were so many times I wanted to use my powers against the Spoilers, but I knew they would hurt my mother and Mia."

"You made the right decision. It'll be over soon. I wish I were going with you. I'd love to see the expression on your mother's face when she sees you."

"Be safe," Erica said. She gave Aaron a hug. She got out of the van and walked over to the line of people. She waved goodbye to Aaron. He drove off down the street with Ivor.

Aaron thought things really hadn't changed that much. He fumbled with the buttons on the dashboard until he found the one to activate the phone. He put the phone on speaker dial. He called out Ling's telephone number.

"Hello," Ling said.

"This is Aaron, Mia's father...Lee told me you are aware of what's going on. He wants us to go to the school. I'm on my way to pick you up."

"I'll be ready," Ling said.

Aaron drove up in front of the restaurant. Ling opened the van's door and got into the vehicle. Aaron explained to Ling that they only had a couple of hours before the satellites collided. If the Spoilers were in the school, they would witness the creatures' last moments on earth. Ling told Aaron there was no doubt in his mind the teenagers would be successful in their mission.

Ling looked around at Ivor perched on the back seat.

"Oh, that's Ivor, Mia's pet," Aaron said.

"An owl is a strange pet to have."

"Mia said to follow him. He will lead us to the Spoilers in the school."

"Well... shouldn't he be flying?" Ling said, amused.

Ivor couldn't resist any longer. "If you let down the window, I will lead you to the school."

Aaron and Ling looked at each other. They both turned and looked at Ivor.

"A talking owl," Ling said.

"Mia left that out," Aaron said.

"Now, let the window down and follow me," Ivor said. He flew out of the opened window. He led them to the school. They parked a few blocks away so no one would think anyone was in the school—especially the Spoilers.

"You know the Spoilers have spent years planning to take over our world," Aaron said. "There are many of them in our world."

"How do you know so much about them?" Ling asked.

Aaron said, "I spent eleven years with them… I can read their minds. What do you know about them?"

Ling said, "Our people tell the story about them in ancient times. It seems they have roamed the earth for centuries. Let's hope their evil spirits will be put to rest."

Aaron and Ling followed Ivor into the school. The door was unlocked. They could see the images of the creatures inside one of the rooms. Ivor would stay there and watch them.

Aaron and Ling continued to walk cautiously down the hall when suddenly the earth shook violently underneath them. The impact knocked them to the floor. The ceiling caved in on them.

They crawled from underneath the rubble to one of the rooms and took cover under a desk. They heard a loud crashing sound. A light pole most likely fell into the school building. Glass blew from the window, hitting the desk. They covered their heads with their hands. Portions of the school continued to fall.

"It feels like a bomb went off," Aaron said.

"It shouldn't last much longer," Ling said.

"Let's hope not. I don't think this school can take much more of this. I think part of the building has already collapsed."

CHAPTER TWENTY-NINE

The frightened people from Citadel made their way down the path. They stayed close to each other. The earthquake had destroyed their world. Parts of the tunnel behind them had collapsed. Large clumps of the earth fell down, barely missing them. The children cried out in fear.

Dr. Ram and Quest were in the front. Nola and Feather followed close behind. Nadia and Marge tried to quiet the scared children.

"Keep your heads down so the dirt won't get into your eyes," Marge said to the children.

"Don't be afraid; just hold on to each other's hands," Nadia said, trying to keep them calm.

Everyone moved carefully around the large holes in the ground. The earth was sinking in.

"Hurry," Moody said. He and Aman ran, with the last of the people, down the path. Hemp and Quest were in the middle. People scrambled to safety when a large chunk of the earth gave way. It was so powerful it threw some of the people to the ground. An elderly woman fell. Moody helped her up and brushed her off.

"What if we're trapped in the earth?" the woman asked, trembling.

"We're not going to get trapped. Don't be frightened. I won't let anything happen to you."

"Is your world a safe place?" the woman asked.

Moody saw the fear on her face. "It will be," he said.

Dr. Ram raised his hand, signaling them to stop. He gazed at the tall mound of dirt in front of them. "This is as far as we can go." He went over and placed his hands on the hard dirt. Their only chance of survival was getting through it. They had no place to go—their world no longer existed. Dr. Ram shouted, "Bring the tools. Maybe the earth has loosen. Start digging. Now! Now!"

The men rushed to the front with their tools and started digging the dirt. Big chunks flew from the mound, as if it was fighting back. "Move the women and children back against the wall," Moody hollered.

Feather rushed over to help Nadia and Marge with the children. "We have to move them farther back," she said in a soft voice, trying not to alarm the children. Chunks of the dirt fell on them. Nadia and Marge covered the children with their robes. Feather, dressed in short warrior clothes, slung her body over a little girl to protect her. She was knocked to the ground with the little girl underneath her. Several people rushed over to help them. They joined the other people huddled in a corner.

Dr. Ram sent a message to Lee on the computer. He let him know they were unable to go any farther. They couldn't dig through the mound of dirt.

The force of the earthquake also hit hard on the path where the teenagers walked to reach their friends. It caused large portions of the earth to fall on them. They had to crawl from underneath the dirt.

Lance and Lee looked over at each other. They turned to Mia, who lay still. Lance called her. "Are you okay?"

"I think so," she said, pushing the dirt and rocks off her body. "Are you guys okay?" She sat up and looked around at the piles of dirt and rocks.

"I'm good," Lee said, standing up.

They rushed over to Lance and helped him move a rock that fell on his leg. Lance tried to stand but his leg couldn't support him. "I don't think I can walk on my ankle."

Mia touched his swollen ankle. "Sit down, don't put any pressure on it." She ripped off a piece of her clothing and wrapped it around his ankle. "This will help keep the swelling down."

Lee grabbed a tree branch from the pile of rubble and gave it to Lance. "Use this to lean on." He and Mia helped Lance stand up. Lance insisted he was okay, but they could see the agony on his face. They held onto his arms and continued down the path, Mia on one side and Lee on the other. They felt the cool wind rushing through the wide hole in the tunnel. It was a pleasant change from the intense heat.

"I wonder if any of the animals in the forest survived," Lee said. He thought back to their journey through the forest to

Orka's mountain. The animals in their final resting place, the wild ones that raced freely through the open field, the talking dinosaur and the three horses that gave them the ride of a lifetime.

"I guess that's something we'll never know. But I do know if Orka can save them, he will," Mia said, very concerned.

Orka's mountain was destroyed. A few displaced animals gathered at the river. They waited on Orka to show them the way. He appeared in front of the dazed animals. He pointed his long, furry finger. "Go down the river."

Animals of all sizes, big, tall, and small, climbed onto the large tree trunks. They drifted down the river. Orka didn't know where the river would take them. He watched the animals until they disappeared.

The teenagers stopped so Lee could check his messages. They were worried about their friends. Lee opened his computer. "Look," he said. "It's a message from Dr. Ram."

"What does it say?" Mia asked. She looked over at Lance sitting on a large rock rubbing his ankle. "Have they reached the mound of dirt?" Lance shouted.

"Hold on, it's scrambled," Lee said. "Okay, here it goes." Lee read the message out loud. "We have gone as far as we can. The mound of dirt blocks us. The earth is slowly giving away. There is no turning back."

"How much longer before the satellites collide?" Lance asked.

"If all goes as planned, about fifteen minutes," Lee said.

"Good," Mia said. "Remember, if the Spoilers are eliminated there's a good chance the ones in that mound will also perish. Dr. Ram and the others will be able to continue on the path."

"We'll know in a few minutes," Lance said.

"Let's go," Mia said.

They reached the shallow water and rinsed the dirt off their faces. They helped Lance take off his shoes and they continued through the stream of water that ended near the tall mound of dirt and put their shoes back on.

Lance used his stick to support himself. He limped over to the mound of dirt and pushed on it with his stick. He placed his ear against it. "I hear movement inside."

"We have to get through it." Lance said, frustrated.

Mia touched the dirt. "It's hard as stone."

"If the Spoilers are in there, they know we're out here," Lance said.

They watched the screen closely. The rocket carrying the satellite raced at full speed to the Spoilers' existing satellite.

The International Rocket Center was in a state of turmoil. The engineers watched in disbelief as their new, powerful satellite was about to crash into another satellite. The Spoilers knew it was the satellite that powered their lifeline. They panicked, hitting different buttons on their space board to change the satellite's course—but it was too late.

"I'll call Dr. Bloom. He'll know what do," an engineer said.

Dr. Bloom was in the room with the other Spoilers and Dr. Ward. They gathered around their lifeline. Dr. Bloom wanted to be there to make sure everything went off as planned. He answered his phone. "Hello. Calm down, I can't understand. What you are saying? What about the satellite? It's what? You must be mistaken... five minutes...do something, do something."

Dr. Bloom observed the clock on the wall. He dropped his phone. Dr. Ward backed away from him. He smiled and walked slowly toward the door. A Spoiler overheard Dr. Bloom. He rushed over to him.

"What's going on?" the Spoiler asked anxiously.

Another Spoiler joined them. It was apparent something had gone wrong. They asked Dr. Bloom repeatedly what was wrong, but he seemed to be in a state of shock.

"Tell us!" the Spoilers demanded loudly. All the Spoilers turned to Dr. Bloom to see him staring at the clock. He watched the minute hand on the clock, showing four minutes left. "We have been betrayed," he shouted. "Those three teenagers."

At that instant the satellites collided in space, causing a massive explosion. The container holding their lifeline shook violently and started to burn. The Spoilers made loud, ear-piercing sounds. They doubled over. Their bodies slithered to the floor, turning into green ash. Dr. Ward stood at the door. He walked back into the room to get a closer look. He saw green ashes covering the floor where the Spoilers once stood.

The lifeline suddenly exploded, setting the room on fire. The heat from the fire caused the glass bottles and tubes to pop throughout the room. Dr. Ward left the burning the room. A thought came to him—had their eggs also been destroyed? He hurried down the smoky hallway to the room where the eggs were stored. He opened the door and saw some of the Spoilers' eggs had hatched because of the intense heat. Smoke filled the room. He could hardly breathe.

Dr. Ward walked among the hatched eggs. Most of the premature Spoilers had perished. The others would soon follow. He felt a little sad. Whether or not he would admit it, he had become attached to these unborn creatures. He often wondered if they would be different. The Spoilers didn't choose to be monsters. They were chosen. Maybe if their offspring had been taken away from them, the next generation wouldn't be evil.

From a scientific point of view, Dr. Ward would have relished the opportunity to find out. He coughed repeatedly. Flames were consuming the room. He looked through the flames and saw a premature Spoiler trying to free itself from its egg. He wanted to save it but couldn't make it around the hot flames.

Dr. Ward made it out of the building. He watched it burn down. He had learned a lot about the animals. Their connection to their lifeline was obvious. Their hearts beat the same rhythm as the green substance in the container. They never once asked him if he had the capacity to convert them into normal humans.

Their only desire was to rule the world. He would always be grateful to the three teenagers for freeing him.

Only slight movements of the aftershocks were felt at Charlton Academy. Aaron looked at his watch. He breathed rapidly. "The satellites have collided."

"Now we'll know for sure if the Spoilers are still a threat to civilization," Ling said.

Ivor flew over to them. "Come, see for yourselves."

Aaron and Ling moved carefully around parts of the school building lying on the floor. They approached the devastated room where the Spoilers were meeting. One of the walls was missing. They could see all the destruction outside. It looked like a war zone. No sign of the Spoiler's reptilian bodies. But Aaron and Ling saw something strange on the floor underneath the rubble in one of the corners. They looked closely. Green ash covered the floor.

"This is all that's left of them," Aaron said. He rubbed his fingers through the ash. "They must have huddled together here during the earthquake.""There was never any doubt in my mind," Ling said joyfully. "I knew they could do it."

"Let's get out of here and see how much damage the earthquake caused," Aaron said. He stopped for a moment and looked back at the room. He thought, *it's finally over.*

CHAPTER THIRTY

There was only one way the teenagers could save their friends. They had to create a passage through the mound of dirt.

"I can blow an opening through the dirt," Mia said.

"Are you sure, Mia?" Lance asked. "The whole tunnel could cave in."

"There's no other way," Lee said. "Besides that, if the Spoilers are still alive in there, we have a problem."

Mia was determined to save the lives of her friends. She positioned herself directly in front of the mound of dirt. Lance and Lee stood next to her. They held their spears in their hands in case they had to fight the Spoilers.

"Are you ready?" Lance asked. He gave Mia a hug. Once again they placed their hands on top of each other's and repeated. "We can do this."

"Just stay focused and control your powers," Lee said.

Mia stared straight ahead at the mound. She concentrated on blowing a hole in the middle. A surge of energy built up inside her. She began to tremble. Within seconds, dirt blew out of the mound, shooting in every direction. The dirt twirled in a circular motion, creating a hole in the middle of the mound. Lee and Lance turned their heads to protect their eyes. Mia's face and clothes were covered with dirt. The dirt continued to twirl, forming a large hole in the center.

Suddenly, black shadowy, distorted figures emerged out of the hole and circled around them.

"What are these things?" Lee asked, his eyes following them.

"I don't know," Lance said, watching them. "But if I were to guess, I would say they are spirits. The evil ones that possessed the Spoilers.

"This is proof, Lance. We did it. We destroyed them," Lee said. They both watched the shadowy figures fade away. They could see the images of the people on the other side. They moved closer to the mound of dirt.

Lee shouted, "Dr. Ram... if you hear me, send everyone through the hole."

"Hurry, hurry," Lance shouted.

"Do you think they heard us?" Lance asked.

"I don't know," Lee answered. He stepped inside, trying to avoid the force of the wind generated by Mia's powers to keep the passage open. "They're coming," Lee said excitedly. "They must have heard us."

All of a sudden, people were making their way quickly through the hole. The children came through first, with Nadia and Marge, then the women. Feather embraced the elderly woman.

Everyone looked at Mia. They watched her magical eyes. They believed she was some type of goddess. Who else could possess that kind of power?

Mia's body weakened ... She fell to the ground. Marge and Feather went over to help her. One of the women brought a container of water. Marge sat her up and placed the container to her mouth. "Drink some water, Mia," Marge said.

People ran through the opening as dirt began to fill the hole. The last men to come through the hole were stuck in the middle. The hole was filling quickly. The men struggled to get out of the dirt. People shouted, "Hurry! Hurry!"

Lance and Lee went farther into the hole. They saw Dr. Ram, Moody, Hemp, Quest and Aman struggle to free themselves. The dirt had risen to their shoulders. Nadia went to the opening. She shouted, "Lee, remember, you wear the bracelet."

Lee could hear her faint voice through the chaos. He paused for a moment. "I'll pull them out," he said to Lance.

"I'll be right behind you," Lance said. They pushed through the heavy dirt until they reached the men. Lee reached out his hand with the bracelet on it. "Grab my hand," Lee said to the men. "One at a time."

The men latched onto Lee's hand. He freed them, one by one, passing them to Lance. Lee was the last one out of the mound. It collapsed within seconds of his departure. Everyone applauded. Lance and Lee smiled. They tapped each other with their fists.

Lance sat down beside Mia. "Are you okay?" he asked.

"Yes," she said.

"The Spoilers are gone forever. We don't have to worry about them anymore," Lance said.

"It's over," Mia said, with a big smile on her face.

Nadia held tightly onto Lee. Dr. Ram joined them. He knocked the dust off himself. "Once again, you three have saved us," he said.

"And just in time," Moody said. "We would have been buried in the earth."

"How far are we from New York?" Dr. Ram asked, looking at the stream of water.

"A few hours," Mia answered.

"We should go now. The tunnel could give way any second," Moody said, looking around at the devastation caused by the earthquake.

Dr Ram asked, "How do we explain the people from Citadel? Where they came from?"

"We'll think of something," Mia said.

"I can't wait to see your world," Feather said to Lee.

"Let's go," Lee said. He spoke loudly and waved to everyone.

There was a sense of relief among the people—the chatter, the smiles the laughter. For the first time in a very long time, they didn't have to live in fear, especially from the creatures in the forest or the Spoilers. They didn't know what to expect in the new world. There would be strange people, strange customs—things they could never imagine. They'd always been one people and they didn't want that to ever change. But then only time would tell.

They entered the narrow river and washed the soil off themselves. The cool water was refreshing. They walked for hours until they reached the ledge outside the waterfall.

"It doesn't look like the tunnel suffered any more damage," Mia said.

"That's a good sign," Lance said. "Everything is quiet again."

"Let's rest here," Mia said. "We don't have too much farther to go."

People chatted joyfully among themselves. They ate from sacks filled fruits and berries. Nadia and Marge fed the children. They stuffed the berries in their mouths, laughing and poking fun at each other.

"Not too many at a time," Nadia said to the children, who snatched them out of her hand.

"They're really hungry," Marge said.

Lance, Moody, Mia, and Lee huddled together. Lance said to Moody, "That creature you saw coming out of the alley was definitely a Spoiler. I just wanted to put your mind at ease in case you had any doubts."

"The scary thing is they made it to our world," Moody said.

"They were powered by a lifeline that was weakening, so they could only stay in human form for a short period of time," Lance said.

"The one I saw was apparently in the process of changing," Moody said. "I'll never forget the look he gave me."

"He was calm because he knew no one would believe you," Lance said.

"Are you sure there aren't any more of those creatures still out there?" Moody asked.

"We destroyed their lifeline. They can't exist without power." Mia added. "You see, Moody, they were spirits. You couldn't kill them."

"The main thing is we don't have to worry about them anymore," Moody said taking a deep breath.

The three teenagers decided to enter the city first so they could see how much damage was caused by the earthquake. They also wanted to make sure no one was around when the people from the Citadel arrived. It should be nighttime but still, a hundred or more people dressed in odd clothing exiting out of a sewer would look freaky, even in Manhattan. It would attract too much attention.

Feather braided her long hair and smoothed her bangs with her hand. She was very excited to see the new world. She wondered if the fast-moving cars could travel faster than animals. And why animals were kept in cages. The only reason she could think of was because they might eat all the food. She carried her bow and arrow to show the kids in the new world how well she could shoot. She watched Mia, Lance and Lee shoot their arrows. She figured the kids in their world must also be good.

After resting a couple of hours, the band of people continued their journey. The temperature rose as they approached the waterfalls, so they removed some of their clothing.

The people from Citadel were amazed by the beautiful waterfall but they were hesitant because of the narrow path alongside it. The water glittered like diamonds from the light shining on it through the cracks in the tunnel. Lance led the way.

One by one people followed behind him. "Walk slowly," Lance yelled. He could see the apprehensive looks on some of their faces—including Mia's. The kids formed a line between Nadia and Marge. They didn't seem to be frightened, just curious. "Who do you suppose lives down there?" Asked a boy.

Nadia answered, "Probably someone who is very thirsty."

"Be careful. It's very slippery," Mia said to Feather with her hand on her shoulder to make sure she didn't fall. Once again the beetles made an appearance. They flew toward them. Several people used their spears to fight them off. Mia, Lance, Lee and Feather shot their arrows, hitting them. They fell into the river.

Everyone was surprised at how good Feather had become with her bow and arrows. She struck the beetles with great accuracy. There was no doubt in anyone's mind that she would be able to take care of herself in the new world.

"I see you continued practicing," Mia said to her. They reached the end of the waterfall.

"Yes," Feather said. "I want the kids in the new world to see I'm also a warrior."

"I don't think you'll have to worry about that," Mia said.

They continued walking upward on the narrow path until they reached the end. The opening in the rocky wall was a short distance ahead. Lance reached the wall. "Wait for us here," he said. "Give us about twenty minutes."

"Moody will lead you out," Mia said. "If there is a problem, he will signal you not to move forward."

Feather was eager to go with them. "Take me with you," she pleaded. "It won't be the same seeing your world for the first time without you."

They looked at Feather bubbling over with excitement. Lee said, "You know the earthquake has also smashed our world."

"We don't know what our city looks like now," Mia said.

"Whatever happened to it, I know you'll fix it," Feather said, looking up at them—her champions.

"Come on," Lance said to Feather. "Let's go see your new world."

CHAPTER THIRTY-ONE

They stepped through the opening in the rocky wall among the crumbled rocks and around the puddles of water on the ground. The path would lead them back to the sewer area.

"We're almost there. The smell in here is not as bad as before. It's good you left the hatch open, Mia," Lee announced.

"It smells like lifeless animals in here," Feather said.

"We're underneath the city," Mia said to Feather. "Don't worry, our world doesn't smell like this. I promise you."

Feather watched the rats running around. "We didn't have these animals in my world," she said.

"Trust me. That's a good thing," Mia said.

Lance pointed. He said, "I think the stairs that lead up to the hatch are over there." He climbed up the stairs. He could see the hatch was still partially open, just like Mia left it. He scanned the area. Nothing appeared but a dark, empty tunnel.

They stepped out of the hatch, happy to be back, regardless of how the city looked. They were back home—that's all that mattered.

"Everything is so dark and quiet." Feather said, looking around.

"It's nighttime," Lance said. "But something's not right. I can feel it."

They hurried through the tunnel. It was unusually quiet. Even at night, you could hear the noisy subways traveling through the city. Lee entered their position on his computer. The screen showed only a few lights in the city. It looked similar to a blackout.

Lee enlarged the area on the screen. "The power could be down," he said. "That could be the reason why the city is so dark."

"Where's the city?" Lance asked, watching the screen.

"It's there but... there's no activity. This doesn't look good," Mia said, looking closely.

"It's surreal," Lance said.

"What's wrong?" Feather asked.

"We should be hearing noise from the streets," Lee said.

Fearing the worst, they continued to the end of the tunnel. They looked out into darkness. Moody, Dr. Ram and the others walked out of the hatch and joined them.

They were all bewildered by the depressing sight in front of them. Water from fire hydrants flowed down the streets, carrying rubble from wrecked buildings. Gas lines exploded, sparking fires throughout the streets. It looked like a war zone. They covered their noses from the strong smell of gas.

"Where are all the people?" Feather asked. She was confused by what she saw.

"I'm not quite sure," Mia answered. She was shocked by the sight of all the destruction. She knew it would be bad but not quite this bad. She wondered if it was like this all over the city. "We need get out of here. It's not safe," she said.

"I agree," Moody said.

"Let's keep moving," Lance said.

Mia turned to the people from Citadel. She reassured them everything was going to be okay. Even with all the destruction around her, Mia managed to hold on to one happy thought. Her mother and father were back.

"It's a good thing people went to shelters," Lance said as he thought about his mother.

"I agree," Mia said.

Dr. Ram told the people to stay together. Lee was still focused on his computer screen. "Follow me; there's lots of activity up ahead."

They wandered through the streets, stepping over fallen electrical wires and broken glass. Mia warned them not to touch anything. "Be careful, Feather," she said. "There are a lot of dangerous things lying on the street."

"I'll be careful," Feather said.

Lee pointed. "Look over there. I can see flashing lights. Let's head in that direction."

"Can we get down that street?" Mia asked, looking at all the bricks and broken furniture from the damaged buildings.

"I think so. Just be careful where you step," Lee said. "Everything around here is messed up."

They went cautiously down the street. They were careful to stay away from shattered glass, exposed wires and fallen bricks. Some of the shops were unrecognizable. Cars had smashed into them.

They reached an area blocked off with orange barricades. Numerous police officers, emergency trucks and firemen surround the area. A policeman yelled out to them not to go any farther. Several policemen rushed over to them.

The people from the world beneath held on to each other. They saw the men dressed in uniforms running toward them. Dr. Ram and Moody assured them everything would be fine—just to stay calm. The policemen were surprised to see them.

One shouted to them, "Watch out. There are live wires on the streets." He looked at all the strangely dressed people. "We thought everyone had evacuated."

The teenager's faces lit up when they realized New York City still existed. However, many of the streets were completely flattened. Mia asked the policeman, "How bad are things?"

"Very bad. There's been quite a lot of damage throughout the world," the policeman said. "We're in a state of emergency."

"Is there a place where we can stay?" Dr. Ram asked. "Everyone is very tired. We need food and water."

"Follow me," said a fireman. "There's a shelter a few blocks away. I'm afraid you'll have to walk."

"Thanks," Dr. Ram said. He waved to the people to follow him. "We're used to walking."

"By the way," said the fireman, looking at the people. "Where were you all? We thought we got everyone out."

Moody had to think quickly. "We took shelter in the tunnel," he answered. "We were rehearsing at the theater." Moody hoped the fireman wouldn't realize the theater was at least ten miles away.

"You know, the show must go on," Lee said.

Dr. Ram and his people followed the fireman down the street. Lee tried to call his family but he was unable to get a signal on his phone. "Does anyone have a phone I can use?" Lee asked. "I need to check on my family."

"None of the phones work. There was some kind of explosion in space, a couple of satellites. It knocked out all communication. Luckily, we have two-way radios."

A fireman covered with soot joined the conversation. He looked tired and worn out. He held a flashlight in his hand.

"A lot of unexplainable things have taken place," he said breathlessly, somewhat overwhelmed.

"Like what?" Lee asked, glancing at Lance and Mia wondering if it had anything to do with the Spoilers.

Wiping the black residue off his face with a rag, the fireman answered, "A lot of people are missing that were in the shelters. No one knows what happened to them."

Lee looked at the fireman. "That is puzzling. Maybe they went into a tunnel like we did. They may still turn up."

"Hold on, that's not all. When, we went into some of the buildings and stores, even parking lots, we found some kind of green ash, like something had burned up in that spot. Now, you tell me... how do you explain that?" the fireman asked.

"No doubt, that is weird," Mia said, "but things happen that can't be explained." She thought about what could have happened if they hadn't wiped out the Spoilers' lifeline. All those people that disappeared would be plotting their next move to destroy them. They would be roaming the streets of New York tonight and what was even scarier was they would have achieved their goal.

The teenagers were eager to see their families. They had to make sure everyone was okay. Lee asked the police officer if he could take them to their families.

"We would really appreciate it," Mia said.

"Sure," said the policeman, "but keep in mind a lot of the streets have been wiped out. It could take some time."

The three were seated in back of the police car. The policeman drove slowly down the streets to avoid large objects on the ground. Parts of the city were in shambles. The policeman steered his car onto the sidewalk to avoid hitting a few misplaced cars. "Luckily, most people evacuated," the policeman said. "The ones that didn't were trapped in the buildings."

"Were many injured?" Lee asked.

"Yes, some critically. We're still digging in some areas," the policeman said. "We set up tents for those people in need of care."

A few people were seen wandering around in the darkness. A pack of stray dogs roamed the street. A feeling of sadness overpowered them, seeing block after block of devastation.

"Is it like this everywhere?" Mia asked, looking through the window at the gloomy sight of what used to be a very upscale area.

The policeman looked through his rearview mirror at the teenagers. "Some areas made out better than others. These catastrophes don't care whether you're rich or poor," he said.

"The city will have to be rebuilt... it'll take some time," Lee said, looking out the window.

"It will happen, Lee," Mia said. "I look forward to spending time with my mother and father, even under these conditions."

"I can't imagine how you must feel having your mother and father back in your life," Lee said.

"I knew they were out there somewhere," Mia said.

"You never gave up," Lance said. He knew Mia was persistent. Once she made up her mind, it was a done deal. She had faced fear close up and challenged herself to overcome her greatest obstacle—acrophobia.

Mia spoke in a low voice. She could see the policeman glancing in his rear view mirror. "Our search to find and destroy the Spoilers led me to my parents. Maybe it was more than just a coincidence."

Mia explained to Lance and Lee how her father and mother had become prisoners of the Spoilers. Her father was a government agent. He was investigating mysterious sightings. Reports of humans changing into animals. Some of the people reported making these strange transitions held high ranking positions in the government. It didn't make any sense to them at first. Then they found a connection between these people and Dr. Ward.

They discovered the facility where Dr. Ward was being held. The Spoilers captured them in the woods. Over time, they learned about them and their plans to take over our world.

"Their plan failed. This country still belongs to us," Lance said.

The policeman stopped the car. He turned to the teenagers. "What do you mean the country still belongs to us?"

"What I mean is worse things have happened. Some countries are controlled by ruthless leaders," Lance explained.

"I see what you mean," the policeman said. "We still have our freedom."

They approached the street where Charlton Academy was located. The once upscale area was now in shambles. Only parts of the school remained.

"Could you please stop here for a minute?" Lee asked, looking at the remains of Charlton Academy. "We want to get a closer look at our school."

"Sure," the policeman said. "Just be careful."

Lance and Mia followed Lee. The sign in front of the school that said *Charlton Academy* dangled sideways on the pole. They stepped over bricks and shingles from the roof of the school scattered on the sidewalk. The large mahogany door was wide open. It was the only thing that didn't seem displaced. The teenagers walked up the cracked concrete steps and looked inside. The upper levels of the school now rested on the first floor.

"I don't feel sad about the school. Only about our classmates, who were looking forward to graduating from here," Mia said. "It all started with Dr. Bloom deceiving us – recruiting us into this school for his devious plan."

"The school will be rebuilt one day. A new beginning," Lance said. "The evil is gone."

They returned to the police car, looking at each other and smiling. "You can move on now," Lance said to the policeman. "Thanks for stopping."

Mia continued to look out the window at the school until it faded out of sight. She had to reassure herself the Spoilers were gone forever.

CHAPTER THIRTY-TWO

For the first time Mia and her family were together. Lance joined his mother, who kept the people in the bunker's spirits up by singing to them. Even though Lee's family's restaurant had been destroyed, the safe room that Ling build kept them safe.

Lee and his grandfather discussed the Spoilers. Ling wrote down verbatim in a journal—the story Lee told him about the Spoilers. He believed future generations must know what happened. Whether, they believed the story or not—they would become more aware of strange things taking place around them.

Six months later a graduation ceremony for Charlton Academy's students was held in a park near the school. The dean of the school wanted the students to move on with their lives, so they could help rebuild New York. The Academy would be torn down, like many other buildings in the city.

Most business had to close. There was very little retail. Many people were forced to move out of the city to vacant lands. They established small farming communities. The people from Citadel were among those people.

They established their own community, using their knowledge and skills. In a way, they did get what they wanted. A place in a world where they could live without fear from anyone or anything.

Even with all the madness that had taken place in their lives the three, Mia, Lance and Lee, were just as excited as their classmates to be graduating from high school. They were far from the danger they experienced and the uncertainty of their future. But their excitement and anticipation of a new beginning overshadowed what they often referred to as a bad scene. Like most people they were busy trying to restore their city.

The wind blew lightly. The smell of ash from burnt down buildings still lingered in the air. It was graduation day. The families of the students were seated in rows of chairs. Irene, Beverly, Erica and Aaron sat together. Next to them were Lee's mother and father, his grandfather Ling and his sister Kim. Nadia and her brother Aman were seated in chairs next to them. Patina and Daily's mother were seated behind them. Seam and a few of her Goth friends, dressed in their Goth attire, were seated next to them.

Feather, Moody and Marge sat under a tree. Ivor was perched above them on a tree branch. The families watched proudly as their sons and daughters accepted their diplomas from the school's dean. Miss Beasley assisted him.

Only a few teachers, including Miss Wilson, attended the ceremony. No one had seen many of the teachers since the earthquake. Dr. Bloom and Miss Finney had been reported among the missing.

Lee's name was called; he strolled up front, smiling from ear to ear, and accepted his diploma.

"Way to go, brother" Kim shouted, drawing laughter from the crowd.

When Lance accepted his diploma, Irene, who now worked in one of the shelters, cried out, "He's going to be a math professor."

Aaron and Erica embraced Beverly when Mia received her diploma. "Thank you, Mom," Erica said. Lance threw Mia a kiss. He and Lee threw their hands up in the air and shouted, "We can do this."

After the ceremony, Daily introduced her mother to her classmates. She told Mia, Lance and Lee, her stepfather is missing. They don't know what happened to him. It was like he just disappeared. She said, his favorite thing to do.

"Maybe one day you'll find out what happened to him." Lance said.

"Maybe," Daily said. She shrugged her shoulders. "One day."

They waved goodbye to Daily and took their familiar walk down what used to be busy Broadway St. Mia held Lance's hand. Lee placed one arm around Nadia's shoulder and carried his backpack with the other.

There was still no electricity in some parts of the city and a shortage of water. They passed by the area where Sam's newsstand once stood. They saw Sam and several other people repairing a building.

"Congratulations," Sam shouted.

"Thanks," the teenagers said together.

They went to the area where the coffee shop once stood. Coffee was being served from under a tent by Seam and her friends. The difference in people didn't matter anymore, only what they had in common—to restore the world.

"Hold on," Lee said. He stopped and sat his backpack on the ground. He fumbled through it until he found a small device.

"What's that?" Lance asked. "It looks similar to the Enhancer."

"I was going to show it to you later but I can't wait any longer...check this out," Lee said eagerly, smiling from ear to ear.

They all looked closely at the device. Lance took it out of Lee's hand and examined it. "What is it? It's got to be special. I've never seen you this excited except when we made it out of the hole," Lance said.

"This powerful device is called the Enforcer," Lee said proudly. He took the device from Lance. "It will allow us to detect any foreign being."

"Really, Lee?" Mia exhaled. "It wasn't enough that we were trapped in another world, fought off deadly beasts, an insane leader and most of all, eliminated immortal animals that were planning on taking over our world?"

"Tell me you're kidding, Lee," Lance said.

"You actually created a device that can track aliens?" Nadia said.

"I don't think so," Mia said.

Lance, Mia and Nadia walked quickly away. They left Lee on the sidewalk, stuffing his device back into his backpack. He quickly caught up with them.

"Okay," Lee said. "Maybe I'm a little premature... but you never know what the future has in store for us."

ACKNOWLEDGEMENTS

I would like to thank those talented people who assisted with the publication of this book; Emmett Hagood for his extensive editorial feedback. Marco Evans, cover art character images and Mark Hagood, continuing support.

ABOUT THE AUTHOR

Marsha Thompson splits her time between her residence in Orlando, Florida and her family in Detroit, Michigan. While spending time with middle graders and teens, she discovered how they are drawn into the science fiction/ fantasy world. This fascination impelled her to write her YA debut novel, Spoilers.

Marsha earned a degree in sociology from the University of Central Florida.

www.marshathompsonbooks.com